EVIL in

EYNHALLOW

B.K. BRYCE

EVIL IN EYNHALLOW

FM-N

Evil in Eynhallow

Chapter 1

'Get off, you brutes,' Marna flapped her arms above her head, protecting her face from the warning swoops and spear-sharp beaks of the Arctic terns. Her flustering rocked the rowing boat she and Sempal were in.

'They are only guarding their nests and eggs, remember,' Sempal repeated the words Marna had said to him that morning. Her glare curbed his laughter. 'I guess we must be near the bay.' He wrenched the oars, sending Marna sprawling.

'Must you do that?' she complained.

'It would help if somebody gave me a hand with the rowing.'

'How can I? I need both arms to prevent us being pecked alive.'

'I thought that was what he was here for.' Sempal nodded at the small dog cowering beside Marna's feet. It whimpered in response.

'Pip is afraid of the water,' Marna reminded him. 'You know his master drowned rescuing him from the loch.' She put a hand on Pip's head and he nestled closer.

'Good thing too,' Sempal replied. 'But that was last year. He can't still be upset.'

'You think because he's a dog, he doesn't suffer from traumatic incidents?'

'I didn't mean that.'

'Let's not talk about it.'

Marna had almost been drowned by the dog's master, Wilmer, in the "traumatic incident". The memory was raw.

Sempal steered the boat away from the cliff with the nesting terns, towards an inlet. It was the only safe landing spot on the island. Eynhallow lay between their island and the busy settlements on Rousay, and the current in the Sound made it difficult to reach. This gave the islanders security from raiders, but it was a hindrance for trading. Marna had only been there once before, and Sempal never.

Marna peered over Sempal's hunched body to the shore. 'I can't see anyone. Are they expecting us?'

'I told Fara, the morning before she left. She should have alerted the look-outs, but she's growing as crazy as her father was. She is constantly doped out of her head, according to Gerk at any rate.'

'Gerk is the one who is the dope,' Marna defended her friend. 'I wouldn't pay attention to what he says. Fara is all right. Jona taught her what plants ease the burden of island life and I don't blame her for using them. Three of her cattle have stopped eating and are giving sour milk. Two of her neighbour's sheep have died and the problem is spreading. The islanders blame Fara.'

'Hopefully your mother's medicine can cure things.'

Marna felt for her bag at the bottom of the boat. The skin was damp, thanks to sea water seeping into the boat. 'Oh no, if the powder gets wet, it will be ruined.'

'If you sat still in the boat, the water wouldn't get in.'

Marna made a face, but clenched the bag to her chest and sat as still as she could. She made cooing noises at Pip, to show Sempal she was annoyed with him, but it wasn't long before she wanted to speak.

'Did you talk with the traders from Wick?'

'I didn't get a chance. They had nothing we wanted, so they didn't wait. They were eager to press on to the Ness.'

'I didn't see them either,' Marna admitted, 'but Henjar mentioned there was a healer with them.'

'Oh, she said nothing to me.'

'No? Then why has your face turned bright pink, the way it does when you are telling tales?'

'It is the strain of rowing. How many of your mother's bere bannocks did you guzzle before we set off?'

'What did Henjar say about the healer?' Marna persisted.

'He has "magic" stones that can draw evil out of people and animals.'

'Evil?'

'That's what Henjar said. She may have misheard or

was using her over-active imagination. She has a thing about sickness and evil being linked.'

'That is ridiculous,' Marna leaned forwards and the boat wobbled again. 'Sorry.'

Sempal pulled the boat in to the bay and looked for a spot to land. The shore was deserted.

'Did she say what this healer was like?' Marna said.

'No.'

'You're lying again,' Marna slapped his knees. 'Henjar will have told you every detail. She has an eye for men.'

'I didn't say it was a man.'

'Oh.'

'But you're right. His name is Aiven and according to Henjar he's "not her type". Mind you, Albar was with her when she said that.'

'He's probably old and hairy,' Marna decided, 'Or bald and wrinkled. People believe anything old, bald men tell them. Even about magic stones.'

'Do I sense you are jealous of Aiven?'

'What is there to be jealous of? He sounds like a work-shy charlatan.'

'Just the sort they love at the Ness,' Sempal was enjoying winding Marna up. 'Patro and his cronies will no doubt be keen to have him stay for a while.'

Marna grunted. 'Keep your eyes on the water. You

almost bumped into a rock.'

The water was shallow enough for them to step out and drag the boat, with Pip in it, up the pebbly beach to the bank. Sempal checked there was no damage to the hull before he secured it to a rock. 'You've been here before. Which way to the village?'

Marna looked round to get her bearings. 'I thought someone would come to greet us,' she said again. 'They must have spotted us approaching.'

'You don't know the way, do you?'

'It's been a while since I was here. Give me time.' Marna began to walk along the path worn in the bank towards the cliff. 'This way,' she called.

It hadn't rained for days and the ground was dry. Marna took a step, caught her foot on a stone and slipped. She staggered several feet, trying to prevent herself falling, but tumbled to the ground and rolled over. Her head and foot hurt as she came to a halt. She lay face down on the grass, assessing her injuries.

'What are you laughing at?' she chided as she heard Sempal approach. 'Make yourself useful and give me a hand up.' She kept her head down, but lifted her arm. A hand with a strong grasp took hold of it.

'Are you all right?' the husky voice asked.

That definitely wasn't Sempal. She looked up to see a startling pair of hazel eyes watching her. 'Who are you?'

she asked, none too civilly.

The eyes were connected to a handsome face, with chiselled cheekbones and chin. The man's dark hair was combed back and tied with a sinew. His beard was short and clean. The lips were smiling.

'My name is Aiven. Can I help you up or are you comfortable down there with the slugs?'

Marna let go of his hand with a jerk.

'Marna does her own thing,' Sempal explained as he joined the man.

'Ah, you are Marna. I have heard people speak of you. And you must be Sempal,' Aiven turned towards him. 'What is that you are carrying?'

'That, is my dog,' Marna answered. She got to her feet, rubbed her tunic then took Pip from Sempal. The dog covered her with drool as he licked her face.

Aiven made a face. 'Can't it walk?'

'Pip doesn't like the pebbles,' Sempal explained.

'He has a bad leg,' Marna added.

'Perhaps I can cure it,' Aiven said, reaching out to stroke Pip. Marna drew him away.

'He bites,' she warned.

'I've coped with worse.'

'Pip has already killed a man,' Sempal said.

Aiven made a sound from the side of his mouth in disbelief.

'A stranger to the islands,' Marna said, tickling Pip's ear.

'We have barely met, yet I sense you have a poor opinion of me,' Aiven rubbed his chin.

'I have heard people speak of you,' Marna was quick to reply. 'If you will excuse us, we have work here.'

'What sort of work?' Aiven moved to block Marna's way. Pip gave a soft growl, but nestled further in to Marna's chest.

'Healing,' Marna replied. 'I don't know how long you have been on Eynhallow, but you surely must have heard about the ailments of the cattle and sheep. My mother has prepared a potion…'

'Can I see it?' Aiven interrupted. Marna was reluctant to show him, but couldn't think of an excuse not to. She put Pip down and opened her bag, bringing out a lidded pot.

'May I?' Aiven raised his fingers towards the lid, but didn't open the pot until Marna nodded. He stuck his thumb in the mixture and removed a sample. After rubbing it between his fingers he lifted it to his nose.

'Dandelions, mint and …what? Clam shells?'

Marna grabbed the lid and thrust it back on the pot. 'My mother is a well-known healer,' she said.

'I do not deny it,' Aiven said. 'Fortunately there is no need of her medicine. The cattle are well. I have cured them.'

'With your magic stones?' Marna jeered.

'My stones have power, yes, but the energy comes from the earth. The stones align the humours in the body and draw out what shouldn't be there.'

'And Fara's cows are now milking?'

'They would provide more milk if they had access to fresh water, but there is a shortage on the island.'

'Your stones can't make it rain?' Sempal said. Marna could tell Aiven didn't know if he was serious or mocking.

'No.'

Marna was tiring of the conversation. Someone as annoying as Aiven really shouldn't be so good-looking and charming. 'Fara is expecting us,' she said, moving past.

'You must be tired after your journey,' Aiven allowed. 'I'll escort you to the village.'

'I know the way,' Marna said.

'Well…' Sempal began, but a look from Marna stopped him.

'I'm heading there anyway,' Aiven answered. 'Would you like me to carry your dog for you?'

'Come Pip,' Marna strode ahead and beckoned to the dog. Pip rose and waddled after his mistress. Sempal and Aiven followed in silence. After five minutes she was lost. The island wasn't large and she should be able to see the village. She stopped and turned sharply. Sempal and Aiven halted in time to prevent a collision.

'I'm going the wrong way, amn't I?' she said.

'It's a circular island,' Aiven answered. 'I thought you were taking the scenic route.'

'Smarty.' Marna stomped round him and back along the track.

'Is she like this all the time?' Aiven asked Sempal.

'No, this is a good day,' she replied, without looking round. She heard Aiven laugh.

As they neared the village, Pip yelped and ran ahead. Marna called, but he disappeared behind a windswept beech hedge. He reappeared with a dead rat in his mouth.

'Put it down,' Marna ordered. Pip looked at her with large eyes.

'Better do as she says,' Aiven told the dog. Pip dropped the half-chewed rodent.

Sempal walked on while Marna was dealing with Pip and he returned with Fara, who was carrying a baby, swaddled in skins. Marna moved to see the child.

'Is it a boy or a girl?' she asked Fara.

'A little girl. We call her Terese. I'm so glad you could come and see her.'

'She is beautiful,' Marna knew that was what Fara wanted to hear. 'At least my journey wasn't in vain. Aiven tells me the cattle are cured.'

'Yes. They have given good milk for two days and no more sheep have died. I'm sorry your mother's medicine was not needed, but it would be good if you could stay with us for a few days. I have a cloak I would like dyed and if Sempal doesn't mind, the villagers would welcome an evening of storytelling.'

'Don't get him started,' Marna pretended to be bored by Sempal's tales, although she loved hearing them.

'You are a storyteller?' Aiven asked.

'Sempal is the best storyteller on the islands,' Fara answered. 'Don't listen to Marna's teasing.'

They walked with Fara into the village. A number of villagers were about, busy at work, or gossip. Gerk invited them in to the house. Marna was about to step in when they heard a disturbance. It sounded like a woman wailing. Pip ran towards the noise with his tail in the air.

'You'd better catch him in case he bites someone,' Sempal whispered to Marna.

Aiven strode ahead of Marna. Most of the villagers were keen to find out what the trouble was. As Marna caught up, she saw an old woman kneeling on the ground. A girl was lying in front of her.

'What is the matter, Wandra?' a villager asked.

The woman tried to answer, but tears stifled her words. She scratched in the dust with her fingers.

'Is the girl ill?' Aiven asked. He reached in the pocket of his tunic for his stones.

Marna bent down to take the girl's arm. It was cold to

the touch and flopped in Marna's hand. Pip nudged beside Marna, sniffed the air and gave a low groan.

'Let me see,' Aiven knelt beside her, holding a stone in either hand.

'You won't need these,' Marna said. 'There is no life in her veins. Her lips are blue and her heart is still. It will take more than some magic stones to raise the dead.'

Chapter 2

'You'd better come inside,' Fara said.

'I'm fine here,' Marna said, getting to her feet. 'I need to ask a few questions. Who was the last..?' Her sentence was cut short by a look from Fara. She put a hand on Marna's shoulder and pulled her away.

'This is a matter for our people to deal with,' Gerk said. 'Meddling from outsiders will not be welcome.'

'I'm not meddling, I'm showing concern.' Marna twisted her neck to see what was happening. There was a crowd round the child's body, but they parted to allow a red-headed man to push through. Fara tightened her grip on Marna and edged towards her home. It was one of the huts behind a stone shed and Marna found her view of the scene blocked. Sempal had picked Pip up and followed behind Fara and Marna, but Aiven remained with Gerk and the villagers. 'He gets to stay,' Marna muttered as she bent to enter Fara and Gerk's hut.

'You can discuss things with him later,' Sempal answered. 'Now he is your new friend.' Marna pretended to snarl and Pip tried to copy her. Thanks to his stone chewing habit, one of his upper front teeth was chipped, which gave him a menacing look.

'I don't think he likes you,' Fara observed.

'He doesn't like anyone except Marna,' Sempal said,

putting him on the ground.

Inside the house, Marna blinked to adjust her eyes to the shaded light then looked round. 'Is that a new dresser?'

'Yes,' Fara beamed. She hesitated for a moment. 'It will be a pity if I have to leave it.'

'What do you mean?' Sempal asked.

'You know about our water problems?'

'How bad are they?' Marna said.

'There used to be two good springs on the island. One dried up a year ago and now the other spring barely gives more than a trickle, on a good day. We have scoured the island looking for a fresh source of water, but so far with no success. Gerk has been talking about moving. Several families have already left the island to live with relatives on Rousay or the mainland.'

'Ah, that explains the empty houses we spotted when we came in,' Marna said.

Fara didn't answer and Sempal moved towards the fire and smiled with approval. 'Something smells good.' He poked his nose towards a cooking pot set at the side.

'I've been making seabird's eggs stew,' Fara said. 'Although you can hardly call it stew, with so little liquid.'

'Seabird egg stew – no wonder the terns were angry with us when we arrived,' Sempal tried to lighten the mood.

'Let me settle Terese in her cot,' Fara said. 'Then we can talk more.' She wrapped the baby in skins with a practised hand and laid her in the bed. There were two polished whalebone sticks resting at the side. She picked them up and clicked them together. The baby giggled at the noise and Marna moved to watch her.

'She's a good girl,' Marna said.

'Some times,' Fara answered. 'She can be worse than three howling dogs when she is hungry.'

'She must tire you out,' Marna put a hand on her friend's shoulder, but Fara slid away.

'Gerk does what he can.'

The baby's eyes closed and she was asleep by the time Gerk returned to the house.

'What sort of host must you think I am?' he apologised to Marna and Sempal, moving to the dresser to lift a pottery jug filled with ale. He gestured to Fara to bring the beakers.

'We'll use the decorative ones,' Fara said.

She handed Sempal and Marna a beaker and Gerk poured the ale.

'What did you find out about the girl's death?' Marna asked, her curiosity getting the better of her.

Gerk glanced at Fara before answering. 'A terrible business.'

Despite further probing, Gerk would say nothing more specific. Marna moved to the corner to think while the others chatted.

'Was it a bad journey across the Sound?' Gerk called

across to her when he noticed she wasn't joining in the conversation.

'Mmm?'

'I'll get the stew,' Fara said. She busied herself ladling stew into bowls while Gerk and Sempal talked about the sea conditions. Marna pulled at tags in her hair. Pip slunk to the corner beside her and curled between her legs.

'Ahem, don't you want any? You must be hungry.' Marna looked up to see Fara standing in front of her, offering a bowl. She stared at her without accepting until the salty smell of the food crept up her nose and down into her mouth, waking her taste buds. She took the bowl, but her mind was elsewhere.

'Do you think it's connected?' she said.

'What is?' Fara answered. Marna didn't reply immediately and Fara walked over to Sempal and gave him the second bowl of stew she was carrying. When her hands were free she removed two wooden spoons from her belt. She handed one to Sempal and took one to Marna. Sempal held the spoon in his left hand and examined it before setting it on the ground and scooping a handful of stew with his fingers.

'The girl's death and the water shortage,' Marna replied, as if Fara's question had taken a minute to reach her brain.

Fara looked towards her husband. Gerk shrugged.

'I mean, if she had been drinking sea water…'

'She wouldn't do that, surely?' Sempal replied. 'That's one of the first things we were taught not to do.' The stew was hot and he shook his burnt fingers, splattering speckles of egg whites across the floor. Fara frowned, glancing at the abandoned spoon.

Marna ran her spoon round the inside of the bowl, dislodging chunks of egg stuck to the sides. The others were watching her. 'I was thinking about the dying sheep and dry cows.'

'I made sure our animals had enough water,' Fara said, addressing Gerk.

'Of course, dear,' Gerk agreed. Fara had brought her husband a bowl of food and he lent his nose over it to savour the aroma and avoid his wife's glare.

'Aiven told us that problem was over,' Sempal said, between blowing on his bowl.

'Tush,' Marna made a noise through her teeth. 'I wouldn't believe a word that man said even if he told me the sun would still be in the sky tomorrow morning.'

'No more sheep are ill and the cows are milking again,' Gerk said.

'It would help if we had more water,' Fara said, sitting down to eat. 'And our missing lamb hasn't returned.'

'It was a weakly one,' Gerk said. 'It must have been taken by a hawk.'

Marna put her bowl of uneaten food to the side and stood up. 'I need to know how the girl died.'

Gerk got to his feet and stopped her before she reached the door. 'I had a word with Wandra before I came in,' he said. 'She was upset.'

'More reason to find out what happened,' Marna said.

'She prodded me and made wild accusations.'

'Like what?' Fara asked.

'It was plain she thought Kayleen's death was linked to the cattle and sheep.'

'Trust her,' Fara grumbled. 'We know who she blames for that.' Gerk moved past Marna to set his bowl on the dresser then put an arm round his wife's shoulders.

'Nobody else believes it is our fault.' He looked to Marna. 'Our cows were the first to take ill,' he explained.

'Did Aiven say what the trouble with the animals was?' Marna asked. Gerk shook his head.

'He thought their dark humours were imbalanced,' Sempal said. 'That's what he told me on the way here.'

'That means nothing,' Marna said. 'It is some fancy phrase he made up to fool "simple" island folk. Use the word "dark" and everyone panics. The elders will be asking for a priest next.'

'I wasn't fooled,' Sempal said.

'I need to speak with Wandra.' Marna stepped nearer to the door.

This time Sempal reached up to stop her. 'Listen to Gerk, it's not the right time.'

Pip gave a growl. He had finished the scraps of stew snaffled from Marna's bowl and was licking his front paws, but stood alert when he sensed his mistress was in danger. Sempal's ankle was the nearest thing to him and he snapped at it, but wobbled and fell back. Marna gasped.

'What have you done to Pip?'

'I didn't touch him.'

Pip was rolling on the floor, kicking his legs in the air and making a horrific squeaking noise. Marna knelt beside him. 'Where's my bag. I need my mother's potion.'

Sempal searched around the room among the skins, but it was Fara who found it crumpled in the corner. She reached inside. 'Is this what you're looking for?'

Marna hurriedly emptied the bag onto the floor.

'Oh no,' she gasped. What was left of her mother's powder was clumped into a soggy splodge of material at the bottom of the bag. As she tried to scoop it up, the remains of the medicine seeped away. 'It must have got soaked in the boat,' she groaned and glared at Sempal.

'Don't blame me,' he said. 'It was fine when you showed it to Aiven. The lid has come loose and the powder has fallen onto the wet bag.'

'And whose fault is it that the bag is wet…?

She was interrupted by a soft whine from Pip and

stroked the dog's head to ease him. She looked from
Sempal to Gerk then Fara. 'What are we going to do?'

Chapter 3

'Well...' Sempal gritted his teeth and drew back his lips. He waited a moment before continuing. 'We could ask Aiven.' He took a step away from Marna. For two slow heart beats it seemed she would pick up the bowl resting at her elbow and toss it at Sempal, but she gave a sob and flopped over the dog in an embrace.

'I'll find him,' Gerk said. He squeezed past Marna and out of the house.

It seemed an age before he returned. Fara finished her stew and although his stomach was full, Sempal scraped at the stew pot to avoid watching Marna. Every few minutes Pip gave a moan to show he was hanging on, but the noises grew weaker.

'Where is the patient, move aside?' Aiven stormed into the house, with Gerk close behind. He managed to stop before tripping over Marna and Pip, but Gerk banged into his back, jolting him forwards. He spread his arms to steady himself and jostled Marna's back. She glared round at him.

'Do you feel sick?' Aiven regained his balance and leaned over her to open her eyes wide with his thumbs pressing on her lower lids and his first fingers pulling the upper lids towards her hairline. He was wearing a ring made from a smooth dark stone on the first finger of his left hand. Marna felt it press against her eye and jerked back.

'Not me, you idiot. Pip,' she said.

'Oh.' Aiven dropped his hands.

'Can you do something for him?' Sempal asked.

'Well…' Aiven nodded towards the heavy quern stone and mimed slamming it down hard. Sempal hurriedly shook his head and Aiven managed to rub his hands together before Marna realised what he was implying.

'What about your stones?' Sempal said. 'Can't they cure him?'

Aiven blew out his breath and looked at Marna who was stroking Pip's nose. He reached in his pocket and drew out two dark, shiny stones. He rubbed them against his tunic then laid them in the palm of his right hand, holding it out flat for Sempal, Fara and Gerk to see.

'Is that them?' Gerk was unimpressed.

'Watch.' Aiven nudged the stones closer together. When they were the thickness of an arrow shaft apart, they jumped towards each other without Aiven's aid.

'How did they do that?' Gerk stared at the stones.

'They are special healing stones with their own power. Now move aside. I need space to work,' Aiven instructed, clasping his hand over the stones.

The others shuffled back. Marna shifted to let Aiven kneel beside her, but didn't take her hand from Pip's head.

'If you'll allow me…' Aiven moved closer to the writhing dog. 'Ugh, what do you feed this animal on?' He waved away the dog's breath with his left hand before reaching with his fingers to take one of the stones from his right hand. He held it in the air between the first finger and thumb, closed his eyes then opened them to balance the stone on Pip's head. He lifted the second stone in a similar manner using his right hand then closed and opened his eyes. He put the stone on Pip's back near the base of his tail. The skin twitched and the fur stood up.

'Stop it, you're hurting him,' Marna accused.

'I'm drawing out the ailment.' Aiven clenched his fists and held them over the stones then worked his hands across Pip's body.

'It's not working,' Marna wailed.

'Give me time.'

Sempal, Fara and Gerk edged closer to see what Aiven was doing, throwing a shadow over Pip. Aiven gave a grunt and turned his shoulders to hide his actions.

'Maybe you need an incantation,' Fara suggested. 'My father swore by them. He knew several for healing. Perhaps I can remember one.'

Aiven placed the stones on the floor, near Pip's nose and eased the dog's head away from Marna. 'I need a little time - and peace - to work.'

Sempal put his hands on Marna's shoulders and gave them a squeeze. Pip's mouth was locked shut, but Aiven managed to insert a thumb between his jaws and prised them open a nail width. He wriggled two fingers inside.

'Ah, oh, ouch.'

'Is that the incantation?' Gerk whispered to Fara.

'I don't think so,' Fara answered.

Aiven pulled his fingers out. One of them was bleeding and he raised his hand to his mouth to suck away the blood.

'I don't suppose he could have been poisoned?' Sempal said.

Aiven dropped his hand. 'Poisoned? What makes you say that?'

'I was thinking of that rat he found. He couldn't have killed it himself.'

'What's that?' Marna pointed at Pip's mouth. 'What have you done?' Foamy saliva was bubbling from one corner. Aiven bent over to look. He reached towards the mouth with his good hand and fiddled at something before twisting and yanking.

'There.' He stood up and held out a half chewed length of fibre.

'What is it?' Sempal asked.

'It looks like a rat tail,' Marna said, peering at it.

'Yuck.' Aiven dropped it.

'Look, Pip's stirring.' Marna tried to cradle the dog in her arms, but he was beginning to recover from his ailment and struggled to rise.

'He must have been choking, like Boda,' Sempal said.

26

'Boda?' Aiven queried.

'My sister's boy. He choked on a stone last year, but he's fine now.'

Marna gave Pip a hug then got to her feet to face Aiven. She wiped away a tear. 'You saved Pip,' she said.

'Only doing my job.'

She stepped forwards and kissed him on the cheek then moved smartly back and wiped her mouth.

'I helped too,' Sempal said. 'I was the one who remembered about the rat.'

'But you said he was poisoned,' Aiven reminded him.

'Your stones didn't do much good, did they?' Sempal grumbled.

'Pip seems to be back to normal. That's the main thing,' Fara said.

'You'd better watch these bere bannocks,' Marna warned. Pip's long nose was reaching up to sniff Fara's baking. She took the hot stone they were placed on and offered the bannocks to Sempal and Aiven.

'Thank you, but I have to go. I was in the middle of speaking to Wandra when you called me,' Aiven said. He turned to recover his stones, but Gerk had picked them up and was inspecting them.

'I was afraid Pip might eat them,' Gerk said, by way of explanation.

'I'd better take them before he does.' Aiven held his

hand out and Gerk reluctantly handed the stones over. Aiven rubbed them on his cloak before putting them in his pocket.

'I'm surprised he doesn't talk to them,' Marna said once Aiven had left. She waited a moment then strode to the door.

'Where are you off to now?' Sempal asked.

'I'm going to follow Aiven. He said he was speaking to Wandra. I need to find out as much as I can about the girl who died.'

'Why?'

Marna screwed her face up in answer.

'I can tell you who she was,' Fara said. 'Kayleen - Borg's daughter and Wandra's granddaughter.'

'Borg? Is he the gruff man we saw? Do you know if Kayleen had been ill? Did she suffer from any childhood ailments?' Marna asked.

'Yes. No. I mean that was Borg you saw, but I don't think there was anything wrong with Kayleen, apart from the stories she made up. I saw her this morning playing tag with the other children.'

'Then it's important that I find out what Wandra has to say.' Aiven had left the door open and Marna took a step outside. She felt Pip's nose nuzzle against her hand.

'Stay here,' she ordered. She hesitated then turned to face Sempal. 'Aren't you coming with me?'

'I thought you told me not to.'

'I was speaking to Pip.'

Sempal followed Marna out. 'We should have asked Fara which one is Wandra's home,' he said.

'There's no need.' Marna pointed to where a group of children had gathered. They were watching Aiven. He was addressing Wandra and although he spoke their language, he seemed to do most of the "talking" with his arms. Two of the children were copying his movements behind his back.

'Show off,' Marna grumbled.

'He saved Pip,' Sempal reminded her.

'That doesn't mean he's not a show off. Where are you going?'

'To join the children,' Sempal answered. 'We'll be close enough to hear what Wandra has to say.'

'Yes, but Aiven will know we are listening.'

'So?'

Marna sighed. She took hold of Sempal's tunic and pulled him round the back of the line of huts. They stayed close to the walls as they crept round, stopping when they reached the side of Wandra's house. The voices were loud and there was no problem hearing what was being said without being seen, but the old woman was crying and her words were garbled. Aiven had to stop her several times and ask her to repeat her answer.

'You said Kayleen was playing with the other children this morning?' Aiven tried to clarify what he was told.

'We know that,' Marna muttered.

'Yes.' Wandra's voice was weak. 'That is until she fell out with her friend Vern.'

'Which one of you is Vern?' Aiven turned to ask the children. Marna saw his face as he took a step closer to them. The lines on his forehead were more pronounced and his eyes were dark. Nobody answered and he took hold of the nearest boy's shoulder. The boy tried to shake himself free, but Aiven's grip was strong.

'Let go of him.' Marna stepped out to confront Aiven.

'What the...?' He released his hand from the boy. 'Marna, what are you doing here?'

'We were passing on our way to gather herbs,' Sempal said.

Marna rolled her eyes at Sempal's obvious lie. 'We want to know what happened to Kayleen,' she said.

Aiven smiled. 'Then please allow me to continue my investigation.'

'*Your* investigation? Who put you in charge? There's no need to shout and throw your weight around.'

'I was hardly doing that,' Aiven looked to Sempal for support.

'You were a bit scary,' Sempal answered.

The children had moved a short distance from Aiven,

30

but curiosity prevented them from running off. They huddled together, feeling secure in a group, like the deer Marna's brother Thork hunted. Aiven stepped towards them and they scrambled a few paces away.

'You don't need to be afraid of me,' he said.

'Why should they trust you?' Marna said. 'The children won't talk now. I suggest we continue questioning Wandra.'

'We?'

Marna didn't answer. Wandra had taken the opportunity to retreat indoors while Aiven was dealing with the children. Marna entered Wandra's hut and bowed her head to the old woman who had crouched beside the hearth.

'Do folk on the Mainland not call or knock before they enter a stranger's home?' Wandra scolded. Her breath held the earthy smell of mushrooms and Marna stayed a few feet away. She mumbled an apology. Kayleen's body had been laid in a cot and a man was standing over it with his head bowed. Marna recognised him as Borg, the girl's father. She hadn't seen his features in detail earlier, but now she could spot the family resemblance between him, Wandra and the dead girl.

Aiven entered the house behind her and closed the door. He nodded at Borg.

'Where's Sempal?' Marna asked. 'Have you shut him out?'

'He's talking to the children,' Aiven said with what Marna thought was a smirk. He moved past her to speak with Wandra. 'You were about to tell me where you found your granddaughter, before we were interrupted.'

Wandra stared at him with large, weepy eyes, but no words came. Borg got up to tower over her and it was clear his presence had a quietening effect on her tongue.

'What good is this doing?' Borg snapped. He banged his fists on the stone of the bed. 'Nothing can bring my daughter back. First my wife, and now this happens. The gods are not happy.'

'What happened to your wife?' Aiven picked up on the comment.

'She didn't recover after having Kayleen. The bleeding wouldn't stop and she died two full moons later.'

'I'm sorry,' Aiven softened his voice.

'That was six years ago.' Marna muttered her thoughts aloud. 'It can't be relevant.' Borg glared at her.

'Six years, aye, and not a day passes without me thinking of her.'

His words were spoken without the passion Marna felt should be behind them. Aiven clearly thought the same. 'I believe Marna is right,' he said. 'I do not think Kayleen's death has anything to do with her mother, or the gods.'

'If the gods are not displeased, why have they not sent us rain for weeks? The island does not have a loch to supply fresh water and for several months now there has been no spring water. We rely on the gift from the sky, which we collect in cisterns, but although we see clouds emptying over Rousay and Westray, our land remains dry. I saw that the spring was giving less and less, but despite my advice, Mooth and the other elders failed to ration the water collected in winter and it is almost done. Neighbours fight for the few muddy drops. I say again, the gods are angry.'

'I understand your problem with the water shortage, but that is not what we are discussing now,' Aiven tried again. 'If we knew where Kayleen was playing before she took ill…'

'Enough. You may be a healer in your own land, but you know nothing about our island and village. You cannot help us. Take your stones and leave.' Borg raised a fist. Aiven ducked although Borg showed no sign of lashing out with it.

'What of the cattle I cured?' Aiven's voice betrayed the irk he felt at Borg's lack of faith in his abilities.

'Cattle are unpredictable. Some days they give good milk, some days they don't.'

'And the sheep?'

'They are not hardy animals, in my opinion. When a spot of illness strikes them, sheep give up the will to live. But all illnesses pass.'

'He saved my dog Pip,' Marna put in before Aiven

could defend his methods.

'Hardly worth the trouble, by all accounts,' Borg snorted. Wandra struggled to her feet and Aiven moved to help her stand. She gripped his arm tightly then gave a shiver and let go.

'What's wrong mother?' Borg said.

Wandra shook her head, her gaze remaining on Aiven. She didn't answer, as if her tongue was held fast by an evil force. Borg's fists tightened.

'I think we should go,' Marna said to Aiven.

'I have more questions.'

Marna took his sleeve and pulled him backwards to the door. He stopped and reached up to touch the main stone above the entrance.

'Thank you for your hospitality.' He bent his head and back. Marna thought he was going to kiss the old woman's hand. Before he could, she opened the door and dragged him out.

'What do you think you were doing?' Aiven stuck his face close to hers as they stood outside. 'It is customary to leave a blessing on a house when you leave – in my land, at least.'

'You heard Borg; this is not your land. Any more questions and he would have knocked you cold,' Marna said. 'He has just lost his daughter.'

'And the longer we delay a proper investigation, the

less likely we are to discover why she died.'

'I'm not an idiot,' Marna answered. She took long strides to march away. He didn't follow.

Sempal was on his own, leaning against a wooden shed a little way off. He was watching her as she walked towards him.

'What's up?' he asked as she approached.

'Aaaah. I have never met such an annoying man.'

'Given your opinion of men, that's saying something,' Sempal answered with a smile.

'Did you find out about Kayleen from the children?' Marna said.

'They are all sad, but frightened as well. She was a healthy girl. There's talk of an evil spirit on the island.'

'Pah. Evil spirits are for story tellers and priests at the Ness. Did you speak to Vern?'

'I did, but she wouldn't answer. She seemed really scared. Her face went white when I asked where they were playing. She knows something, but she didn't tell me.'

'She knows about the evil spirit?'

'I don't think so, but I sensed she and Kayleen had a secret. She's frightened of getting into trouble from the adults.'

'And she considers you an adult,' Marna scoffed.

'It must be the beard.' Sempal stroked the few light hairs on his chin.

'Is that what they are?'

'Ha, ha. So what do we do now?'

'I don't know. I'm out of ideas. My head is whirling from seeing Fara again, with little Terese, arguing with Aiven, worrying about Pip and now Wandra and Borg. It has been a strange day.'

'Most days are strange when you're around,' Sempal joked.

'I haven't even got over the journey. I'll think of something after I've rested.'

'It seems a shame to waste the long evenings,' Sempal said.

'I need to sleep, but why don't you and your "new friend" Aiven take a stroll round the island?'

'What do you mean?' Sempal looked at her quizzically.

'Do I have to explain everything? Find out what he knows, and I mean *everything* he knows. Feel free to push him over a cliff afterwards, if he gets too obnoxious.'

'He saved Pip, remember.'

'You keep saying that. It is his only redeeming feature,' Marna allowed. 'We know nothing about him. My heart tells me he has more to do with this affair than he is letting on.'

Chapter 4

'What did you find out?'

Marna was eager to question Sempal the following morning, but she waited until they were alone. After breakfast, she made the excuse of searching for ochre to explore the island although she didn't expect to find any on the hilly moorland where they found themselves. Pip had been left with Fara, who was trying out the new whalebone needles Gerk had made. As well as collecting plants and rocks to prepare dyes, Marna wanted to do some snooping and the dog would get in the way.

A constant wind blew over the hill and Sempal raised his hand to his ear. Marna couldn't tell if he hadn't heard or if he was pretending he hadn't heard to tease her. She repeated the question with irritation.

'Nothing much,' Sempal answered, pausing to examine a pile of stones. 'It looks like this may be the opening to a tunnel or a cave. We aren't far from the coast.'

'Careful you don't fall,' Marna said, edging him closer to the hole then grabbing his arm, pretending to save him. 'Tell me what you learned about Aiven.'

'I didn't stay with him for long. He was keen to visit the brothers Serel and Bryne to throw gaming dice. They invited me to join them, but I made up an excuse. The tanner, Froink, was there. He stank like a week-dead seal. I couldn't bear sitting next to him.'

'The village needs a tanner. It isn't his fault the skins smell,' Marna said.

'No, but he could have washed after working. He's got a whole sea to do it in.' Sempal could tell Marna wasn't taking his excuse. 'It wasn't just that, I'm pretty useless at throwing dice. I never know when my luck is in and I should bet big.'

'Gaming isn't the only thing you are useless at.' Marna didn't hide her irritation.

'They said Borg would join them when he finished chopping dead branches. I could hardly start asking questions about his daughter, could I?' Marna made a face to suggest she didn't see why not. 'There was something I did find out that might interest you. Aiven came over from Wick with the traders we met in Barnhouse.'

'I already knew that,' Marna interrupted.

'To study at the Ness,' Sempal continued.

'Study what? Who with? For how long? Why isn't he there now instead of interfering here?'

'Slow down,' Sempal said. 'I can only answer one question at a time. He's here to study potion-making. I don't know who with, possibly Jolty or Quint. He is already an experienced healer, so when he heard about the trouble on Eynhallow, he thought he could help.'

'Naturally,' Marna scoffed.

'I got the impression he wanted to show off what he could do to the priests at the Ness.'

'That bunch of brainless, bald bampots.'

Sempal laughed. 'Be fair. People travel from far off to visit the Ness, bringing valuable flint, amber and woods to the island. The priests do have a reputation for their knowledge, especially of the stars.'

'What have lights in the sky got to do with healing?' Marna argued, but she made a face to show she grudgingly accepted what he said. 'Did Aiven tell you anything about the trouble here? Has he found out what killed the sheep?'

'You know what sheep are like. They don't show signs of illness until it is too late to save them.'

'That's what Borg said, but I get the feeling everyone is hiding something.'

'Aiven believes the sheep that died had been drinking sea water.'

'What makes him think that? Did he cut open a dead sheep?'

'Ugh!' Sempal stuck out his tongue, pretending to be sick. Marna rolled her eyes. 'I don't think so,' he said. 'But his conclusion makes sense. It hasn't rained on the island for weeks – what else can the sheep drink?'

'You shouldn't be complaining about a lack of rain,' Marna chided. 'You usually moan about getting wet.'

'No I don't.'

Their squabbling continued as they made their way back to the village. Sempal reminded Marna what she looked like when she fell in the stream. 'I thought I was seeing a dancing whale playing the drums,' he laughed.

'Be quiet,' Marna said.

'I'm only joking. I was concerned, really.'

'I said, be quiet. Something is going on over there.'

They had passed through the gates to the village and Marna pointed at the house ahead of them.

'That is Wandra's house,' Sempal said.

'And that is Aiven standing outside. I should have known. Wherever there's trouble, he's sure to be involved.'

'You don't know there is trouble…' A look from Marna quietened Sempal before he could finish.

A number of the villagers had stopped what they were doing, trying to look on without appearing nosy. Aiven was unsteady on his feet and was holding his head. Borg stepped out of the hut with his fists raised. When Aiven managed to steady himself, Borg lashed out, landing a punch in his opponent's midriff. Aiven crumbled to the ground. The onlookers took this as their cue to surround the men.

'Come on,' Marna rushed towards the fray.

'You always say you hate fighting,' Sempal groaned as he hobbled after her.

Marna edged her way to the front of the crowd, earning

disparaging looks and comments. Aiven was rolling on the ground holding his stomach, with no intention of getting up. There was blood clinging to the end of his beard, running down from a slit on his bottom lip. Borg stood over him, swinging his leg in preparation for a kick to Aiven's groin.

'Stop it,' Marna spoke up. When Borg ignored her she rattled her fists against his muscled arm. He would hardly have felt it, but he stared at her with burning eyes.

'Keep out of this, girl,' Borg said. He completed his kick, but with less force than initially intended. Aiven gave a grunt.

The disturbance had brought most of the village from their houses and workshops. Marna spotted Gerk and strode over to speak with him. 'Is this how your people resolve disputes in Eynhallow?'

Her voice was loud and there was mumbling among the villagers. One of the older men separated from the crowd and took steps to stand between Borg and Aiven. Borg was shaking with rage, but he moved back and gave the older man a curt nod.

'The girl is right,' the older man said. 'Arguments that cannot be solved between you without violence should be brought to the elders.'

'Is he the village priest?' Marna whispered to Gerk.

'That's Mooth, our oldest inhabitant. He is a wise man, but no priest. We have no need for priests on the island.'

41

'Until now,' Sempal added. He had joined Marna and Gerk at the front of the group of spectators.

Aiven had been helped to his feet by two of the women. He stood a few feet away from Borg and dusted down his tunic to hide his embarrassment.

'What made you hit our guest?' Mooth puffed up his bony chest and tried to sound important.

Borg stared round at his neighbours, catching faces with angry eyes. 'Jael, you have a daughter on Rousay with three children. Bryne, you want your son to carry on producing oil from the whale carcases that wash up, don't you?' The men muttered agreement. 'So why has our island started welcoming enemies who wish to harm our children?'

'I was offering to help,' Aiven raised his voice to speak over the crowd.

'You are the one causing the trouble.' Borg poked a stubby finger at Aiven.

'I don't understand. You shall have to explain yourself, Borg,' Mooth said.

'We know there was a problem with our livestock. Our sheep were dying and our cattle had stopped milking.'

'And I cured them,' Aiven said.

'You laid your magic stones on them, aye. No more sheep have taken ill, but at what price?'

'Two of my lambs have gone missing,' a woman in

the crowd spoke.

'And my daughter is dead,' Borg spoke over her. 'She bore the same dark marks on her skin that we saw on the faces of the sheep.'

'Many ailments show the same marks of body decay. You can't think…' Aiven began, but Borg hadn't finished.

'This wizard boasted about how he saved a dog from choking, before placing a hand on my mother. This morning my mother almost died. I watched helplessly when her face turned blue and she struggled for breath.'

'There was a hazelnut stuck in her gullet,' Aiven tried to make his voice heard over the grumbling. 'I needed to thump her back to dislodge it.'

'You wanted to finish your deadly deed,' Borg urged the villagers to jeer.

'Why would I harm your mother?' Aiven said.

'No doubt to steal the whalebone that was on the dresser. How can we know what evil is in your heart? We know nothing about you. Where did you come from? Why are you here?' Borg challenged.

The onlookers hushed and Mooth looked to Aiven for his reply.

'I am not a thief.' Aiven took a step towards Borg, but quickly retreated. 'I heard about the island's problems when I arrived at the Ness, from no less a man than Patro. We were discussing imbalances of the humours. Patro believes they are related to the movement of the moon, but I argued…' Mooth gave a loud cough, making it clear he had no interest in academic arguments. 'I have Patro's permission to be here,' Aiven finished.

At the mention of this the crowd began murmuring again. Marna made a disparaging noise with her tongue. 'He gives people permission to travel now,' she grumbled.

'If Patro of the Ness agreed…' Mooth began, unsure of what to say.

'We have only his word for that,' Borg interrupted. 'Anyone can claim to have Patro's permission. No doubt this girl would too, if it helped her friend here.' He nodded towards Marna. 'Although in her case it would be likely the priests sent her here to get rid of her.'

'Marna is a wise woman,' someone called from the crowd. 'She discovered who was responsible for the death of Fara's father.'

Others agreed and Marna was about to step forward, but Sempal held her back.

'Leave me alone, I have a plan,' Marna said, shaking free.

Sempal groaned and moved closer to Gerk. 'I hate it when she starts thinking.'

'That's because you have never tried it.' Marna overheard him.

'Actually, I do have an idea.' He shouldered his way

past Marna and stood before Mooth, with his back to Borg. 'There's a simple way to find out if Aiven was sent by the Ness.'

Mooth looked from Sempal to Aiven then Borg. 'Go on,' he allowed.

'Someone should go to the Ness and ask Patro.'

There was a communal gasp from the villagers and they took a step back. Borg gave a forced laugh and put his hands on his hips. 'I'm tired of listening to "simple" advice from strangers.'

'He has a point,' Mooth said. 'What is your name, boy?'

'Sempal.'

'We don't know this Simple,' someone in the crowd spoke. 'If we send him to the Ness, how will we know we can trust him to tell us what Patro says?'

'No, I didn't mean I should go,' Sempal clarified. 'I meant Borg could go there and ask about Aiven.'

'Fool, I can't leave my mother. Not after what happened to Kayleen.'

'Then send someone you trust from the island,' Sempal said.

The villagers turned their heads away and shuffled their feet in the dust. A few decided it was time to return to their work. No-one volunteered for the journey.

'Sempal's idea is a good one. What is the problem?'

Aiven asked. 'Why is no-one willing to go to the Ness?'

'That is proof that he has been lying,' Borg told the others. 'If he **had** met Patro at the Ness, he would understand why the priests are best avoided.'

'The Ness is a wonder to behold,' Aiven protested. 'The buildings rise from the earth like mountains spouting fire. Inside, the walls are as colourful as meadows of summer flowers. The men there are welcoming and intelligent. There is great wisdom in their words.'

'What about the women?' Marna raised her voice.

'The women too,' Aiven corrected himself. 'There were a few female scholars.'

'The priests welcome folk from foreign lands who bring them new knowledge and rare gifts, but I'm afraid your welcoming and intelligent men are too high and mighty to entertain the likes of us,' Mooth said. 'We are no closer to a solution.'

'What do you say, then?' Borg demanded.

Most of the onlookers were tiring of the show. There was silence while they waited for Mooth or anyone else to come up with an alternative suggestion. Ideas flirted through Marna's head, but she couldn't keep hold of one long enough to speak it. She knew it was ridiculous to think Aiven could transfer ailments from the animals to people, even with "magic" stones, but without an answer the islanders would accept, it was wiser not to voice her opinions.

'If no-one has anything else to say, I shall leave.' Aiven took a step away, but three hefty men blocked his path with folded arms. It was Gerk who broke the deadlock.

'I will travel to the Ness. Fara's brother Kali is studying there. He will give me a welcome, if Patro's priests do not. While I am there, I can ask about our drought problem. Perhaps one of the intelligent men studying there will have an answer to our problem.'

'Patro is clever, but I doubt even he can make it rain,' Aiven said.

'I wouldn't put it past him to think he can,' Marna whispered. The woman beside her gave a smile.

'I can set off this afternoon,' Gerk said.

'Can you?' Borg shoved past to stand close to Gerk, towering over him. 'You intend missing my daughter's funeral?'

'Surely the internment of the bones will not be for several months?' Marna's voice was loud enough for most of the crowd to hear. Several eyes turned to stare at her, but no-one answered.

'I will be back as soon as I can be. The journey would be faster if someone travelled with me,' Gerk answered.

'It only takes one man to row across the Sound,' Sempal said. 'And two can walk no faster than one.'

'Yes, but a companion keeps the spirits up. The

journey to the Ness is not such a harsh one at this time of year, but no-one can foretell if an accident will happen on the way. There is also the meeting with the priests,' Gerk said.

'Are you scared of them?' one of Gerk's friends quipped.

'Are you, Olan?' Gerk snapped back.

'I'm afraid of no-one, especially not big mouths who can't eat without someone lifting a spoon to their gullets.'

'Good. You can do the talking at the Ness.'

Realising he had somehow volunteered, Olan agreed to go with Gerk.

'What about the rope you were making for my boat?' the man Borg had called Jael asked.

'Your rope only needs to be greased. It will be ready before your next fishing trip,' Olan reassured Jael.

'We won't be away long,' Gerk said. He faced Borg. 'We will be back for Kayleen's funeral rites.'

Gerk and Olan avoided further questions by leaving the gathering to make preparations for the journey. Mooth puffed out his cheeks and blew out the air. This was a signal for the villagers to disperse.

'What about him?' Borg raised his voice to ensure Aiven wasn't forgotten as the others moved about their business.

'Ah, yes,' Mooth looked at Aiven. 'I shall have to ask

you to remain on the island until Gerk and Olan return.'

'I thought you might,' Aiven said. 'How long will "not long" be?'

Mooth moved his tongue around his mouth, dislodging seeds between his teeth. It was obvious he had no idea. He looked to the sky, but failed to find inspiration. 'I haven't ventured off the island since I lost my wife, but I don't expect Gerk and Olan will need more than three or four visits from the moon to complete their task,' he said.

'It took Marna and me two days from Skara Brae,' Sempal said. 'My cranky leg slows me, so Gerk and Olan should travel faster, but it will depend how long they are detained at the Ness. Patro may not agree to see them at once or he may be away on one of his many travels. I wouldn't expect them back for five days at least.'

'Five days for Kayleen to lie in the burial cairn before her spirit can be allowed to depart,' Borg grunted. He pointed a stumpy finger at Aiven and Marna noticed the tip was missing. 'In the meantime, we have to put up with him.'

Aiven turned his head and Marna couldn't see the response on his face, but Borg did. He raised his fists and took a step towards the stranger before catching Mooth's eye. 'Don't try to escape,' he warned. 'I'll be watching you.' He stood staring at Aiven for a moment before dropping his hands and striding back to his house. Marna spotted Wandra's face peeping round the door and looked away.

Mooth flapped his arms at the few remaining villagers, encouraging them to return to their activities. A younger woman approached him and linked arms, leading him to his house.

'His daughter, Neela,' Aiven explained as Marna watched them.

'Do you know everyone here?' Marna asked. She and Sempal were the only ones left with Aiven.

'Just about, and I'm not looking forward to another five days with them,' Aiven said.

'I reckon it will be more like seven or eight,' Sempal said. Aiven gave a groan.

'There's no need to thank us for saving you from a thrashing,' Marna said.

'You think I couldn't have held my own against that thug?'

'Do you want a serious answer?' Marna said. She didn't wait for his response. 'Will you try to leave the island?'

'I'm not afraid of Borg, but I respect Mooth and I believe in obeying the rules of the people I am living with. It would be wrong to leave before Gerk and his friend return from the Ness and prove my innocence. How long will you and Sempal stay here?'

'As long as we want to.' Marna's reply was sharp. She didn't like his tone. 'What is it to you?'

'Nothing,' Aiven tried to calm her. 'I have no wish to influence your plans.'

'We intend going home tomorrow,' Sempal said.

'But our plans have changed,' Marna added.

'Oh?' Sempal twisted to face her and his weak foot gave way beneath him. He stumbled forwards, but managed to right himself before landing on his face by grabbing onto Marna's shawl. The bone clip holding it sprang loose and fell off. Aiven hid his laugh by bending to retrieve it. She snatched it from his fingers and inspected it.

'With Gerk gone, Fara will need help with the baby,' she said.

'When did you become keen to help with babies?' Sempal said.

'They are no different from clumsy adults,' Marna answered. The brooch appeared undamaged and she fastened it to her shawl. 'I look after your nephew Boda for Henjar when she is tired. I can prepare food. My mother taught me about flavouring plain foods with herbs. I can also make sure the fire doesn't go out while it cooks,' she explained, jerking her head towards Aiven as she spoke, as if he couldn't see her.

'I see,' Sempal said, but his expression spoke otherwise.

Chapter 5

'If I could interrupt your cosy little chat,' Aiven stepped
between Marna and Sempal. 'I wondered, since I don't
seem to be welcome anywhere, if you could persuade Fara
to let me stay with you.' He looked at Sempal rather than
Marna. 'There should be space, with Gerk away and I'm
sure he wouldn't mind.'

'Wouldn't he? I don't know Gerk that well,' Sempal
began.

'But obviously Aiven can tell what people are
thinking,' Marna said. She took Sempal by the arm and led
him a few feet away. 'Don't encourage Aiven. The heather
is dry. He can make a bed on the moor.'

'It may be dry, but the moor is open and the winds are
strong. He has nowhere else to sleep.'

'That doesn't mean he has to tag along with us.' Marna
didn't lower her voice. She was aware Aiven was listening,
but he didn't interrupt them.

'He did save Pip,' Sempal said.

'Why do you always bring that up?' Marna said. 'All
right,' she relented. 'I'll speak with Fara.'

'Thank you.' Aiven gave her a smile. 'I'll try not to tag
on to you, but I sense you are keen to find out what
happened to the girl, or am I wrong?' Aiven said.

'Her name was Kayleen.'

Aiven inclined his head. 'Of course, I meant no disrespect. Since I will be here for the foreseeable future, I would like to assist you. I too am interested to know how…Kayleen… died.'

'Interested? Kayleen's death isn't a puzzle for you to work out while you wait to leave.'

'I am sorry for the girl and her family, but we can't bring her back. Finding out what happened may help the others.'

'The others?' Sempal said. 'You think more people are at risk?'

'It's what he wants,' Marna answered. 'That will give him an exciting tale to tell when he gets back to the Ness. He can boast about how he solved the mystery to Patro.'

'You have a poor opinion of me. I want to help.' Aiven forced a smile that was too broad to be genuine. 'It's what I do.'

Marna snorted and walked off. She expected Sempal to follow. When he didn't, she turned round.

'Hey, it's raining,' Sempal said. He had his arm out, grasping at the air. It took a moment before Marna felt a speckle of water on her face.

'Maybe the gods aren't so angry after all,' Aiven said.

'Or maybe this is their little joke,' Marna answered. 'You can't call three drops of water rain. I don't see dark clouds overhead.'

'Still, we should take shelter,' Sempal said. He allowed Marna to walk ahead, following a short distance behind with Aiven. She heard Aiven remark that he admired a fiery woman. A caustic reply was on her tongue, but she decided to pretend she wasn't listening. He wasn't worth wasting time over. They returned to Fara's house.

Fara had placed a bowl outside to collect the rainwater, but the drops amounted to little more than a covering of the bottom.

'Every little helps, I suppose,' she said.

Gerk was packing a spare tunic, stone knife and dried meat into a sack. Fara handed him a skin to collect drinking water from the lochs on the mainland. Marna caught a glint of annoyance on Fara's face when she spotted Aiven, but she turned away to hide her displeasure. She wasn't overjoyed at the idea of having him stay, but Gerk agreed, so she busied herself making space and sorting heather and skins for him to sleep on. Pip followed her round the house, his nose touching her legs, until he decided to make a nest among the skins.

'That's me ready to go,' Gerk said. Fara was re-arranging seating stones, but she stopped to attend to her husband, brushing some dirt from his tunic.

'You can't present yourself at the Ness looking like a country bumpkin. Have you got everything you will need?'

'I'm as prepared as I ever will be. I remember what

54

your father told me about the Ness.'

Fara smiled.

'Oh, what did Jona have to say about it?' Marna was curious.

'Unfit words for sensitive ears,' Gerk replied. Marna made a tutting noise through her teeth to show she wasn't as naïve as he imagined.

'I have heard about Jona from other priests,' Aiven said. 'I wish I had met him.'

'He would have eaten you for breakfast,' Marna grumbled.

'My father was known for speaking nonsense,' Fara said. She gave Gerk a kiss on the cheek and he put a hand on her waist. 'At least the Sound isn't too rough at this time of year. You should have a safe crossing.'

'I'll return to you and Terese as soon as I can.' Gerk moved to smile at the sleeping child, but Fara gestured to him not to wake her.

The door opened and Olan appeared swinging his bag. The room was full and it hit Sempal. 'Sorry, didn't see you,' he apologised.

'Come on, let's go,' Gerk said.

The men clattered out of the house. The farewells had disturbed Terese and she began crying. Fara lifted her from her cot and rocked her in her arms.

'We should give you peace,' Marna hinted to Aiven

and Sempal.

'No need for that now,' Fara said, cuttingly.

'If the rain is off, we could take a walk round the island,' Aiven said. 'We could watch Olan and Gerk's boat leave.'

'What good will that do?' Sempal said. 'It won't speed their journey. Besides, I walked around the island earlier.'

'You could try to work out what has happened to our spring,' Fara suggested. 'Some of the older people in the village believe it may not have dried up, but merely altered its route underground.'

'Your folk have already searched the island,' Sempal said, trying to think of a reason to avoid the exercise.

'Perhaps with Aiven's stones…'

'…They are not all-powerful,' Aiven interrupted. 'But we can keep our eyes open. What about you, Marna? Will you come with us?'

'I have Fara's cloak to dye,' she said.

Aiven laughed. 'It's clear the women don't want us hanging round the house with them.'

'Ah.' Sempal looked round the room, crowded with seal skins, cooking pots and baby's toys. 'Do you want us to take Pip?' he asked Marna.

'Not today. He can stay with me.'

'You spoil him. He'll grow into a fat house dog,'

Aiven said.

'I don't trust you to look after him,' Marna said bluntly.

The men left. The rain had been nothing more than a light shower and the sun had dried the ground. Marna expected Aiven and Sempal to stay out most of the day, but they returned an hour later. She had been crushing ochre into powder and her hands were stained brown. Fara had shooed her outside to wash in the sea before she left marks on the dresser and she met Sempal and Aiven as they approached the house.

'I thought you were dyeing,' Sempal said, nudging Aiven to laugh with him at his joke. Aiven thought it wiser not to.

'Fara is preparing dinner,' Marna said. 'She doesn't want it tasting of pigment. Besides, I've disturbed her enough, asking questions.'

'What questions?' Aiven said, trying not to sound too eager for an answer.

'About the island funeral rituals. At Skara Brae we leave the bodies on the dunes until the vital tissues are removed and only the bones remain.' Sempal curled his tongue and stuck it out in disgust. He had always been squeamish about such things. Marna continued. 'We place these in tombs and celebrate the spirit's departure to the after world.'

'As we do in my village,' Aiven said.

'It seems the custom is different here. The villagers bury the whole body in their cairns, not long after they have died. They preserve them with fresh smelling plants.'

'That's why Borg was annoyed that Gerk and Olan were leaving the island,' Sempal said.

'It is longer to wait than usual, but it gives the villagers time to make funeral vases,' Fara said. 'Sorry, I couldn't help overhearing.'

'Funeral vases,' Sempal said, moving his hands to indicate whole bodies being squeezed into them. 'I haven't heard of those.' He looked to Marna and Aiven.

'Me neither,' they said together.

'They are clay pots with tiny holes. We fill them with oil and burn them in the cairn,' Fara explained. The smoke flows out the openings. The movement can be beautiful to watch and sweet smelling if the right herbs are burned.'

'At least you have plenty of whale oil on the island,' Aiven said with a hint of envy.

'Indeed. Dinner won't be long,' Fara said. 'I've made broth, with cheese and hazelnuts on oatcakes.'

Sempal licked his lips. 'Just as well we came back early,' he said. 'I wouldn't want to miss that.'

'Why **are** you back so soon?' Marna asked. 'Has anything happened?'

'We were followed round the cliffs by Borg,' Sempal

said. 'I got the impression he thought I was trying to help Aiven escape in my boat.'

'Escape in *your* boat? Nobody is that desperate,' Marna said.

'Thanks.'

'It is going to be a long five days,' Aiven said.

'Why don't you tell us adventure stories after dinner, Sempal?' Fara asked. 'I could invite Gora over with her pipes. She is Gerk's cousin and a brilliant musician. Everybody says so, even people from Rousay and they know how to make a tune.'

'That sounds good, but Aiven is further travelled than I am,' Sempal said. 'He has celebrated mid-winter at the Stones of Callanish. I imagine he has wondrous tales to tell of the veil between the worlds there.'

'That's settled then,' Fara said before Aiven could object. 'You can both entertain us.' She stopped stirring the broth and handed Sempal the spoon. 'Watch the soup while I nip across and ask Gora and her family.'

'Can't you do that after dinner?' Sempal said.

'I need to do it before you change your minds.'

'We hadn't actually agreed,' Sempal argued, but Fara was already out of the hut. He stuck the spoon in the pot that was resting on the fire and swirled it in the glutinous mixture. Drops of broth splattered up onto his tunic and he jumped back.

'It will just be a family gathering, won't it?' Aiven asked.

'Of course,' Marna answered with a glint in her eyes. She took the spoon from Sempal, smelt the soup and reached for a bowl of dried, chopped leaves sitting near the hearth. She added a generous handful of leaves to the pot and stirred.

'I don't think I trust you,' Aiven said.

'These are herbs, to add flavour,' Marna explained.

'I meant about it being family only tonight.'

'The trouble is, everyone on the island is related in some way. It's one big family,' Sempal said.

'I thought as much.'

'It will be a chance for you to get back on good terms with the islanders,' Marna said. 'And show how clever you are.'

Aiven gave a grunt then sniffed the air. 'Are you sure you know what you are doing with that broth? Shouldn't there be liquid in the pot?'

'Aargh,' Marna cried.

Fara returned to rescue the broth and the pot. She took the spoon from her and whirled it round the mixture, releasing the crusts forming on the sides. 'Everything is arranged,' she said. 'Gora and the others are happy to come along.' She removed the spoon from the pot. A dollop of something black stuck to the edges. 'Now, who wants…soup?'

'Not for me,' Aiven said, holding his abdomen. 'I have stomach cramps. I feel sick.'

'That's what you get when you mess with Borg,' Fara said. She scraped the soup from the pot and served the others portions with the oatcakes. They ate in silence until Terese began bawling.

'She's been fed,' Fara said. 'She may need fresh air. I'll take her outside, away from the smoke for a while.'

Marna waited until Fara left before calling Pip to her side and feeding him her uneaten broth.

'What have we got ourselves into?' Aiven asked Sempal. 'I don't know what these storytelling evenings are like here, but back home they can be wild nights, usually ending with a fight and someone being seriously injured. I've got a weird feeling on this occasion it is likely to be me.'

'We are civilised people,' Marna said. 'We can enjoy ourselves without resorting to violence.'

'Really?'

'Marna is right,' Sempal said, allowing Pip to take the burnt scraps from his dish. 'We tell a few stories, drink ale and sing. It only gets wild if there's dancing – and it is the women to blame for that.'

'If women are involved, then there is bound to be fighting,' Aiven said. He looked round the room. 'There will hardly be space for everyone to sit in here, never mind dance.'

'It's a nice evening. We can gather outside,' Sempal said.

Fara had been thinking much the same while she was taking her daughter for a stroll. She returned to catch Sempal munching the piece of cheese she'd kept for Gerk's return. 'The villagers are assembling in the centre,' she told them. 'Mooth has instructed some of the youngsters to mark out a circle with loose stones.'

'Why?' Aiven asked.

'If we gather inside the circle, it will seem cosier,' Fara answered, clearly thinking her guest was an idiot not to know. 'You could light a fire, Marna. We don't need one for warmth, but I like watching the flames when listening to tales of far-off lands and sea monsters.'

'There will be no tales of monsters. A young girl has died. I shall tell a story suitable for the occasion. A story set here in Orkney,' Sempal said.

'We do have some good island tales,' Fara didn't hide her disappointment. She turned to Aiven. 'What story will you tell?'

'You will have to wait and hear it with the others,' Aiven answered.

Marna washed the soup pot and bowls while Fara wrapped Terese in warmer skins for the evening. Before she left Fara combed her hair with a whalebone comb then offered it to Marna.

'You're lucky having pots of whale bone,' Marna said.

'The whales often get into trouble coming up the Sound from the ocean,' Fara replied. 'The currents are deceptive. We trade the excess oil and bone with the farmers on the mainland. It is how we survive.'

While they waited for Marna and Fara to get ready, Sempal and Aiven discussed which stories to tell. There was a moment of tension when they realised the Mighty Mammoth in Aiven's story was the same as the Fantastic Fish in Sempal's. Fara solved the problem by suggesting they combine the story and each take a role.

The children of the village had laid out a stone ring, as Fara described. The circle bulged at one point and a number of the smaller stones were hard to see among the dried out vegetation, but everyone admired the handiwork. Mooth was standing beside two larger stones that had been laid further apart to make an entrance to the make-shift arena. The villagers arrived in family groups. They offered Mooth greetings and handed him small gifts. Beads and arrow heads were cheerfully accepted.

'Why are they doing that?' Marna asked Fara.

'It's a tradition on the island,' Fara explained. 'Every family has to give the eldest villager a dash or they don't get in. It doesn't have to be valuable. A handful of last autumn's barley heads or a painted stone will keep him happy.'

Mooth had his hands out as they approached him. He smiled a toothless welcome.

'We're the ones telling the stories,' Sempal said.

Mooth's grin narrowed and he raised his cupped hands higher towards Sempal's face.

'I don't think that matters,' Marna said. 'Does anybody have anything we can give?'

'Here,' Aiven searched in the folds of his tunic and found a handful of berries. 'I gathered these on the hill earlier today.'

Marna looked at him accusingly. 'Eating berries, no wonder you had stomach cramps. It doesn't look like you intended sharing them.'

'I meant to. It slipped my mind that I had them until now.'

The berries were squashed from being in Aiven's tunic, but Mooth accepted them with a nod and allowed them to pass into the circle. As well as marking out the circle, the children had gathered dry twigs and driftwood and placed them in a heap in the centre of the ring, stuffing moss between the gaps. Marna knelt beside the bundle and lit a fire with her wooden drill.

'Mmm…want any oil…mm.' Mooth was munching on the berries and his advice was lost.

'Need help?' Sempal asked, fearing Marna was taking longer than usual to kindle the flames.

'If I do, I'll ask,' Marna replied brusquely.

The dried moss caught a spark and Marna nursed it into a flame. While the fire grew, Fara introduced her guests. Most of the villagers had heard of Sempal's storytelling ability and he was the first to speak. He stood with his back to the fire and the flames created a lively background effect. His story was set in Westray, one of the northern islands in the group. It involved a young girl who talked to the seal people. Marna had heard it several times, but Sempal always changed the ending to add variety. She wondered which one he would use – obviously not the version where the girl drowned. Her attention was drawn to a disturbance at the edge of the circle.

A group of the older children were bunched round something writhing on the ground, an injured bird or animal, she suspected. She crept towards the spot without interrupting the story, but a number of the villagers had also spotted what was going on. Their muttering rose over Sempal's story.

'It's Mooth,' a young woman cried.

'What's wrong?' Sempal stopped his tale to look over. Marna gave up crawling and rushed to the old man's side, shooing the children away. Pink saliva was bubbling from his mouth and his eyes were rolled back in their sockets to

65

show the whites.

'A devil has possessed him,' one of the boys said.

'Nonsense,' Marna said. She tried to raise the old man's head, but it was heavy and flopped to the ground. She leant over to listen for his heart, but heard nothing.

'Someone should call for Borg,' Gora said. 'He is a village elder.'

There was no need. Borg and his mother weren't at the gathering, but they had heard the disturbance and had come out of their house to see what was happening. Borg ran to where Mooth lay. Marna moved aside as he leant next to Mooth and poked two fingers against his eye sockets.

'Is he dead?' Marna asked.

Borg wiped the saliva that had dribbled from the old man's mouth to his chin with the sleeve of his tunic. He rubbed the gooey material that stuck to his wrists on the ground then stood up to address the gathering. He raised his arms and held them in the air until he had everyone's ear. 'Mooth is dead. He has been poisoned by the berries he ate.'

'The ones Aiven gave him?' Sempal asked.

There was a hush, broken only by a hiss from the fire. Borg searched for Aiven with his eyes and gave him a cold stare. 'Mooth is dead,' he repeated, slowly directing a finger to point at Aiven. 'And there is the culprit.'

Chapter 6

The jolly mood of the story-telling gathering changed to
one of anger and fear. Aiven was set upon by several dark-
faced villagers who restrained his arms behind his back
until others brought ropes. He tried to reason with his
attackers, but no-one wanted to listen and hearing his voice
increased their hostility. He managed to jostle his arms free,
but the victory was short-lived. Out-numbered before he
could flee, he was forced to the ground where his hands and
feet were bound tight.

'Shouldn't we help him?' Marna said to Sempal, who
was keeping back from the action.

'I don't think that would be a good idea,' Sempal
replied. 'Not unless you want us tied up and beaten too.'

'Don't be stupid.' She stepped forward and appealed to
the villagers. 'You should wait until Gerk comes back with
word from Patro before you do anything rash.'

'What does Patro know or care about what happens
here?' Borg replied.

'He will pay attention if you kill a stranger he has
welcomed as a guest.'

Borg moved his bottom jaw from side to side as he
considered Marna's words. The others were watching him,
waiting for an answer. 'Throw the devil in the pit,' he
ordered.

Aiven was manhandled to his feet by three men and dragged out of the village towards a pit that the islanders had dug to trap wild pigs brought over the previous autumn to forage on the hillside. The crowd followed and cheered as Aiven was pushed over the edge and landed face down on the hard ground. He lay there, winded by the attack. The pit wasn't so deep that Aiven couldn't have escaped, if his hands weren't tied behind his back and if his feet were free and Borg felt the need for a guard. He instructed a man called Serel to take the first watch.

'I guess that's the evening's entertainment over,' Fara said, once she found Marna and Sempal.

'Not for some people,' Marna said. A number of the village youth were crowing over the pit, spitting on Aiven and hurling insults.

'He did give Mooth the berries,' Fara said. 'Perhaps the reason he didn't share them with us was because he knew they were poisoned.'

'Why would Aiven poison Mooth?' Marna asked.

Fara pushed out her bottom lip and shrugged. She was carrying Terese and the baby began to cry. 'I'd better put her to bed,' she said.

'We could all do with a good night's sleep,' Marna agreed.

'What about Aiven?' Sempal asked.

'There's nothing we can do. I'll think of a plan in the

morning,' Marna ran her fingers through her hair. The wind had tangled it into a knotted mass that had captured goose grass seeds. She wasn't convinced herself, but her confidence persuaded the others. They left the pit and walked back to the house.

Marna spent a restless night coming up with ideas that fell apart when she thought of the problems. By sunrise she had to admit she was no nearer finding a way to help Aiven, but she was unwilling to admit this to Sempal. She rose before him and pretended to be busy arranging seal skins while he slurped the gruel Fara prepared for breakfast.

'What's the plan?' Sempal asked.

'I need to see where Aiven found the berries,' Marna decided. 'You were with him. Did you pick any?'

Sempal took another mouthful of gruel and swallowed while he thought. 'I can't remember where they were - up the hill, somewhere. Most of the bushes were shrivelled due to the lack of rain and the birds had snaffled whatever berries there were. Aiven found a bush partly hidden between two boulders. He ate a handful of the berries, said they were good then stuffed the rest in his pocket.'

'He didn't offer you any?'

Sempal shook his head. 'I think he wanted to keep them for you. They would have been good with this porridge.'

'Poisoned berries - humph,' Marna made a noise in her

throat. She picked up her shawl and walked to the door. Pip followed Marna out and she didn't stop him. Sempal scurried after them, munching on a slice of flat bread. He had dipped it in the remains of the gruel and sloppy pieces of cereal dribbled onto his tunic. He stopped to wipe his chin and clothes. Marna reached the edge of the village before him and waited, leaning against a wood shed.

'The pit isn't far away. Shouldn't we see how Aiven is?' Sempal asked.

'What good will it do? I can't ask questions with a guard standing over him.'

'I thought he would want breakfast. I can't imagine Borg providing any.'

'His stomach will have to wait.'

'He didn't eat dinner yesterday.'

'That was his fault.' Marna was unsympathetic.

'You think it was the berries that gave him the stomach pains he complained of?' Sempal said.

'That's what happens when you guzzle in private. So, where did you find them?' Marna repeated.

'Up there.' Sempal pointed to the small hill in the centre of the island. Marna strode off, with Sempal close behind. The heather and scrub were dry and they brushed against Marna's ankles. She stopped to rub her skin and Pip gave her a helpful lick.

'Oh no, what does *he* want?'

Sempal looked round. Borg and a man she recognised from the night before marched up to them.

'Where are you going?' Borg demanded.

'I'm looking for club moss,' Marna answered, giving Sempal a look that he knew meant not to argue with her.

'That takes two of you, does it? What do you want it for?' Borg said.

Marna hesitated. The moss had been the first plant she'd spotted when she looked down.'

'Bedding,' Sempal answered. 'The cots in Gerk's house are horribly hard.' He gave his back a rub.

'I heard Mainlanders were soft,' Borg's companion said.

Borg laughed. 'You'll find some alongside the shore.'

'I've found some here,' Marna said.

'You can't come up here,' the second man said.

'Why not?' Marna asked, trying to squint past the men to see what they were protecting.

'No-one is allowed on the hill,' Borg said.

'That isn't an answer,' Marna said. Her voice had an aggressive edge which Pip picked up on. He snarled at the men from between her legs. Borg eyed the dog darkly. Sempal put an arm on Marna's shoulder to pull her away, but she pushed it off.

'There is evil here,' Borg's companion said.

'You don't believe that,' Marna said. Most of the evil

71

was coming from the man. He stank of rotten flesh and sour ale.

'You can mock, if you wish to end up like Mooth.'

Marna realised the man believed the story. She turned to Borg.

'Froink speaks the truth,' Borg said. 'The land here has been touched by a plague.' He thrust his hands out to demonstrate, as if he were addressing the village council. 'It is clear now that was the reason our animals took ill. It is why our people are dying.'

'I thought last night you blamed Aiven,' Sempal said. 'What has a plague got to do with him?'

Borg curled the side of his lip.

'You can't think he cast a spell on the land. Your cattle were ill before he arrived on the island,' Marna said.

'We'll find out what his intentions are after we question him,' Borg said. Froink sneered and fingered the stone knife at his belt.

'I think we should leave,' Sempal said to Marna.

Marna stood her ground, but she could think of nothing to say that would get her past Borg and Froink. There were a few stunted trees dotted on the hillside, but most of the ground was open, making it difficult for them to slip round the back and sneak up out of the view of the men. Borg would make sure every approach was protected.

'Some people just don't want to be helped,' she

muttered to Sempal, loud enough for the men to hear. Sempal took hold of her arm and urged her away. She could feel Borg's eyes on her back as they made their way down the hill. When they neared the village, Fara came running out to greet them.

'What's wrong? Is it Terese?' Marna couldn't see the baby in the folds of Fara's shawl and she felt a lump in her throat.

'She's fine, asleep in her cot. I've come about my neighbour Jael. He has taken ill through the night, shaking with fever. His family are afraid. I thought of your mother's potion.'

'It was all ruined by the water, remember,' Marna admitted.

'Can't you make some more? I told his wife you would sort things out.'

Marna sensed her disappointment. 'I do know something of my mother's methods. Perhaps I can find plants on the island that will help. Has Jael been sick or are his bowels overactive?'

'No.'

'Has he brought any green phlegm up from his throat?'

'I don't think so.'

'Does he have headaches or hear ringing in his ears?' Marna asked.

'I don't know,' Fara admitted.

'What is the problem?'

'His appetite has gone and his limbs are stiff. He can't move his lower body,' Fara said. 'Can you help?'

'I'm not familiar with the signs. I don't have my mother's skill, but I can do my best.'

'Can I tell Jael's family you will look at him?'

Marna agreed and Fara rushed off.

'My mother would know which plants to use,' Marna said to Sempal. 'I've seen her use mint and feverfew in her mixtures. They might not cure Jael, but they won't do any harm.'

'You could ask Aiven for help,' Sempal suggested.

'He is accused of poisoning Mooth. What would people say if I took his advice and Jael got worse?'

'I didn't think of that.'

It wasn't long before Fara was back, keen to hustle Marna to the patient's house.

'Let me see what plants you have at home,' Marna said.

Apart from dried dock leaves and thrift, there weren't any medicinal plant ingredients in Fara's house.

'I can gather what you need,' Fara volunteered.

'I'll speak with Jael and his wife first. Hopefully I can narrow down the possible causes. Where does he live?'

Jael's house was next to Wandra's. Fara went with Marna to help. News travelled in the village and neighbours

74

were curious to know what was happening. A small group had gathered at Jael's door. Fara had exaggerated stories of how Marna had solved problems in her own village and had even nicknamed her the Wise Woman of Skara Brae. The islanders were keen to see what she could do.

Jael was lying with his body prone. His legs were too large for the cot and were raised to balance on the stone bed-end. He had thrown aside the skins covering him and his wife had tried to replace them. Marna questioned his wife, but her answers were vague and confused. She said he was hot and cold, restless and sleeping, thirsty and unwilling to take water.

Marna took her time examining the house before turning her attention to her patient. The room was bright and tidy. Pots were covered and stored on the dresser. The room was warm and the hearth fire unlit, allowing air to circulate round the house. The reed mats were brushed free of mud and sawdust. Jael was the village carpenter and odd pieces of boxes and benches carved from drift wood and hazel branches leant against the wall

Jael's symptoms were hard to assess. He was no longer a young man, but he couldn't be regarded as old. His face was lined, but the skin looked healthy. He had kicked away the skins with his feet, despite his wife claiming he couldn't move his legs. It was hard to come to a conclusion.

'Is it the same as Mooth?' Jael's wife asked with a

shaking voice.

'I don't think so,' Marna answered. There was certainly no pink foam at his mouth. She rubbed her chin, trying to remember what her mother taught her. 'Did he eat any berries?'

'He hasn't eaten anything. That's the problem.'

A voice in her head told Marna she should look in his mouth, but she wasn't keen, especially after leaning over him and being knocked back by the smell of rotten fish from his breath.

'My husband was one of the men who captured and tied up the wizard. Have the demons he consorts with put a curse on him?'

'Aiven is not a wizard and there are no demons on this island.' Marna said, exasperated. The woman pulled her shawl close and gave a look to show she not only didn't believe Marna, but suspected her of being in league with the dark forces. Marna turned to Fara who was standing at the door, relating what was going on to the on-lookers. 'I'll need mint,' she said.

'I know who has some,' Fara answered. She gestured to the gathering to clear a path. She was barely out the door when she bumped into Gora. It took a moment to untangle limbs.

'Is Marna here?' Gora spoke quickly, looking over Fara's shoulder into the room.

'Why do you want to know?' Marna stepped towards her.

'My mother is sick. Her hair has turned white overnight.'

'Overnight?' Marna looked puzzled.

Fara turned to ask, 'Will you need more mint?'

'No,' Marna said. 'I need my mother.'

Chapter 7

It took Gerk and Olan an hour to battle the waves in the
Sound and steer their craft along the coast to land near
Evie. The tide made manoeuvring difficult, but Olan was an
experienced seaman. Gerk rubbed the blisters on his fingers
as Olan pulled the boat onto the bank.

'Give me a hand,' Olan called as he gathered seaweed
to cover the boat.

'I don't see the point,' Gerk said. 'We will be back for
it soon enough.'

'We'll be away long enough for the local youths to
think it fun to take it out fishing one evening,' Olan
answered heaving a strand of kelp over the bow.

Gerk made a show of helping and when the job was
done they both collapsed on the sand. Gerk was breathing
heavily.

'You farmers are like girls,' Olan laughed. 'No
stamina.'

Gerk sat up and sniffed his clothes. Olan's boat was
constructed from cattle skins stretched over willow and he
made it watertight using animal fat. It worked well, except
that by the end of the journey Gerk smelt like a cow and the
seaweed tang clung to his skin.

'We can't go to the Ness like this,' he protested.

'There's no point bathing here,' Olan answered.

'We've got a hike over the moor, between the hills, round the loch and through the bog before we get to the Ness. We can wash in the loch when we get there.'

Gerk wasn't persuaded. 'If, as you say, we have a long trek, the sun will have gone down before we reach the loch. There are currents in the water and weeds to tangle round limbs and drag bodies under. It isn't safe bathing at night.'

'Then the priests will have to take me as I am,' Olan declared. 'My parents never complain and I can be out at sea for longer periods than this.'

Gerk imagined his friend's parents must have lost their sense of smell years before. 'No wonder you haven't found a wife,' he said.

'I'm waiting for someone special.'

Gerk left Olan lying on the beach while he washed in the sea. The afternoon was warm and his clothes would dry while they walked.

'I don't suppose you know anyone who lives along the way?' Olan asked. 'One of Fara's family or friends? I wouldn't mind stopping for a bowl of stew and a beaker of ale.'

'Fara has friends in Barnhouse, but that would add another mile to our journey. We need to get to the Ness as quickly as we can.'

Olan chuckled.

'What is it now?'

'Listen to yourself. Why do we need to get to the Ness as quickly as we can? To persuade some big-headed, self-appointed High Priest who has no time for anyone but himself that a stranger nobody knows anything about is innocent of… what, witchcraft? Patro will laugh in our faces, if he bothers looking at our faces, which I doubt. We should turn back now.'

'And tell our people what? We said we would try,' Gerk answered.

'This might be funny if Patro didn't have an army of armed priests at his disposal. After he has amused himself at our expense, he will have us beaten as an example to others who come wasting his time. No-one would know if we spend a couple of days here then rowed home and said Patro refused to speak with us.'

'They might not guess straight away, but Fara and her brother are close. The next time they get together she will ask Kali about the meeting and he will tell her we didn't show up.' Olan wasn't convinced. Gerk thought of a new argument. 'If Aiven *is* a magician, his band of goblins will have followed us to keep watch.'

'Why don't *they* rescue him?' Olan huffed. He took a moment to consider who he feared more, Patro and his priests or Aiven and his magic. 'We'd better get started,' he said gruffly.

The men kept a good pace, stopping only to refill their

water pouches from the loch and eat the food Fara had packed for them. The sun was low, but it was nearing mid summer when the days extended into the night. The view ahead was still visible as they reached the top of a small hill.

'Is that it?' Olan sounded disappointed as he pointed towards to a raised area of land containing hewn stones surrounded by a ditch.

'That must be the Ring of Bookan,' Gerk said. 'Fara told me about it. There's a causeway from it towards the Ness.'

'I'm not going in there.'

'You'd rather sink in the bog?'

'Maybe.' Olan walked ahead of Gerk towards the top of the hill to look down to where the loch of Stenness and the marshland of Harray loch could both be seen. He stopped.

'Wow.' His eyes were wide. He rubbed them and looked again. 'Wow, wow, wow.'

Gerk caught up with Olan and surveyed the scene. He had seen the Ness once before, although the priests were constantly adding or changing buildings. He knew his friend hadn't been there. Although the settlement was often spoken about on Eynhallow, it had more the status of a dream world, that didn't properly exist.

'It's like…' Olan was lost for words. 'As if our village

81

covered our whole island and stretched into the sea,' he said. 'Whoooa' His eyes widened. 'I didn't think so many cows existed in the world.'

'They need cattle for their feasts,' Gerk explained.

'I hope one is planned for some time soon,' Olan said. 'Hey, what is going on there?'

'It looks like a work party building an earthen wall,' Gerk replied.

'Let's speak with them.' Olan strode ahead, but after a few minutes his feet sank into the ground.

'I warned you of the bog,' Gerk laughed, offering his friend a hand to free himself.

They retraced their steps and made their way to the ring where the raised land was drier underfoot. It wasn't long before they passed the new ring of stones being constructed at Brodgar. Olan blew out his breath in wonder, taking a detour from the path to touch each stone in turn.

'Marna's brother Thork helped raise one of them,' Gerk boasted.

'He would,' Olan said. 'The mainland folk have nothing better to do with their time.'

'We'd better get moving or the priests will send a delegation to arrest us,' Gerk said.

Olan and Gerk rejoined the path and made their way towards the walls of the city. The people they had seen working on the dyke being built across the peninsular had gone. Olan spotted some stragglers making their way to a group of buildings outside the main area.

'We could spend the night there,' he suggested. 'Have hot food and a good sleep before meeting the priests.'

'Putting it off won't help,' Gerk wasn't fooled. 'I'd rather get it done with and return to Fara as soon as we can.'

'We should have brought an offering,' Olan said. 'Did Fara give you anything?'

Gerk checked in his bag. 'It's not like her to overlook something like that, but her head has been all over the place since the baby was born. I was hoping having her friend Marna to stay would help.'

Olan opened a felt pouch attached to his belt. 'I have two flints.'

'That's like offering a blade of grass to a cow,' Gerk said. 'Still, if the priests don't want them, Kali can use them. He's learning to be a fire-maker.'

'Shouldn't he have learned that by now? Hasn't he been here for a year?'

'I suppose,' Gerk said. 'He's not the brightest member of Fara's family. I think he is more interested in the stars and aligning stones to capture the sunlight than domestic tasks.'

'What good does that do?' Olan said. 'It sounds like a waste of time. Are you sure your brother-in-law isn't just afraid of real work?'

'I would keep that opinion to yourself while you are here,' Gerk warned. 'Patro and his priests are easily upset by criticism.'

'Like big children.'

Gerk made a face. 'Come on,' he said. They walked to the main entrance and Gerk battered on the door with his fist. They had to wait for several minutes before they heard the clatter of the bar being removed and the door opened. Gerk took a step back as they were greeted by five armed men, none of whom had the shaved heads and scented beards of the priests.

'What is your business?' one of the men asked. He stepped closer to Gerk and Olan, raising his axe in an attempt to drive them away.

'We are from Eynhallow,' Gerk answered.

'I asked what you want, not where you are from,' the man said.

'They are islanders,' one of his friends sniggered.

'They must have left their brains there,' a third man added.

'Islanders don't have brains,' the second man answered.

'I am related to the trainee priest Kali. His sister is my wife,' Gerk said. When this didn't impress the men he added. 'My wife Fara is Jona's daughter.'

Jona's name had an effect on the men. They lowered their weapons and talked among themselves. One man was sent to fetch Kali. Gerk bit his thumbnail and Olan shuffled from foot to foot until a young man appeared. It took a double take for Gerk to recognise his brother-in-law. Kali had shaved his fine head of red hair and polished his scalp. His beard was dyed with ochre and twisted into a plait. He wore a yellow and red tunic with a sealskin cloak fastened by a whalebone pin. He resisted Gerk's attempt to greet him with a bear hug.

'Is this your brother-in-law?' Olan suppressed an urge to smirk.

'Yes, what's this?' Gerk asked, pointing at the young man's head.

Kali didn't answer, but instead asked, 'Why are you here? Is my sister ill?'

'Fara is well, as is Terese,' Gerk said. 'I am not here on family matters. We have been sent on official island business.'

'What business on your obscure island could concern us?'

Gerk tilted his head towards the guards, implying the matter was too important to discuss in front of them.

'Who is he?' Kali twisted his lip as he pointed at Olan.

'Olan is my friend. I couldn't have rowed the Sound without him.'

'Couldn't have rowed the Sound,' one of the guards repeated, mocking Gerk's lilting accent and slouched stance.

'Mind your manners,' Kali said. The guard stood to attention. Kali tugged on his beard before accepting Gerk's explanation. 'Come, you must be tired after the journey.'

Kali instructed the guards and they stepped back to allow Gerk and Olan to enter.

'No weapons,' the first guard said as Olan passed him. Reluctantly, Olan handed over his stone knife.

'I want it back undamaged when we leave,' he said. Gerk and Kali had walked ahead and Olan hurried to catch them. Kali negotiated the numerous passageways between the buildings with ease, while Gerk and Olan marvelled at the architecture. Several buildings had flagstones as tall as Gerk marking the doorways. Olan ran his hand along the walls of one, only to be glared at by Kali.

'Don't touch,' Kali ordered.

'Just testing the stone,' he said, drawing his fingers away before Kali removed the stick he carried in his belt and whacked them.

A fire was burning between the entrance stones to one of the larger buildings. Anyone wishing to enter had to walk through the flames.

'What's in there?' Gerk asked.

'It's a place of revelation and transformation,' Kali

answered. Olan made a noise through his teeth and Gerk decided revelation and transformation wasn't worth getting burnt for.

Shaven-headed priests moved about the buildings in silence. Gerk and Olan kept their gazes fixed on the ground as they passed. Gerk did so out of respect, but Olan was trying to stifle his sniggers.

'Are we going anywhere?' Olan asked as they turned a corner for what he reckoned was the third time.

'Guests are housed separately from the priests,' Kali said.

'They would be,' Olan said.

Kali led them into one of the rougher constructed buildings, beside a byre for sick cattle. There were four stone beds, sparse of heather or coverings. 'You can sleep here,' he said. Olan dropped his bag on one of them.

'We need to speak with Patro,' Gerk said.

'Patro is the Head Priest,' Kali said. 'What is so important on Eynhallow that you need to bother him? He is a busy man with many thoughts on his mind. He has recently returned from a gruelling trip south and needs rest. It is likely I can solve your problem, or one of the juniors.'

'Since when did you start making decisions?' Gerk accused.

'I am a priest, as my father was,' Kali answered.

'Your father detested the priests here.'

'He didn't understand them. My father's ideas were old-fashioned and frankly misguided. I repeat, what is your business? Hey, leave that alone.' Kali moved to snatch a small figurine from Olan's hands.

'My instruction from our village council is to speak with Patro,' Gerk repeated.

Kali gave a forced laugh. 'You are an ignorant farmer from a forgotten lump of rock in the Sound. What makes you think you can demand to speak with our High Priest.'

'Patro is a farmer,' Gerk reminded his brother-in-law. 'He may be a wealthy farmer with a herd of hundreds of cattle and twice as many sheep, but a farmer none-the-less.'

'If you come on farming business, you should arrange a meeting with one of the stock managers. You can't imagine Patro attends to the cattle himself.'

'He wouldn't,' Olan muttered in an accent suited for Gerk's ears.

Gerk was tiring of Kali's self-important posturing. Being a priest had changed him and not for the better. 'The matter concerns the magician from Wick. The man called Aiven.' He tried to copy the tone Borg used when addressing the villagers at home although he thought it better not to thrust his arms in Kali's face. 'He arrived on our island without warning some moons ago. We welcomed him as a friend, but dark deeds followed his footsteps.'

Kali rolled his eyes. Olan put a hand on his shoulder.

'We've travelled since midday. You could at least listen.'

'To hocus-pocus nonsense of dark deeds?' Kali shrugged off Olan's hand. 'I'll see you are brought supper.'

'Aiven has been accused of casting evil spells on the island. He claims he was sent to us by Patro,' Gerk said.

'That being the case, we have a right to call on Patro either to renounce the wizard or defend him,' Olan finished.

Kali took a step back. 'You are accusing Patro of being in league with evil doers?' He stared at Gerk and Olan.

'We have open minds, but since the consequences are severe, we would be obliged if you would let Patro know we are here,' Gerk said.

Chapter 8

Kali rubbed his bald head. 'I'll see what I can do. Wait here and don't upset anything.'

Kali hesitated, as if about to say something more, but decided against it. When he left, Olan slumped onto his bed. There was an ominous noise as the stones surrounding the pile of skins wobbled.

'Kali warned us not to upset anything,' Gerk said.

'What is there to upset? The sheep have a better pen on Eynhallow.'

Gerk checked there was nothing he could break before lying down in the next cot. He took his time wriggling his body into a contorted shape before he settled.

'Do you think your brother-in-law will remember supper,' Olan said, giving a yawn.

Gerk covered his face with skins and his answer was indistinct. They were asleep when Kali returned. He shoved Gerk's shoulder to wake him.

'Is it morning?' Gerk asked.

'No. I have managed to persuade Patro to see you before supper,' Kali said.

Gerk sat up and leaned over to nudge Olan.

'Not him,' Kali said. 'Patro has only agreed out of courtesy, since you are Jona's son-in-law.'

'We go together or not at all,' Gerk insisted. Kali

screwed up his eyes. 'If that's what you want...' Gerk let his sentence trail as he lay back down.

'You can't refuse to see Patro.'

'Can't I?' Gerk turned his back on Kali.

'Very well, follow me - both of you. You will need to wash before you enter the council chamber.'

'Can't you bring us water to wash here?' Olan asked.

'You will purify yourselves in the loch, as all visitors do,' Kali answered.

The sky was darkening, with the embers of a red and purple sunset in the distance, silhouetting the half-finished ring of stones to the north. A half moon and a blanket of stars guided them to the loch. Kali didn't think it worth lighting a torch and wasting oil on them. Gerk stumbled along the path, drowsy from his nap, but the cold loch water woke him. They removed their clothing and waded in up to their thighs. Olan splashed handfuls of water at his friend's face, hoping to hit Kali who was waiting on the bank with his arms folded. When Kali was satisfied they were presentable, he signalled that they could leave the water.

'Two baths in one day is not good for a man,' Gerk grumbled as he dressed. 'I need to dry myself.'

'You can do that inside,' Kali said.

Gerk and Olan followed Kali back to the settlement. He led them to a chamber with benches placed round a fire. Scraps of soft hide were lying on the benches and Gerk used one to towel himself dry while Olan hogged the fire.

'Patro is waiting,' Kali reminded them.

'We're ready,' Gerk said.

Kali marched in front, striding towards one of the larger buildings. The door was open, but he stopped before entering. Olan peered over his shoulder to look inside. He nudged Gerk. 'Wow, look at that. The priests have brought the stars indoors.'

The room was lit by a vast number of small lamps set on shelves and tables at different levels, glowing like sheep's eyes in the moonlight and casting shadows. Olan's pupils were wide, transfixed by the tiny lights and following the movement of the beams.

'It smells,' Gerk complained, trying to conceal his wonder.

'Aye, there must be nose to tail whales in the lochs here to get that much oil to burn,' Olan agreed.

'You don't get whales in lochs,' Gerk began until he realised Olan had regained his senses and was joking.

While they were speaking, Kali had stepped into the room, bowing his head. He expected Gerk and Olan to follow.

'Where are these visitors you spoke of?' a voice boomed from the far end of the room. Kali turned to introduce them, but Gerk and Olan remained at the door, gazing in awe. He gestured them with his arms, as if trying to pull a stubborn ox. Olan pushed Gerk into the room first. There were tables lined on either side with the remains of a meal. A feast, more like. Gnawed cattle bones were piled on a plate with fat and sinews still clinging to them. Berries were squashed into the wooden surfaces, ale dripped from upturned beakers and nuts gathered on the floor from where they were dropped and kicked below the tables. There was sufficient food left over to feed the villagers in Eynhallow for three days, but there were only five priests and two bodyguards in the room.

'This is before supper?' Olan whispered to Gerk in approval.

The Head Priest was perched on a stone chair surrounded by four of his acolytes. They were dressed to impress, or intimidate, in well-sewn skins dyed in vivid colours with their faces painted to match. Their cloaks were held by carved whalebone pins, twice as long as was needed for the material and dyed red. Gerk supposed he should be impressed by the show, but the effect was lessened by a dollop of grease on the lips of the Head Priest's chief adviser and crumbs folding into the beards of the other two.

Patro was more particular in his grooming. Any traces of dinner had been wiped clean. He held his willow staff close, but the intricate patterns depicting the stars in the sky could be made out.

Everyone waited for him to speak, but now that the newcomers had arrived, he chose to ignore them, whispering to his men instead. Gerk's stomach rumbled. A bubble of gas was making its way down his bowels. He tried to hold it in, but that made matters worse when the noise erupted. Patro looked up.

'This is the delegate from Eynhallow,' Kali said. He sounded embarrassed.

'And I'm his friend,' Olan added.

Patro moved his tongue round his mouth. 'Eynhallow.' He chewed on the syllables, as if trying to place the island. 'Isn't that where a school of whales beached at the beginning of spring?'

'I believe so.' The priest nearest Patro bent down to answer.

Patro pushed out his bottom jaw and looked to Gerk. 'Who is your priest?'

'We don't have one,' Gerk replied. He knew Patro was aware of that, but the High Priest turned to his followers and grasped his chest as if Gerk had mortally wounded him. 'We haven't needed one,' Gerk added.

'Until now,' Patro said coldly.

Gerk wanted to object, but Patro's air of authority tightened his tongue. 'Aiven, the man you sent to the island, has been accused of wrong-doing.' He paused to gauge Patro's reaction. The side of his lips turned down, but he nodded for Gerk to continue.

Gerk tried to explain as well as he could. He was a spokesman in his village, but here at the Ness he found it difficult to organise his words.

'Make yourself plain. Are your animals ill or not?' Patro asked.

'The animals are recovered, but a young girl has died.'

'And you fear others are at risk?'

'Marna is there to help if they do,' Olan blurted in. He had lifted one of the cattle bones and as he spoke gobbets of fat splurged from his mouth. Patro glared, as if he considered the rope-maker to be no more than a pilfering aide, whose duty was to clear up the dinner remnants. Olan replaced the bone on the nearest table, but it slid to the floor.

'Marna?' Patro repeated. He tightened his grip on the staff and his little finger twitched.

'Thork's sister,' Kali answered. He was cut off from saying more by a piercing stare from beneath Patro's clipped eyebrows.

'There was the business with Wilmer in Barnhouse last year,' one of his priests reminded Patro.

'That stupid girl.' Patro spat the words out.

'She is a wise woman,' Gerk objected.

'I know who she is.' Patro rapped the bottom of his stick on the ground three times. He was thinking and everyone in the room knew not to disturb him. Embarrassed by his greasy hands, Olan looked around for somewhere to wipe them and spotted a faded strip of felt hanging from the wall nearest him. He leaned across and ran a hand down it.

'What is that fool doing?' Patro bellowed. Olan jumped back. 'That wall hanging was made for my great grandmother by the people of the Firth.'

'Is that the village that was covered by the sea?' Olan said. Patro nodded and Olan drew his hand back and mouthed an apology.

Patro was about to respond, but deciding he would be wasting his breath he rolled his eyes and returned his attention to Gerk. 'Is the illness contagious?' he asked.

'Conte what?' Gerk looked blankly at Kali.

'Patro wants to know if the disease will spread,' Kali explained. Gerk hesitated and Kali turned back to Patro. 'I believe the old woman who choked was the girl's grandmother,' he explained.

'So she would have …touched…the body?' Patro drew back as he spoke.

'As did a number of other people, including her father,' Gerk answered.

'You said your people blame Aiven – is that because he is a stranger?'

'It's because he is a wizard,' Olan said.

'He cured the cattle with his magic stones and

afterwards Kayleen died,' Gerk explained. 'He saved Marna's dog from choking and when he touched Wandra she too found a nut lodged in her throat.'

'Marna again,' Patro muttered. He tapped his stick on the ground again, but with less force. The light behind him threw a shadow and in contrast his face appeared lit up.

Olan's mouth fell open. 'Is he going to let an ancestral spirit possess him so he can divine what the problem is?' He whispered over-loudly to Gerk.

Patro gave an exasperated sigh. 'I hardly think that is necessary.' He stood up and after a brief pause his followers rose to stand round him. 'It does not take communion with the spirits to realise where the problem on your island lies. You have allowed indiscipline to get out of control', Patro declared. 'It was my opinion that the gods had simply forsaken you, but it appears they are now angry.'

'Why would the gods bother about Eynhallow?' Gerk said.

'How else can you explain your lack of rain when the other islands have plenty?'

'How did you know about that?' Gerk couldn't restrain his wonder.

'Our concerns are not restricted to events here at the Ness. We have eyes and ears throughout Orkney, including Rousay. Your neighbours talk about you. The gods of the

97

sky are withholding their blessings from you therefore your animals, children and old people are suffering.' Patro flung his arms wide. His eyes rolled in their sockets and his voice changed, dropping lower as he proclaimed his prophecy 'It will not be long before your entire population is struck down.' The words echoed off the walls and several of the oil lamps flickered. Gerk and Olan fell to their knees. Patro looked to the roof. 'This calls for drastic measures,' he announced. The four lesser priests beat their chests and gargled bubbling noises as saliva gathered in their throats.

'Are they ill?' Gerk looked to Kali, but his brother-in-law was thumping his chest too.

'We must send a party to Eynhallow. The gods must be pacified. Sacrifices must be made.' Patro was in full flow.

Gerk and Olan had not experienced intense religious rites and they looked at each other for support. Olan had fallen to his knees and it was up to Gerk to speak.

'All we require is for you to say that Aiven travelled to Eynhallow with your blessing. Borg won't dare defy you by holding Aiven. He'll allow him to leave the island and everyone will be happy.'

Patro signalled to his men to stop their chest beating, but he didn't look convinced by Gerk's words. He brought his staff down, to swipe the air a hand span from Gerk's face. He inhaled deeply and held his breath until Gerk wanted to exhale the stale air for him. His face turned deep red then purple and finally blue before he allowed the air to whistle out his nose. 'I shall visit Eynhallow myself,' he decided. 'It is time to set up a new priesthood there.' He turned to his nearest advisor. 'Do we have a suitable candidate?'

'Kali knows the island,' the man answered. Patro turned his gaze to Kali. He had taken a breath at the same time as his leader and was still trying to hold the air in his lungs. By the time he had recovered, Patro looked away.

'Someone will be found,' he declared. 'We shall have a sacrifice at the stone circle.'

'Which stone circle?' Olan asked. 'The old one at Stenness or the brilliant new one at Brodgar?'

'I'm glad you approve of our new circle, but I meant on Eynhallow, fool.'

Olan nudged Gerk. 'What stone circle on Eynhallow?'

'Shh.' Gerk didn't have the heart to tell Patro there was no stone circle on Eynhallow. Since he planned travelling to the island, he would find out in good time. 'Our folk will be delighted to welcome you for a celebration. Olan and I shall return home tomorrow and organise the preparations for your visit.'

'I think not. You will stay here until we are ready to depart,' Patro commanded.

Gerk gulped. He had tasks waiting at home and Fara would be concerned. There were crops to tend and sheep and lambs to protect. Patro noticed his concern.

'While you are here, why don't you spend the time learning about our culture? You may find it useful, even on Eynhallow. Tonight we intend reading the movement of the stars to the north in order to discern their effect on the land.' He glanced at Olan who was beating his chest the way the priests had done. 'Or you could at least trim and scent your beards.'

The meeting was over. Patro sat down and began talking to his priests. When one of them realised that Kali and the visitors were still present, he shooed them from the room.

'Who do they think they are?' Olan muttered on his way back to the sleeping chamber, but Gerk detected admiration in his voice.

'Patro can be heavy-handed, but he is no fool,' Kali answered. 'He has studied the sun and the stars. He knows how they affect the weather, the tides and the growth of our crops. He knows about the seasons and the cycles of the land. The stone circles are a way of deciphering the sky. They are an integral part of everything.'

'He is certainly keen to spread his ideas with his travels,' Olan said.

'Even to Eynhallow. Most people find excuses not to visit us,' Gerk said, pointedly.

Kali grunted, but didn't speak.

'What's your problem with Eynhallow?' Olan probed. He nudged Gerk, 'Or is it just your family you are avoiding?'

'You are from the island you must know what is said about it,' Kali answered.

'A great deal is said about it, very little true. What story have you heard?'

'People say that when a group of travellers visit the island, one of them will not return. The faerie folk take them.'

'Ha, you told us you study the weather and the stars. Now you say you believe in the faerie folk.' Olan gave a laugh.

'My father spoke with them on several occasions.'

'After he had been chewing salvia and drinking the ale from stale bread,' Gerk chuckled.

'Be like that if you want.' Kali strode ahead and round a corner.

'Wait.'

Kali had disappeared by the time Olan and Gerk reached the corner and looked round to face a choice of routes.

'Can you remember where the sleeping room was?' Gerk asked Olan.

'I wouldn't mind supper,' Olan replied. He sniffed the air. 'Can you smell roast duck?'

'And mushrooms,' Gerk agreed, 'With a hint of dandelion and burdock.'

'You're making that up.'

'Aye, the fancy folk here wouldn't deign to eat dandelions,' Gerk said.

'They surely can't be eating again,' Olan said.

They were discussing the matter when two helpers carrying clay pots with lids scurried along the track between the buildings towards the High Priest's chamber.

'No wonder the doorways here are so wide,' Olan said. 'What will they make of our houses?'

'I don't want to think. Come on, let's find a bed. There will be no supper for us, I fear.'

'If you hadn't upset Kali…' Olan moaned as they trudged along the corridor.

'If there are any nuts left in my bag, you can have them.'

They reached the bed chamber and were preparing to settle when a woman appeared. She was dressed in a coloured tunic with a polished stone necklace and her face was dyed, but she sported a good head of hair. Gerk noticed the red, whalebone pin and took her to be one of the higher order priests. She bowed in greeting.

'Patro has asked me to invite you to join us for supper, if you are not tired after your journey,' she said.

Olan smiled. 'That is far more like it.'

Chapter 9

It took two days for Patro and his men to organise a party suitable for travelling to Eynhallow. After an initial meeting with a group of trainees, Gerk and Olan decided against taking Patro's advice of studying with the priests. Olan made friends with the workers building the wall who lived outside the main settlement. He spent most of his time there, helping with the making of ropes, learning new techniques and fishing in the lochs.

Gerk visited Fara's friends in Barnhouse. He marvelled at the ancient circle at Stenness and the other-worldly tomb at Maeshowe. To please Fara, he paid a trip to the loch side where her father was murdered and laid his flints as an offering.

They both returned to the Ness in time for the trip home. Three priests, including Kali, were selected to journey with Patro, along with lay-helpers. They collected and packed bowls of sweet smelling plants, coloured powders, bone figures and ceremonial robes. When the morning of their departure arrived, Gerk was surprised to see a number of stone knives and axes among the items placed on the stretcher. The finer ones were for ritualistic purposes, but the heavier blades looked sharp and strong enough to kill a man.

'Are you expecting trouble?' he asked one of the

helpers. The man ignored him. 'You would be wiser to pack drinking water and ale,' Gerk said. 'They will be of more use to you on Eynhallow. Water is in short supply unless it has rained there since we left.'

'It will take days to get to Evie carrying all that,' Olan moaned. 'And at least five journeys in my boat.'

'We have our own boats.' Kali had overheard the conversation. 'They were built by the best craftsmen on the island.'

'Do we have to carry them from here to the north of the island? How long will that take?'

Kali laughed. 'Not everywhere is as backward as your little island. We have people here who do things for us. They feel it is a privilege. It will take less than a day to reach Evie. We'll set up a shelter on the coast this evening, ready to launch the boats in the morning. We will be on Eynhallow in time for breakfast tomorrow.'

'If the tides are fair,' Olan grumbled, not wishing to be outdone by Kali.

'Who has the honour of carrying Patro?' Gerk said. 'I can't imagine he will walk to Evie.'

They were waiting outside the walls of The Ness while the priests made sure they had everything they needed. Kali pointed past Gerk to the entrance. Patro was on his way out.

'What sort of beast is that?' Gerk spluttered. 'It is like

104

no ox I have seen.'

The Head Priest was sitting astride a shaggy beast with a long neck and pointed ears. His legs straddled its back to reach just above the level of the weeds on the path. He held onto a rope fastened round the animal's nose and over its neck, but the animal's head was being steadied by one of the helpers. The man tried to coax it forwards, but it was keen on tugging at the weeds on the bank. It let out a strange neighing sound like the rumble of a spring tide.

Two drummers fell into line in front of Patro and beat their instruments. The animal was startled by the noise, but Patro calmed it by leaning over to stroke its neck.

'Haven't you seen a horse before?' Kali answered Gerk's question.

'We don't have anything like that on Eynhallow. Does it fly?' Gerk asked.

'Of course not.'

'Won't it throw him off?' Olan's voice betrayed his eagerness to see that happen.

'Hansibar is accustomed to processions,' Kali said.

'It has a name!' Gerk was already bewildered by the customs at the Ness. Giving a dog a name was bad enough, but giving such a beast a human name was madness.

'It was a gift given to our leader during his journey south to Avesbury last autumn,' Kali said. 'It is a great honour to be offered such a beast, testament to the awe and

105

respect the people there had for Patro.'

'I'm afraid we have no such wondrous gifts to offer on Eynhallow,' Gerk said.

Olan strode up behind the pony and raised its tail. The pony lifted a back foot and kicked Olan sharply on the shin. Patro looked round to see Olan staggering back, grasping his lower leg.

'It bites too,' he warned, with a smile.

Olan hobbled back to Gerk. 'You had better not laugh,' he snapped.

The drummers beat a roll in time, and the procession set off. They hadn't reached the dyke before two priests hurried through the gates from the Ness and hastened towards the group. When Patro was made aware of them, he held up a hand to stop the procession until they caught up.

'What have they forgotten now?' Olan said to Gerk. 'We'll never get away.'

The appearances of the two men were similar although one of them was several years older. They were senior members of the community. Gerk and Olan had seen them in the Ness, they remembered remarking on the brownish birthmark the younger man had on his right cheek, but they hadn't spoken to them.

The newcomers stood in front of Patro, preventing the horse from walking on. The older man seemed out of breath and stroked the long nose of the horse until he regained his breath.

'What is it?' Patro sounded impatient. Gerk and Olan edged closer to listen.

'It is almost mid-summer,' the younger of the two men said.

'I know the skies better than you, Quint. I am aware of the sun's travels.'

'Yet you seem to have forgotten our celebrations.'

'Not at all. I am going to Eynhallow, not Ireland. We shall be back in time for the final preparations. I trust you can see to the minor arrangements.'

The two new priests made faces at one another, communicating without words.

'Besides, I'm sure you could manage the rituals if I did happen to be detained,' Patro addressed the younger man, Quint. He didn't hide his disdain.

'Quint has a point,' the older priest said. 'There have been rumours about the healer. This isn't the first time he has stirred up trouble. Is travelling to Eynhallow at this important time really worth it?'

Gerk couldn't make out Patro's muttered response, but he thought he heard the word "whale".

Patro leant down to whisper in the younger man's ear and he responded by mouthing a curse which Gerk had not expected from a priest.

'We need the oil and bone,' Patro said, nudging the horse into a trot with his feet and brushing the men aside.

The older man moved out of the way and watched as the priests, two guards and the helpers carrying three boats and the stretcher with the supplies increased their pace to follow. Gerk and Olan hung back, trying to hear what the older priest and Quint were saying to one other, but the men were whispering. Quint spotted them watching. He curled his lips into a snarl and raised his arm to shoo them off.

'I thought Patro was bad, but I wouldn't mess with that Quint,' Olan said as they jogged to catch the procession.

Olan was the faster runner and ran past Gerk to reach the back of the group first. He turned his head to see how far back Gerk was, hoping to tease him about his lack of fitness. Gerk was not alone. He was talking to the elder of the two priests, who was keeping pace.

'Stop, wait a moment,' Olan called to the men and women in front of him. He grabbed the back of the nearest man's cloak.

The man stopped, but his forward leg kicked the woman in front's ankles. She turned and knocked an elbow into her neighbour's face. The resulting commotion reached Patro who drew up his horse. Gerk and the priest quickened their pace to reach the group. Despite the priest's age and previous breathlessness, he made his way to the front ahead of Gerk. Patro didn't speak, but his face displayed his displeasure.

'I'm coming with you,' the older priest said in a voice that warranted attention. Patro glared at him and the man glared back. Patro was first to look away.

'Very well,' Patro said. 'Have it your way.'

The new arrival took his place with the other priests behind Patro.

'This is weird,' Olan whispered to Gerk as they made their way past the dyke towards the Ring of Brodgar. Patro raised his stick to salute the workers.

'The Ness is growing in size and importance. There is need for a new circle, cairns and mounds. Everything has to be bigger and more modern for the Ness folk. I don't mind the wall it's the stones that unnerve me. They are a bit creepy, standing there watching. Imagine what they look like at sunset when they throw their shadows towards the loch against a crimson sky.'

'I agree, but that's not what I meant. I was talking about this.' Olan pointed a finger at the procession in front of him. 'There are priests in fancy coloured skins, armed guards, drummers and the High Priest himself on top of a fantastical beast. I hope they don't intend to start humming. Our people are in for a surprise.'

'More like a shock,' Gerk answered. 'Did you sense the friction between Patro and that priest, Quint? Patro clearly isn't happy the older priest has joined us. He wanted him to stay and keep an eye on things at the Ness.'

'Why do you think they all want to go to Eynhallow? It has nothing to do with us…has it?'

Gerk ran his tongue round the inside of his mouth. 'No, I don't think so. But I don't think it has much to do with Aiven either.'

Chapter 10

Despite Marna's ministering, the sick in Eynhallow did not appear to improve and by evening two new cases had developed.

'We need your mother here before someone else dies,' Sempal told Marna as they slurped their lumpy broth with Fara that evening.

'You think this illness is related to the deaths of Kayleen and Mooth?' Fara asked.

'We don't know what caused those,' Marna said.

'And you don't know what is making the villagers ill, so it seems likely the answer is yes,' Sempal answered.

'It is too early to say,' Marna huffed.

'We don't have time to waste. I can take you across the Sound tomorrow. We could be in Skara Brae by evening to speak with your mother.'

'Can't you go on your own?' Marna argued. 'I'm needed here to give whatever help I can. Besides, if anyone is able to persuade my mother to travel in a boat, it will be you.'

'I don't know which potions to ask her to bring.'

'I'll tell you.'

'I'll have forgotten them by the time I land my boat at Evie. I'm useless at remembering lists.'

'Really? How do you remember the tales and sagas

you recite at the gatherings?' Marna said. 'They have records of families going back for generations, much longer and more complicated names than those of a few common plants, yet you don't forget them.'

'That's different.'

'You could make the names into a song, if that helps,' Fara suggested. She began humming a tune and Marna joined in adding the ingredients of her mother's potions.

'Willow bark to ease the ache, meadowsweet found by the lake.'

'Thank you,' Sempal moved away from the din until the girls stopped. 'I get the picture - you don't want to come with me. You'd rather stay with Aiven.'

'Don't be silly…' Marna began.

'It will be nice to see your mother again,' Fara put in, to prevent her friends quarrelling.

'Will it? I thought I was getting peace for a week,' Marna mumbled into the remains of her soup.

The next morning she accompanied Sempal to the shore and helped him prepare his boat.

'Tell my mother she will need fever-few, elderflower and milk thistle. She can get hawthorn and willow bark here. Can you remember that?'

'I don't need you to sing it,' Sempal answered, but she made him repeat the ingredients three times before she was satisfied he would get it right. 'The symptoms are vague, so perhaps she should bring rose hips too.'

'Elderflower, milk thistle, rose hips, hawthorn,' Sempal tapped on a finger for each plant.

'No, I said fever-few. She can get hawthorn here.' Marna sounded exasperated.

'Maybe you should come with me back to the village,' Sempal said, with a smile bursting out from the edge of his mouth.

'I can't,' Marna asserted. 'I'm needed here to do what I can and I want to keep an eye on things.'

'There, you've said it,' Sempal grabbed hold of her hand.

'Said what?'

'You want to keep an eye on Aiven. That's the real reason you won't come. Don't deny it. Pip woke me and I saw you sneaking out last night.'

'I was taking him food. The guard wouldn't let me speak with him.'

'I'm sure you'll manage to get round that problem, while I'm away.'

'What do you mean?'

Sempal smiled. He gave her hand a squeeze then let go and scrambled into his boat. Marna gave it a shove out as he arranged his oars in the water.

'Mind the rocks,' she called as she waved him off. She watched the boat bob on the waves until it became too small to distinguish. Her mother would no doubt moan about having to travel, but she would know they would only call her if there was a real need. Despite her show of confidence for Sempal and Fara, the situation scared her and she hoped she would be able to control the disease until her mother arrived.

After Sempal left she returned to the village to check on Jael, Gora's mother and the others. Thankfully, their symptoms were no worse and there were no new patients. Afterwards she decided to take a walk round the island and search for the plants her mother might need.

The land round the coast was the most fertile and despite the lack of rain there were a few flowers growing. The land was salty, which only suited certain plants. Marna was able to gather horse tail and goose grass. The leaves and seeds of the goose grass stuck to her fingers and clothing. Every time she removed one piece, another would hang on. When they were younger, Sempal used to stick pieces on her back which she couldn't get at and her mother would tell her off for playing in the bushes. It wasn't just when they were younger. He still did.

Marna hoped Borg and his friends would have grown tired of patrolling the hillside – everyone in the village was aware of the danger, so there was no need for a guard - but a look-out blocked her access to the centre of the island. It was the leather tanner, Froink. Marna didn't want to argue with him although the situation was stupid. There were people in the village taking ill, who hadn't been near the hill or eaten anything grown there. She was beginning to think the berries had nothing to do with Mooth's death. He was old; perhaps the excitement in the village was too much for him. Perhaps he choked, like Wandra.

'Nice day.' She smiled and pointed to the sun as she passed Froink. He grunted in return and she noticed a bruise above his right cheek that hadn't been there before. Someone had given him a black eye.

'You'll need some meadow eyebright for that,' she said. 'My mother might bring some over.'

'We don't need more incomers telling us what to do,' Froink grumbled. 'Get back to the village and make yourself useful.'

Froink was not averse to using his fists rather than his tongue and Marna knew it was best not to cross him. He watched her leave, following her down the path. It wasn't as much that she sensed his gaze on her back, but that she smelt the lingering odour of his trade. He stopped at the foot of the hill and Marna made her way along the coast path to the rocky shore.

Four of the island children were there. Two boys threw stones into the sea, watched by a couple of inquisitive seals that kept far enough out of reach. The other two children, both girls, had picked up top shells and poked twigs through the air holes in the undersides, spinning them with their fingers. The game was to see who could keep their shell spinning the longest.

'Hello,' Marna called.

The two boys tossed their stones into the water, shouted something and ran off. One of the girls hesitated before following them, but the other girl stood still, as if frozen with fear. The shell she was playing with dropped from her hand. Marna walked towards her.

'Don't be afraid. I'm Marna. I'm a friend of Fara and Gerk.'

'You are the Wise Woman,' the girl said in a quiet voice.

Not that wise, Marna thought, but she was flattered by the title. She bent to pick up a stone. 'I saw you throwing stones in the water earlier. Could you show me how to make this bounce across the waves?'

The girl looked at the stone in Marna's hand and giggled.

'What's wrong?' Marna pretended to be surprised. She had been playing the game since she could walk and was much better than Sempal at it.

'That stone will simply plop,' the girl answered. 'You need a flat stone.' She bent to examine the rocks on the shore and selected a stone. She ran it between her fingers then drew her arm back before thrusting the pebble out to sea. Marna watched as it skimmed the water. The seals dived beneath the surface as it bounced four, five, six times before sinking.

'Impressive,' Marna said. 'I heard Vern was the best stone skimmer in the village, but I think you must be better.'

The girl giggled again. 'I am Vern,' she said.

'Oh.' Marna paused. 'I am sorry about your friend Kayleen.'

'She wasn't my friend,' Vern said coldly, turning away from Marna to look where the other children had run to.

'I heard you had a row, but all friends argue.'

'They don't say what she said,' Vern replied. She gave a sniff and although Marna couldn't see her face she guessed the girl was stifling a tear.

'Her gran said Kayleen was your special friend. You went everywhere together. I had a special friend when I was your age. We used to play in the meadow beside the loch where we live. Where did you and Kayleen go to play?' Vern gripped the sides of her tunic and rolled the material through her fingers. Marna knew she was treading on dangerous ground. Vern was clearly upset.

'That was our secret. Kayleen said she would hold my head under the water until my hair curled if I told anybody.'

'I know how important secrets are,' Marna agreed. 'Sempal and I have lots of secrets.'

117

'Is he the storyteller?' Vern swung round. 'Is Sempal your special friend?'

Marna had been thinking of Sempal's sister Henjar when she mentioned playing in the meadows, but she supposed Sempal was a special friend too. 'Yes,' she agreed.

'Are you going to marry him?'

The question surprised Marna and she blushed. 'No, we're not that sort of friends.'

Vern thought about the answer then gave a grin. 'Do you like the wizard?'

'You mean Aiven?'

'I don't know his name. I mean the stranger with eyes like the ocean on a morning when the sun smiles on the waves.'

Marna wasn't sure how to answer. She wanted Vern's trust. 'I didn't notice his eyes,' she laughed.

Vern stared at her face, as if wondering whether she was blind. 'What did you notice?' she asked.

'His hands,' Marna said after a moment's thought. 'He has the hands of a healer. The skin is smooth and the fingers long.'

'A healer wouldn't kill anyone,' Vern said.

Not deliberately, Marna thought. She had known cures that went wrong and ones where patients took odd reactions, but she nodded. 'No and I don't believe Aiven has killed anyone. He saved my dog.'

Vern's mouth broke into a wide grin and her eyes sparkled. 'Is your dog the little one with the bad legs? He's so cute.'

'His name's Pip.'

'Can I play with him?'

Marna was about to refuse, but she couldn't break the look of delight on Vern's face. 'Yes, but only if you are careful. He isn't like other dogs. He doesn't like rough and tumble and he isn't good with too many people. He gets scared.'

'Dogs aren't meant to get scared,' Vern said. 'They are meant to protect us.'

'Not every dog is the same, just as every person is different.'

'Dogs aren't people, silly.'

'No, they are a lot wiser than us,' Marna answered. Vern was relaxing and Marna tried to steer the conversation back to Kayleen. 'Pip likes to be in quiet places.'

'I could take him to the secret place. There wouldn't be people there to scare him. The other children don't know about it.'

'You don't play with the other children often, do you?' Marna asked.

'I was playing with them when you came.' Vern dug her foot among the pebbles and shuffled them around.

119

'Of course, and you liked playing with Kayleen, until you fell out. She knew your secret place.'

'She was the one who showed me. She told me not to tell anyone...'

'...or she would hold your head under the water until your hair curled.' Marna showed she was listening. 'You could tell me, though.' Marna wheedled. 'Since Kayleen isn't here. Is it up that hill?' Vern nodded. 'This side or the other?'

'This side,' Vern said in a small voice.

'Where the men are, Borg and his friends?'

'No, the men are stupid. They won't find it. Neither will you. Not on your own.'

'Will you show me?' Marna asked, but instantly knew she had made a mistake.

'Why?' Vern said. She stopped smiling and took a step back.

'Please Vern, I need to know what happened to Kayleen.'

'She died,' Vern said, in a matter of fact voice that she must have overheard from her mother. She made a choking sound and bowed her head to stare at the stones. Marna could tell she was crying again. 'I can't tell you,' she croaked.

Marna wanted to put an arm around the girl, but feared that would frighten her. If she jerked back or tried to run away, she might fall on the rocks. 'I'm sorry,' she said, backing off.

'Can I still play with Pip?' Vern asked.

'Of course you can.'

'Today?'

'If you want.'

'Now?'

'Will your mother let you?' Marna asked. Vern nodded. 'I'll fetch him.'

Marna made her way back to Fara's house to find Pip. He was keeping guard at the bottom of Terese's cot while Fara ground dried bere heads into flour.

'I need to borrow the babysitter,' Marna said. Pip gave a whine as she tried to pull him away. 'Don't be like that. I have work for you - important work.' She turned to Fara. 'Do you have any animal fat?'

'There should be some in the stone box by the dresser.'

Marna found a lump of congealed sheep fat. 'And some mint?'

'I'll get it.' Fara wiped her hands before walking to the dresser to take a sprig of mint from a pot.

'I'll need it cut up,' Marna said.

'What is this for?' Fara began pulling the leaves from the mint. Marna rubbed the fat onto Pip's paws and stuck bits of mint onto the sticky pads.

'Pip hates mint,' Marna explained. 'It will stop him

licking the fat off.'

'Why do you want fat on his paws?'

'Because I want to know where Vern takes him.'

Fara looked blankly at her.

'Vern asked to play with Pip. She'll take him to her secret place. Pip can't tell me where, but he can gather plant seeds and material and I can work it out from that.'

'Won't Pip pick up bits and pieces from all over the island? How will you know which ones are the ones from where you want, if you know what I mean?'

'You know what Pip is like. He won't walk far, especially not on pebbles or heather. He will whine until Vern picks him up and carries him there - and back.'

'I didn't think of that. Gosh, you really are a wise woman.'

Marna finished pasting the minted fat onto Pip's legs and lifted him in her arms. He gave her a soggy lick on the cheeks.

'You can take these nuts and bannocks to Aiven while you are out,' Fara said.

Marna reached out to accept the food, sneaking it into her pouch to prevent Pip from stealing the bannocks.

'Anybody would think I didn't feed him,' Marna moaned.

'Just about everyone in the village has been feeding him,' Fara said. 'I even saw Wandra throw him scraps this morning.'

Marna made a face. 'She must be feeling better,' she said, grudgingly. She made her way with Pip back to the shore, but Vern was nowhere to be seen. She called the girl's name, but there was no answer. One of the boys she'd seen earlier told her that Vern's mother had come for her. She pondered whether to find Neela or not, but decided to continue to the pit to check on Aiven. She carried Pip, in the slight hope there would be a chance her plan with the fat could yet be put into action.

'Back again.' The guard was getting used to her visits and dispensed with the usual questioning. 'Have you brought any of Fara's bere bannocks?' he asked.

'Would you like one?' Marna felt in her pocket and brought out a bannock. It was the one Pip had managed to take a bite out of before she could hide it from him and the guard declined.

Aiven's hands and feet were free of the ropes and he was sitting cross-legged on the ground. His back was straight, he held both hands in front of him with the palms raised and his eyes were closed. Marna was afraid she was disturbing some odd ritual. She waited a few seconds, admiring his dark ring, a little surprised the guard hadn't taken it from him. Perhaps he was afraid of some evil attached to it.

When Aiven didn't stir she gave a loud cough. As if to

make a point, Pip repeated the sound in his doggy way, splattering saliva down onto Aiven. He opened his eyes and looked up, squinting against the sun.

'Is that you, Marna? And Pip too. Any news from the Ness?' he asked.

'No. I wouldn't expect Gerk and Olan to be back today. It is only three days since they left.'

Aiven made a grumbling sound in his throat and bent to swipe the dust at his side. 'Do you carry that dog everywhere?' he complained.

'You don't need to take it out on Pip because you are annoyed,' Marna said. She wanted to continue holding Pip to show she wasn't swayed by his words, but her arms were getting stiff. She cradled the dog for as long as possible, but was forced to put him on the ground. Pip gave a whine.

'What has been happening on the island?' Aiven asked. 'I've been deafened by the noise and talk coming from the village, but I can't see what is happening. Has it something to do with the funerals?'

'I should let you work it out for yourself,' Marna teased. 'It will give you something to occupy your time. What were you doing just now? Sleeping at midday?'

'I was meditating.'

'What does that mean?' Marna was suspicious.

Aiven laughed. 'You tell me what is happening in the village and I will explain meditation to you. I think you will be interested in it.'

'I doubt that. Do the priests at the Ness medi… do what you said?'

'I don't think so.'

Marna wished she had agreed to learn about Aiven's medi-whatever. It would be one up on the Ness priests if she knew about something they didn't. 'Many of the villagers have taken ill,' she said. 'It has affected one in three families and the people who are healthy fear they will be next to suffer.'

'Has anyone died?'

'No, thankfully. Sempal has returned to our village on the mainland to fetch my mother.'

'The healer?'

'There's no need to scoff,' Marna said.

'I wasn't mocking,' Aiven placated her. 'I would love to discuss ailments and their treatments with her.'

'If anybody else dies, you won't get the chance. Borg will have your neck slit open.'

'I'm sorry if I've upset you.' Aiven got to his feet. The top of his head was a foot lower than Marna's toes. She guessed he could escape when Serel or one of the others chosen to guard the pit weren't paying attention, but it would be difficult for him to leave the island if he did.

'Did Serel remove the ropes?' she asked.

'I managed that myself. After the third time Serel

decided it wasn't worth re-tying them.'

The ropes had been fastened tight with strong knots. Marna was curious to learn how he had freed himself. 'Was it something to do with the methylation?' she asked.

'Meditation,' Aiven corrected her. 'No, simply practise.'

'You mean you get tied up a lot.'

'I'm a traveller. People are wary of strangers in their towns and villages.'

Marna accepted his answer although she guessed people were more wary of him than of the more usual traders or pilgrims. 'You were made welcome at the Ness,' she said. 'You weren't tied up there.'

'Patro is a wise man.'

Marna interrupted him with a laugh.

'He, at least, was keen to learn about meditation,' Aiven continued. He sat back down and crossed his legs, resuming his former pose.

'Do you want to know what I've found out?' Marna asked. Aiven didn't answer. 'Don't you want something to eat? I've brought bannocks.' Again Aiven didn't reply, but she heard a humming noise. For a moment she thought she saw him rise from the ground, in his sitting position. She rubbed her eyes. 'Be like that then.' She offered Pip a bannock. He gulped it down. When he finished eating, she picked the dog up. 'You won't want to know what I find when I examine Kayleen and Mooth's bodies tonight either,' she said and walked off.

'Wait,' Aiven called from the pit, but she didn't stop.

Chapter 11

Marna had no intention of examining the dead bodies until the thought danced into her head as she spoke with Aiven. She was looking for something to impress him with, but her words had surprised her too.

She couldn't go to the cairn on her own, without Sempal, could she?

Why did she need him, or anyone?

Her mind was bursting and she wanted to tell Fara when she got back, but Gora was there and Marna suspected she would tell Borg. Gora didn't like Borg, but Marna knew she was keen to be one of the village elders and would use any information to gain favour.

'I've invited Gora to stay for dinner,' Fara said. 'Her mother is sleeping and shouldn't be disturbed.'

'I've brought my pipes,' Gora said.

'Great.'

After they finished eating, Fara played with Terese as Gora practised her music. She was trying out new tunes, some of which reminded Marna of the Irish woman, Erin, she had met the previous summer. Erin spoke with imaginary faerie folk who taught her how to play her pipes, or so she said. Gora stopped playing to gather her breath and drink from a beaker of ale to wet her lips.

'Do you believe in faerie folk?' Marna asked.

'Faerie folk - here on Eynhallow? I don't think so,' Gora answered.

'But you do believe in them?'

'Of course not,' Fara answered from the other side of the hut. Marna hadn't realised her voice had carried.

'What about spirits?' Marna asked, thinking about her planned trip to the cairn where Mooth and Kayleen were laid out. The stone door hadn't been pushed closed as the villagers were waiting for Gerk and Olan's return for the final farewells.

'Spirits are a different matter,' Fara agreed. 'My father was careful not to upset those.'

'How did he manage it?' Marna tried not to sound too eager to know.

'He would offer them gifts.'

'Sacrifices of cattle?'

'Sometimes, but more usually it was small things that would please them, like flint axe heads, coloured beads and stone balls.'

It sounded as if the spirits were children, pleased with baubles, but Marna was relieved she wouldn't have to kill anything to keep them happy while she examined the bodies. It was darkening outside. Marna gave a yawn and stretched her arms.

'I should see how my mother is,' Gora said, taking the hint.

Marna didn't try to stop her leaving. She would have left the food bowl sitting until morning, but Fara liked things cleaned and put away. She helped Fara then snuggled in her cot with Pip at her feet. She could smell the remainder of the mint on his paws.

It wasn't long before Terese was sleeping and Fara settled for the night. Marna kept her eyes open, afraid she would fall asleep and not waken until Fara stirred in the morning. It seemed an age before the whistle of Fara's snoring echoed round the walls. Pip had wormed his way up the bed to lie on her chest and she stroked his muzzle, giving time for her friend to fall into a deep sleep.

'You stay here,' she whispered to Pip as she pushed away the coverings. Pip gave a whine that grew into a howl as he realised he was being left. 'Quiet.'

It was too late. The noise had disturbed Terese and she let out a cry.

'Terese,' Fara called sleepily from her cot. 'Gerk…'

'Gerk has gone to the Ness, remember,' Marna answered. 'I'll see to Terese.' She tiptoed over to the baby and lifted her in her arms, rocking her and making cootching noises until the baby's eyes closed and she nodded off to sleep. Marna replaced her in the cot with care. She looked down at Pip who was staring up at her.

'Guard the baby,' she commanded, in as stern a voice as she could muster. Pip wagged his tail and settled down beside the cot.

Marna put on her shawl and prepared a torch with the whale oil Fara kept in a pot on the dresser. She lit it from the embers in the fire and sneaked out. A gentle breeze blew, but the village was still. Marna didn't expect anyone to be about, but she was on edge. The bodies had been placed in a chambered cairn, a few hundred yards along the coast path from the village in the opposite direction from the pit. Unfortunately for Marna, that meant it was in the direction of the nesting terns. She would rather face Borg and his dice playing friends than a colony of angry birds.

It was verging on mid summer and there was a glower of light in the sky even though the moon was little more than a slit, but a mist crept across the island from the sea, blurring the view. The torch was for use inside the tomb, but Marna was glad she had it with her as she checked her footing on the coast path. Remembering Fara's mention of gifts, she searched among the pebbles for coloured stones. There were some attractive red and yellow ones which she collected.

She was half way towards the cairn when the first tern spotted her. It circled overhead, dropping in height until it was only a few feet above her head. Another bird joined it then another. Their shrieks alerted the others in the colony. Marna increased her pace, but the birds clustered above her, diving at her nose. They pulled up inches before striking.

Marna lashed out with her arms, waving the torch at the birds. The flame drove them higher, giving her time to scurry towards the cairn. She was breathless by the time she arrived at the tomb and leant against the entrance to regain her breathe. The terns were content that she no longer posed a danger, but kept a watch at a distance.

There had been talk, or so Fara said, of rowing the bodies over to Rousay to inter them there. It was rumoured there were more cairns on Rousay than people with brains, but Marna guessed that was the Eynhallow folk's way of looking down on their neighbours. Her people in Skara Brae said much the same about Barnhouse. It was decided to keep the bodies on Eynhallow, although there were a limited number of burial cairns and most were full. Borg had insisted he wanted his only child kept close to him and with some re-arranging and building of internal partitions, space had been found.

A stone as large as Marna had been dragged to the side, allowing access to the narrow corridor. Marna bent her back until her nose was inches from the ground. She shone the torch along the passage. Her hand was trembling and the shadows from the flame stretched up the walls. She heard the scurry of a rat and wished she had allowed Pip to come, but he would have been a menace with the terns.

She tried to gulp the saliva that suddenly gathered in her throat, but her mouth was dry from the smoke and she spluttered and choked. The echo sounded like a laugh, bouncing like wind-blown straw from the walls to the ceiling, transforming to produce a dirge for the dead. Marna was reminded of her last experience inside a tomb. That was at Maeshowe, when the bones of her friend's husband were laid to rest. They had found more than they expected then – the body of Roben the fire maker - but this time she knew there would be corpses in the crypts. She tried to picture the figures of Mooth and Kayleen to lessen the shock of coming face to ashen face with them.

Kayleen had been dead for several days, but Wandra had dressed the body with horse tail and scented herbs and placed bog myrtle in her hair to ward off fleas and flies. Marna imagined that Neela would have done something similar to her father's body.

It was necessary to crawl on her knees along the first stretch of the passage. This wasn't easy carrying a torch and trying to keep it alight in the closed space. She could feel her own hot breath on her arm and tried not to feel afraid. Her father had told her that the spirits of those who died in mysterious circumstances called out for revenge. She had thought he was making up stories to feed their childish delight, but what if the tales were true?

Nonsense - she was scaring herself for no reason.

She reached the end of the tunnel and was able to stand upright in the central chamber. The cairn was a good size for a small island. The internal area was rectangular, rather than circular as in Maeshowe, with six separate chambers leading off from the middle, three on either side. Five of them were sealed with stones. Only the chamber at the end on her left was open. The lichen covered walls pressed in on her, guiding her towards the open chamber. Marna forced herself to pause before walking ahead.

What was she looking for?

She couldn't put it into words, but she knew she would recognise it when she found it.

If there was anything to find.

She needed a plan of action, to avoid having to stare at the bodies for any length of time, but the clawing air in the tomb seemed to weaken her brain. It took effort to recall the events in order.

Kayleen had collapsed and died in her grandmother's arms. It was reported she had been poisoned, but had she? Might there be some mark on the body?

One - examine Kayleen's body for wounds.

Mooth had eaten the berries Aiven gave him, she had seen that herself, but what else had he eaten? Could he have choked? Was he suffering from a bad heart, tooth abscesses or stones in the kidneys?

Two – look in Mooth's mouth.

Her knowledge of the effects ailments had on bodies was poor. Perhaps she should have allowed Aiven to come with her.

Three – take note of anything unusual to discuss with Aiven or her mother.

A swish of what she hoped was wind through the entrance tunnel disrupted her thoughts and she decided three points were sufficient. She looked towards the end chamber and placed a foot in front of her, then another. Being scared was stupid. The dead couldn't hurt her.

As she neared the chamber the smell of decomposing flesh tore at her nostrils and she covered her nose with her sleeve. She could see over the top of her arm and peeked in at the bodies. They were laid on slabs with their feet nearest to the door. There were no grave goods. Borg had forbidden any until Olan and Gerk returned and the villagers could have a proper ceremony, but Marna spotted a grass doll on the floor and guessed Wandra had left it for Kayleen. The sight of the doll made Marna smile and she ventured nearer.

The eyes of the corpses were closed, with pebbles holding the lids down. She was glad of this. It was enough to have the spirits watching from the walls.

She was about to retrieve the coloured pebbles from her pouch when a rumbling rose from the ground. Her heart jumped. Her hand was shaking as she shone the torch on the floor to see red eyes glowing back at her.

'Argh,' she screamed. The rat ran between her legs. Marna exhaled then laughed. The noise had been her stomach rumbling. She remembered in Maeshowe how sounds swirled around the walls, with little clue where they came from. Wilmer had tried to explain it to her in terms of air movement, but she preferred Jona's idea of the dead playing games with them. She liked to think of Kayleen being happy. It made it easier to examine her body.

She lifted the cold arms. They were heavy and wouldn't rise far, but there was no evidence of broken bones. The skin was clammy. She felt along the girl's legs and was about to look in her mouth when she heard a thud. She felt her blood stream round her limbs. Her fingers trembled and the torch dropped onto the stone floor. She watched helpless as the flame petered out in the dust.

She took five deep breaths to regain her thoughts. The sound was coming from the outside passage. Someone was entering the chamber; more than one person from the different voices. The noises were distorted and difficult to make out, but assuming they were alone, the newcomers made no attempt to conceal their presence.

No-one in their right mind would visit a tomb in the middle of the night.

Marna panicked. Was she the one who was mad? She put a hand over her mouth to make sure no involuntary gasps or groans escaped. There was no place to hide. All she could do was squeeze as close to the wall as she could, stay in the shadow and hope whoever was coming stayed in the central chamber and didn't enter the burial compartment. The footsteps grew louder until she sensed they were standing outside. Torchlight shone into the chamber to light the faces of the dead.

'Are you sure this has to be done?' one voice said. It was pitched too high for a man and too low for a woman. Marna shuddered.

'Serel overheard the girl say she was going to examine the bodies,' another voice spoke, as if unattached to a mouth.

'In here? She wouldn't dare.'

'She's not from the island. She is stupider than you think.'

The voices stopped, but Marna guessed the speakers were communicating in silence. They were talking about her, but she was too shaken to be angered by their remarks. Fearing discovery, she closed her eyes and held her breath, knowing that this made no difference.

'Do it quickly,' the not-man-not-woman voice said.

She felt a splash then heard rustling followed by a hiss and a crackle.

'Let's go.'

'We should wait until it catches.'

Until what catches?

Marna couldn't hold her breath any longer, but she waited until she heard the footsteps retreating before opening her eyes. She opened her mouth and gagged.

Smoke.

Something unnatural was burning. The fumes were acrid. She put her shawl over her nose. Her eyes smarted and tears were blurring her vision. It took a moment to realise she shouldn't have any vision. She had dropped her torch and the people had gone, but the tomb was lit up.

Flames were rising from a bundle of dried heather and grasses strewn on the floor at the entrance to the chamber. She recognised the stench of burning whale oil. The fire dazzled her and she stood, unable to move as the flames ran across a line on the floor towards the bodies.

Kayleen and Mooth would catch fire. She had to protect them.

In daylight, she would have realised her initial reaction was unwise, but caught up in the world of spirits and darkness she went with her guts. The fire had already reached Mooth's wrinkled toes and the dry skin caught like thatch. His woollen leggings smouldered. Marna beat at them with her shawl, but succeeded in fanning more life into the fire. A cloud of smoke rose to choke her.

Looking across, she saw that Kayleen was also burning. The dried herbs intended to purify the body were alight. Marna reached for her throat. She had to get help. It was then it donned on her that the doorway was blocked by the fire. It was stealing whatever air there was in the tomb and she felt dizzy.

She should have told Fara where she was going, but if she had, Fara would have stopped her.

She struggled towards the exit, wobbling against the wall. There was a growing heat in the chamber, concentrated, like in the potter's oven. It pushed her away from the only escape route. The smoke dulled her eyesight, but she imagined she could make out the central chamber through the fire.

Surely it would only take a few brave steps to reach safety.

She had seen the old priest Jona walk through fire at one of his special ceremonies, but she had no way of soaking her feet first and there was no salvia to chew on that could numb the senses.

The flames had reached Mooth's tunic and were advancing to attack his beard. Marna covered her nose and mouth and lunged forwards, forgetting about the doll on the floor. Her foot slipped and she fell, banging her head against the wall as she tried to right herself. Her mind went blank as she slid to the ground.

Chapter 12

Marna had no idea of the passing of time as she lay unconscious. When she came to her senses she was lying on the ground with twinkling stars above her. Her throat and mouth were dry and it felt like a wild beast was scratching at the lining of her nose. There was a buzzing in her ears. She sat up and held her head. A skin pouch was shoved under her nose.

'Here, drink this.' She drew back. 'It's water.'

Marna steadied the pouch between her fingers and sniffed. Her nose was numb. She took a sip. Realising the speaker was telling the truth she gulped, dripping more down her chin than into her mouth.

'Not so fast,' the voice warned.

Water was scarce on the island, she remembered. The villagers were now trying to capture the water that flew in the air when they boiled sea water for salt. The dried peat from the hillside provided fuel, but it was a hot and tricky task. Marna felt guilty drinking too much, but the water tasted good. It lacked the brackish tinge she had come to expect.

'What happened?' Marna croaked. Her vision was returning and she could make out a blurred figure.

'You were in the tomb,' the voice said.

'Yes, I remember.' She closed and opened her eyes

several times until they regained their focus. The guard, Serel, was kneeling beside her. 'There was a fire. Are Kayleen and Mooth safe?'

Serel bent his head. 'I do not believe the fire will have prevented the gods from accepting them.'

'Their bodies were burned?'

'As yours might have been. You should have been more careful with your torch.'

'Did you rescue me?' Marna asked.

'Aye. What were you doing there?'

'I wanted to examine the bodies,' Marna said. It was clear Serel believed her to be responsible for the fire. She wanted to tell him about the voices, but a thought made her think better of it. 'What are you doing here?' she countered.

'I had handed over the watch of the wizard to Froink and was heading home when I heard the terns arguing like fury. I went to see what was going on and I saw a light and smoke coming from the cairn. People say I'm a nosey type, but you're lucky I am.'

'Thank you.' Marna took a final mouthful of water before handing him back the skin. She struggled to her feet. Serel offered her a hand, which she accepted. They were near to the shore, not far from the cairn. There was no sign of a fire. 'What will you tell Borg?' she asked.

Serel rubbed his chin and Marna saw burn marks on the back of his hand. 'He won't be happy.'

'Does he have to know?'

Serel gave a half laugh. 'He'll find out soon enough. For the moment, I need to get you back to Fara.'

Marna allowed Serel to guide her along the path to the village. There were questions that needed answers, but he didn't speak and neither did she. Marna remembered that the terns had quietened when she reached the tomb. They would have been disturbed a second time by the people she heard.

If Serel heard the birds, he must have seen the people. Had he spoken to them – or was he one of them? If that were the case, why had he rescued her?

The sun was coming up, but the village wasn't awake. Serel left Marna at Fara's hut after she insisted she was fine. Fara was out of her bed and attending to Terese. When Marna entered she looked surprised and glanced towards the cot where she should have been sleeping. The skins were piled in a bunch. 'I didn't know you were out.'

'I needed fresh air.'

Fara frowned. 'You don't need to explain anything to me, but don't lie.'

'I'm sorry.'

'You look awful. What happened to your hair? Are those burn marks?'

'I'm tired. Can we speak later?'

Relieved of his guard duties, Pip had curled up at the

end of Marna's bed with his nose under his front paws. It didn't take long for Marna to join him in a dreamless sleep.

She slept late into the morning and even Terese's bawling for food didn't wake her. Fara was out when she finally stirred. Her head hurt and her stomach rumbled. The events of the previous night came back to her as she thought about what she could eat and her eye caught the pot beside the fire.

She was keen to know what Serel had told Borg and the others and was relieved that there wasn't a band at the door demanding an explanation from her. She planned what she would tell them as she searched Fara's shelves and storage boxes for ingredients to make fritters and was rolling balls of seaweed and breadcrumbs mixed with egg between her fingers, watched by Pip, when Fara returned.

'I saw Serel. He asked how you were,' Fara said, lifting the cooking pot. She added a dollop of fat and positioned it on the fire.

'Did he say anything else?'

'No,' Fara replied nonchalantly.

Marna dipped the fritters in flour and placed them in the melted fat until they sizzled and turned golden. She prodded them with a hazel stick and breathed in the aroma. 'These are Sempal's favourite,' she said.

'Perhaps Aiven would like some,' Fara said.

'Aiven? What makes you mention him?'

'Serel says you've been seeing a good deal of him.'

'Only to find out what is going on. He knows things he isn't telling anyone.'

'So do other people in the village.' Fara removed the pot from the heat and rescued the fritters before they burnt. 'Maybe they just aren't so attractive.'

'Who do you mean? Who knows something?'

'Nothing gets passed Wandra.'

Marna grunted at the suggestion. She helped herself to a fritter, juggling it between her fingers until it cooled.

'If you don't want to talk to Wandra, there is Neela. She keeps her thoughts to herself, but she joins the gaming evenings with Borg and his friends. She must hear things when their tongues are loose from drink. Vern will tell her mother secrets too.'

'Ah, now that is someone I want to speak to,' Marna spoke with her mouth full.

'Neela?'

Marna finished the fritter and licked her greasy fingers before answering, 'No, Vern.' She had been kneeling by the fire, but got up. 'It's time I took Pip out for his exercise.'

'If he worked, you wouldn't need to take him for exercise,' Fara said. 'He isn't a puppy. It's time you trained him. He could help drive the sheep and cattle when they need to be moved.'

'His parents were hunting dogs, not farm dogs,' Marna

said. 'And that's what we are going to do right now.'

'Hunting without a spear or a bow?' It was clear from her look that Fara didn't believe her, but she wrapped a couple of the fritters in burdock leaves and handed them to Marna. 'In case you don't catch anything.'

Marna headed out of the village to where she knew the youngsters practised throwing techniques. She didn't expect Vern to be with them, but they might know where she was. They were full of suggestions, but no-one could agree.

'Why do you want to find her?' one of the lads asked.

'She wanted to play with my dog.'

The boy laughed. 'Dogs are meant to work, not play.'

'You look old enough to be working and all you're doing is tossing a stick at a piece of driftwood,' Marna countered. The youth took offence at her tone and raised his stick, pretending he would throw it at Marna. Pip growled and the boy backed down.

'Hey, Borg is coming,' another of the boys called. Marna looked round. There was no-one in sight and the boy laughed. 'Fooled you.'

The youths were keen to show off, trying to impress her with their hunting skills. Marna decided it was time to leave. She had more important matters to attend to.

Chapter 13

She was unable to find Vern that day or the next. Everyone she asked denied seeing her. Even Neela, her mother, was vague about her whereabouts when Marna asked.

She hadn't gone to Neela's house to look for Vern, but to ask about Mooth's burial. She wanted to know what Serel had told Borg about the happenings at the tomb, but feared asking Borg or Wandra directly. Neela spent a good deal of time with Borg, on official island council business. She would have been told about the fire. The villagers had been strangely quiet about it although on occasions she heard them muttering behind her back.

'Fara told me about the funeral urns. Will you need help preparing them?' she asked.

'No,' Neela said curtly, but softened her tone. 'Borg decided Kayleen's internment should be an intimate affair for her family and their close friends only. I had no wish for my father to be moved for a public ceremony, so I agreed the ritual farewells should be performed together. The rites were performed yesterday evening and the stone has been replaced over the entrance.'

'Yesterday evening? I didn't know that. Why didn't you wait on Olan and Gerk's return?' Marna queried.

'Neither of them are close relatives of Borg's family.'

'He was the one who complained about them leaving

the island. It doesn't make sense.'

'You do not know what it is like to lose a child,' Neela said. 'Borg's emotions have been tested. His thinking has been skewed. Now that Kayleen has been allowed to pass to the next world, he can perhaps find peace.'

Marna didn't push the point. Borg clearly had his reasons for hiding the fire in the tomb. She tried to remember the voices

– could one of them have been Borg's? Why would he have started it? Did he know who had? What had Serel told him?

She stood for a moment, thinking of something to say. 'Would you like me to dye this shawl for you?' she asked, picking up the material next to her.

'Mooth liked it that colour,' Neela said, taking the shawl from Marna.

'I'm sorry about your father,' Marna said. 'I lost my own dad when I was young.'

Neela accepted her condolences, but from the way she fiddled with the trinkets on her dresser it was plain she wanted her visitor to leave. Marna obliged.

Since Borg and the elders were still patrolling the hillside, Marna collected the plants she found along the shore to make potions and salves for her patients. After checking on the ailing villagers, Fara insisted she bathe in the sea before she was allowed to play with Terese. She

147

feared some of the evil would be transferred through Marna to her child.

The baby was too young to take part in proper games, but she was skilled at crawling into awkward spaces when Marna was distracted. After rescuing her from behind the dresser for the third time, she was pleased when Fara returned from attending to her animals and put her daughter to bed for an afternoon nap.

'I wish Gerk would return,' Fara said. 'I'm worried about him.'

'He'll be fine. He has Olan to watch him.'

'That's what I'm worried about. Olan has a reputation for bravado which some people call stupidity. He likes taking risks and he doesn't think before he speaks. His tongue can get him into trouble.'

'I doubt he will have much chance to speak at the Ness,' Marna said.

'There was also trouble last winter. Certain people thought Olan was stealing from village supplies. He always had more fire wood, nuts and whale bone than anyone else. Neela lost her beads and Mooth had words with Olan. It was nothing. The beads were found, but...'

'These *certain people* won't let it rest. They wouldn't be Borg and his gambling pals, would they?'

'Olan likes to play dice too.'

'It seems like it is a major part of island life,' Marna

148

said.

'Don't even think about getting involved in the games,' Fara warned.

'Sempal likes throwing dice.'

Fara shook her head. 'Don't let him. Not here. He can't afford to lose.'

Marna was keen to find out more, but Fara changed the subject. 'After dinner we can have a natter about home,' she said to Marna. 'How are Thork and Caran getting on in Orphir?'

'Thork is training to be a priest. He wants to study at the Ness, but Caran won't let him. I'm glad she is the one who has to listen to his boasting rather than me, but I miss him at home. Odd isn't it?'

'I haven't seen Kali for almost a year. We used to be close and I often think about him. I agree that brothers can be pains though. Kali likes making up pointless rules...'

'...so does Thork,' Marna interrupted.

'Kali loves studying at the Ness. They make ten new rules there before breakfast.' Fara laughed.

Marna was about to add her own comment when they heard shouting outside. There was the sound of running footsteps and odd clashes and thumps.

'What's going on now?' Fara's laughter changed to irritation. 'I hope whatever it is doesn't wake Terese.'

'She's fine, but I'll take a look,' Marna answered.

'Perhaps Gerk and Olan have returned.'

'Oh.' Fara jumped up, but Marna put a hand on her shoulder.

'Let me go.' She was at the door before Fara could object, bumping into a group of women as she exited backwards to blow a kiss towards Terese's cot.

Most of the able-bodied villagers left on the island were making their way to the shore. Even Chifa who needed a stick to help her walk was hobbling along the path at the back of the small crowd, not wanting to miss anything. Marna squeezed past the chattering women and overtook Chifa to catch up with Gora.

'What's going on?' Marna asked. Gora was walking at a smart pace and it was difficult for Marna to make out what she said as she puffed along beside her. 'Could you stop a moment please?' she was forced to insist.

'Froink was on watch on the hill when he spotted four boats approaching the island,' Gora answered.

'Four?'

'He ran down to warn us. He says three of them are large and they carry several men. The elders fear they are pirates.'

Chapter 14

'Pirates? Here in the Sound?' Marna had heard of sea folk raiding villages near the coasts, but not in Orkney, not in her or her parents' lifetimes.

Gora gave a firm nod and raised her arm to show the hefty stick she carried before setting off again. Looking around, Marna became aware of the wooden rods and stone implements in the hands of the other islanders. Chandra, a timid young woman Marna had spoken to while looking for Vern, held fast to a strong stick her mother used for prodding the fire. Even the children carried handfuls of stones and clods of earth.

The folk lined up in three ranks along the bank. Borg was at the front, arranging the men according to their fitness and what weapons they carried – bowmen at the front, axe wielders behind them. The women, children and older men were ordered to the back, but many of the women pushed their way forwards, curious to see what was happening.

By the time the three larger boats were steered to the shore, the party waiting for them was far from welcoming. No-one moved as two men jumped from each boat and dragged the vessels the final few yards into the shallow water. They steadied the boats to allow the other travellers to climb out. Marna was disappointed. They didn't look like

151

pirates or warriors. Their appearances and robes suggested they were priests from the Ness.

'Is this the sort of barbaric welcome you give visitors on Eynhallow?' The speaker was a tall, shaven-headed man with a painted beard. He was carrying a carved willow staff which he held at arms' length. It was no thicker than a walking stick, but the rest of his party sheltered behind it.

No-one on the shore answered his question. The villagers peered at the strangers in perplexed silence until someone spotted the fourth boat being rowed haphazardly to the shore.

'What, by the power of the seas, is that?' Serel asked, raising the spear he was carrying and aiming it towards the boat.

Despite being hampered by his ceremonial robes, Patro was quick to move between Serel and his line of fire. He held his arms apart to shield the target.

'It's Gerk,' Marna called. 'Gerk and Olan.'

Oblivious to the potential danger, Olan and Gerk jumped from their boat. As the experienced seaman, Olan had been charged with transporting Patro's horse across. He held the body of the boat fast, while Gerk attempted to entice the horse to jump out into the shallow water. The animal dug its hooves into the skin lining of the boat and whinnied. Gerk pulled the rope round its neck harder and the animal thrashed its head, knocking Gerk into the water.

'Idiots,' Patro sighed. He raised two fingers to his lips and gave a low whistle. The horse pricked up an ear then leapt from the boat, knocking Gerk back into the water as he scrambled to his feet. It trotted to Patro and the priest stroked its nose while it shook the water from its coat onto the nearest helper. 'Haven't any of you seen a horse before?'

'A what?'

'Did he say gorse?'

'It looks like a stunted ox. Is it diseased?'

'It's a devil.'

'A HORSE,' Patro repeated.

'It's a pony,' Marna muttered under her breath. 'I saw one last year. Traders from the south had one. They said a horse was much larger – as big as an auroch, but without the horns.' She didn't mean anyone to hear, but her voice carried.

'Hansibar is from noble blood stock,' Patro said, glaring at Marna. 'The sire came from North Africa.'

The villagers hadn't heard of Africa, but they gazed in wonder at the strange, fiery tempered beast that seemed to quieten at the head priest's touch. They lowered their weapons, but Patro's men, gathered in a defensive huddle, fingered the knives at their belts.

Marna sensed the tension. She looked towards Borg, who was about to step forward with his stone axe raised.

153

Taking a deep breath, she pushed her way to the front.

'Welcome to Eynhallow, Patro of the Ness.' She gave a small bow.

Patro frowned, but assessing the situation he was wise enough to acknowledge her greeting with a tip of his head. He lowered the hand holding the staff. 'We have come in peace, in response to your messengers.' He gestured towards Olan and Gerk. Olan had been trying to dry Gerk's tunic with beach grass. They looked up sheepishly when they realised they were being stared at by everyone in the village.

The islanders laughed at the sight and one by one they dropped the stones they were carrying and returned their knives to their belts.

'Trust Gerk and Olan to make fools of themselves in front of the priests,' someone called from the back. The village wits added their comments while others leapt to Olan and Gerk's defence. The situation threatened to deteriorate into a battle of insults until Borg stepped out of the group and pushed Marna aside to stand in front of Patro. He was holding his axe, which he made a show of placing on the ground. In turn, Patro reached for the ceremonial mace secured in his belt and dropped it beside the axe. The villagers hushed.

'I am Borg, son of Wandra and Hiras,' Borg declared. Patro showed no sign that he recognised the names. 'My father was a skilled boat maker and seal hunter.'

'Ah.' Patro gave a small smile.

'Our elder Mooth has died, so I am leader of this community,' Borg continued. There were grumbles of disagreement from the gathering, but no-one spoke up. Borg ignored the interruption. 'It was Mooth who decided you should be informed of our business. He was egged on by the stranger called Aiven.' He paused for Patro to respond, but the priest tilted his head, expecting him to finish what he had to say before he replied. 'Did you send the man, Aiven, here?' Borg asked.

Patro narrowed his eyes to look at the villagers one by one. Marna could tell he was judging their mood before committing himself. 'As Head Priest, I serve in an advisory role. I give no orders,' he said in a tone that would have been convincing had she not known him better. 'What is the charge against Aiven?'

'He is the man responsible for Mooth's death,' Borg declared. 'He poisoned our leader.'

Patro's jaw dropped. He hadn't expected such a reply. Olan and Gerk had left the island before the gathering and Marna realised they wouldn't have known about Mooth's death. It took less than the blink of an eye for the priest to regain his composure and Marna guessed she was the only person to notice his shock.

'I suggest we discuss the matter somewhere more

appropriate,' Patro said in a voice that implied he and Borg were old friends.

'Aye,' Borg agreed with a cold tone. He remained still and Marna counted the waves breaking against the shore for several heart beats. Patro stood opposite Borg, trying to suppress his irritation as the new village leader eyed him up and down. He kept his back straight, chin high and forehead back. Marna feared Patro would order his men to advance, but Borg turned and gestured to the gathered villagers to clear a path for the visitors. They shuffled aside and Patro signalled to his men who formed an orderly procession behind their leader, ready to march to the village. Hansibar gave a snort and Patro took hold of its halter. One of the helpers stepped forward to take the rope from him and lead the pony, once it was under control.

Borg leant to pick up the mace and axe. He scrutinised the mace before handing it to Patro.

'Please, keep it,' Patro said.

Borg nodded and stuffed it with his axe in his belt. He walked ahead between the uneven lines of watching villagers. Patro and his men followed.

As they passed Marna, she couldn't help reaching out a hand to stroke the pony's neck when Patro wasn't looking. There was a thick covering of muscle, the hair felt warm and smooth and was well groomed. The pony neighed and Patro looked round. Marna quickly drew back her hand.

The villagers fell into line behind the priests as if taking part in a mid-summer dance ritual. Marna took her place at the back.

She had been away longer than anticipated and curious to know what was happening, Fara had disturbed Terese, wrapped her in her shawl and carried her outside. Marna spotted her at the entrance to the village, talking to Olan's mother. Pip had followed her out and was sitting at her feet. Fara was rocking Terese in her arms and Marna guessed the baby was crying. Olan's mother poked a finger into the shawl to soothe her.

'They are coming now,' Olan's mother said.

'Look, it's Kali.' Fara recognised her brother marching at Patro's side. 'Kali,' she called, lifting Terese up for her brother to see. The baby wriggled and drooped in her arm. Olan's mother grabbed at the shawl.

Kali looked across and scowled at his sister. When Fara raised Terese, Pip jumped to his feet and started barking. When no-one paid him attention the barking changed to a growl. Olan's mother tried to calm him, but the commotion stopped the parade. Everyone, including Patro, glared at Fara and Pip. Marna gave a sigh and rushed over to calm her dog. Pip pawed her feet, hoping for a treat, but she didn't have anything.

Patro glared at Marna. 'Is that your…dog?'

Marna wasn't sure if the question referred to Pip's

species or her ownership of him. 'Yes,' she answered defiantly, covering both queries.

'I should have known.' Patro peered at Pip. 'It looks familiar.'

'Pip used to belong to Wilmer, the jeweller from Barnhouse,' Marna answered.

'Wilmer, yes, a good man drowned, trying to save you I heard.'

Trying to kill me, Marna thought, but she didn't contradict him.

Patro moved closer and knelt to stroke Pip. He put out a hand.

'No, don't,' Marna warned, fearing Pip would bite the priest. To her astonishment, Pip sniffed the man's hand then allowed Patro to tickle behind his ear. He rolled over to have his stomach rubbed.

'Not much of a guard dog, is he?' Patro stood up. Marna was too surprised to answer. 'I have heard other stories about his former master,' Patro admitted. Before Marna could decide how to respond, Patro twitched his left eye in what Marna thought for a moment was a wink then walked off. He took his place at the head of the group from the Ness. Marna realised Fara was staring at her.

'That was Patro,' Fara mouthed, but the words didn't come out. She gulped a mouthful of air. Her voice was squeaky when, 'he spoke to you,' tumbled out.

'Should I be honoured? He's just a man.'

'Kali didn't even smile at me,' Fara complained. 'And he's my brother. Wait until he wants new sealskins or some fish stew.'

'Will he be staying with you while the Ness folk are here?' Marna asked.

'I don't think I want him too, if he's going to be all haughty and priest-like. He hasn't finished his basic training. What will he be like when he wins his red cloak pin?' Fara shot a look at her brother's back before marching towards her house.

Marna thought about waiting to see what developed, but Borg and his friends had taken over the organising and she knew there was nothing she would learn until later. She picked Pip up and wandered after Fara.

Marna was not known for her patience, but fortunately she didn't have to wonder where the delegation would be housed for long. She took the long route round the village, which gave her the chance to assess where there might be space. As she circled round towards Fara's hut, she spotted Wandra a short distance off, arguing with a younger woman. Vern was standing with them, but she wasn't interested in the conversation. Marna thought she was looking out towards the sea, until she realised her eyes were on Patro's pony.

Marna put Pip on the ground, facing Fara's house. 'Go

159

find Terese,' she said, giving him a gentle nudge with the side of her foot. 'I won't be long.'

She waited until she saw the dog trundle indoors then sidled towards Wandra. Closer up, she could see the other woman was Neela. She leant against the wall of a house, pretending to rub dirt from her sandals while she listened to the conversation. From the snippets she managed to grasp, she concluded that although many of the empty houses could easily be lived in, Patro had his eye on taking over Mooth's house for his stay. Borg had agreed. It was the largest in the village and seemed the most practical for housing the head priest and his senior colleagues. Apparently Patro's first comment had been that the walls were 'horribly drab'.

Mooth's daughter and granddaughter had no wish to stay and act as serving maids so were forced to find alternative accommodation for the period.

Neela was screaming at Wandra. Her flapping arms did most of her talking, but Marna heard her say 'Borg won't dare send us away.'

'My son is a fool,' Wandra spat. 'And your husband was a bigger one.' She would have said more, but she spotted Borg coming towards them. Marna crept round the side of the hut, out of sight, but able to see what was going on. Borg stopped and put a hand of Vern's shoulder. Marna saw the girl cringe and had to prevent herself from stepping

160

out and intervening. While she was fuming at Borg, she missed the words that were spoken by Wandra and Neela.

'They stay with us and you will make them welcome,' was Borg's final judgement, which he delivered with a finger prod to Wandra's chest.

One of the priests, an older man with a jolly face, strolled towards the group. 'Are there problems?'

While Borg re-assured him that everything was in order, Marna made her way back to Fara's house. She met Gerk as she reached the door. She was desperate to ask him about the Ness; what new buildings there were, what the priests were discovering in the night sky, if the delegation that had returned with Patro from Avesbury had brought new dyes, pottery or building techniques; but Fara preferred to welcome him home with hugs and kisses. Marna left them alone and went outside. She loitered around the village, watching as places were found among island families or in the abandoned houses for the workers and helpers from the Ness.

'Hansibar will need shelter, good food and fresh water,' the man in charge of Patro's pony insisted.

The villagers were initially excited about the animal and willing to offer help, but the pony reared and lashed out with its front hooves whenever a stranger tried to approach. The islanders backed off and the handler found himself alone.

'I know somewhere you can house it.' Marna came to the man's rescue.

'I shall stay with the horse and guard it,' the man replied.

'Who from?' Marna said. 'Nobody can get near it apart from people it knows.'

She led the groom to the sturdy shed at the edge of the village, used for storing driftwood. She had noticed it was empty the previous day.

'I can fetch straw and heather,' she offered.

'Is there nothing better?' The man kicked aside a shrivelled branch of wood on the floor.

'Find somewhere yourself then,' Marna answered smartly and walked off. Her tummy was rumbling as she made her way to the house and she hoped Fara and Gerk were ready to eat. She thought of the clay-baked duck her mother made over a gorse wood fire and licked her lips before realising there were no rivers nearby to get wet clay. They would have to make do with the usual stew.

Gerk wasn't keen on speaking about the priests in case word reached Patro, but he had more to say about the rich food and furnishings at the Ness. He described the meats and fish, the lighting and the decorative pottery and coloured beads over dinner. Marna could tell from Fara's darkening expressions that she was jealous.

'…And Olan wiped his hands on one of the precious

wall hangings,' Gerk laughed.

'They haven't taken long to make themselves at home here,' Fara commented. 'No doubt Mooth's hut will be unrecognisable by the time they've decorated it to their satisfaction.'

'Don't worry, it won't be long until your brother comes to see us,' Gerk said, realising what was causing his wife's foul mood. 'Don't you want to hear about my journey? How the pony almost tipped our boat up in the middle of the Sound.'

'Of course,' Fara answered. 'But I warn you, I will compare what you tell me to Olan's version.'

'He is bound to invent wild beasts, hurricanes and other dangers we didn't encounter. I'm afraid I'm not such an interesting storyteller as he is, or Sempal. Where is Sempal, by the way? Drinking and gaming with Froink?'

'He has gone to fetch Marna's mother,' Fara answered. 'I haven't told you about what has happened here.' Her voice implied she hadn't time to get a word in.

'I heard Borg speak about Mooth. What happened? Why does he blame Aiven?'

'Mooth is only part of the story. Others are ill, including Gora's mother.'

'She is improving, thankfully,' Marna put in. 'Tell us about your adventures.' She edged the conversation away from her failings as a healer.

Gerk started to tell about the horse, but Marna wanted to hear everything, from the beginning.

'We were midway across the Sound after leaving Eynhallow when I discovered a hole in the boat,' Gerk related.

Marna gasped or laughed, depending on the occurrence, but her mind was on the meeting Patro and his priests were having with Borg and the elders in Mooth's house.

'Can you believe that?' Fara was looking at her, but she had missed what Gerk had said.

'Believe what?'

'Gerk says the priests at the Ness walk through fire without first sucking plant saps to dull the senses.'

Marna shivered, recalling the events in the tomb. She didn't want to think about fire or walking through it. Fara hadn't spoken to her about her nocturnal visit, but Marna knew she must have learnt something from island gossip. She supped a mouthful of stew to avoid speaking, but Fara was waiting for an answer.

'I have heard if you bathe your feet in water then go fast enough, the flames don't have time to scald them,' Marna said. 'My question would be; why would anyone want to walk through flames?'

'My father told me the only way to commune with the spirits in the world of the dead is to purify the mind,' Fara said.

'Jona was a wise man,' Gerk put in before Marna could spurt out opinions she would later regret regarding the former head priest of her village.

'I don't see how burning your feet purifies the mind,' she grumbled.

Gerk was about to impress them by describing the burning candles that lit up the Ness like the night sky, when the door of the hut swung open with a bang that woke Terese. Kali strode into the house as if it were his own and looked round.

'Where is Sempal?' he demanded.

Chapter 15

'It's nice to see you too, brother,' Fara answered. She stood up and stepped towards him. 'What sort of manners do they teach you at the Ness? How to ignore your family and then treat them like your servants?'

Kali's face reddened. He pulled at his fingers before noticing Terese and moving over to her cot to look at her. 'Is this your baby?'

'No, that one was washed up on the shore after a storm. Whose baby do you think it is?' Fara advanced to the cot and lifted Terese, holding her away from her brother.

'I imagine Kali is kept busy at the Ness,' Gerk said, stepping across to stand beside his wife. He put a hand on her waist. 'I'm sure your brother would visit us if he had more time for travel.'

'He could make time.' Fara wasn't appeased. 'Father has been gone a year and we still haven't discussed what will happen to the house in Skara Brae. If we don't, the elders will make the decision and it may not be to our favour. Horan will give us three cows and two sheep for it. His household is expanding with his daughters both giving birth. I feel we could demand more.' She looked to her husband. 'You thought, perhaps, the cows and four sheep.'

'There are other people interested in the house,' Marna

166

said. 'Henjar is now married to Albar and they are expecting a child.'

'Her mother's house is large enough for them.'

'Sempal lives there too,' Marna countered.

'Enough,' Kali interrupted the argument. 'I know you want the business settled, Fara, but this is not the time or place.'

'When and where will that be?'

'Patro can be demanding,' Kali said with a sigh.

Marna couldn't prevent giving a chuckle at this. Kali threw her a glance. He paused for a moment then said, 'Does Thork still have my father's staff?'

'I don't see what the fuss is about some old stick.'

'*You* wouldn't,' Kali grumbled. 'You hold everything about our priesthood in contempt.'

'Thork's staff could be in the house, propping up the table or down the back of a bed, but he may have taken it to Orphir with him. You'll need to ask my mother.'

'I'll do that, next time I see her.'

'Which won't be long as she will arrive soon,' Fara said.

'Your mother is coming to Eynhallow?' Kali addressed Marna, not believing his sister.

'She has been sent for,' Gerk answered, 'Or so I gather.'

'Patro doesn't intend staying long. We may be gone by

the time she gets here,' Kali said. 'So, where is Sempal?'

'Why does Patro want to see him?' Marna asked, before Gerk or Fara could answer.

'Who said it was Patro that wanted him?' Kali challenged. Marna put her hands on her hips and made the face her mother did when demanding which child in the village had knocked over the water barrel or broken a pot during their games. 'Well it could be, but the matter has nothing to do with you.'

'Then I won't tell you where Sempal is.'

Kali turned to Gerk, hoping his brother-in-law would intervene, but he was enjoying the stand-off and gave a grin. 'Patro wants to speak with him because he was with Aiven when the poisoned berries were found, satisfied?'

'Patro wants to interrogate him, more like,' Marna said. 'What has Borg said? What is Patro doing here anyway? Why is Aiven important to him?'

'I've given you the answer to the question you asked. It's your turn to tell me where Sempal is,' Kali said.

Marna removed her hands from her waist and slowly folded them in front of her.

'I don't have all day,' Kali continued.

'I do.'

'At this rate it would be quicker searching the island for him.' Kali turned to the door.

'Do that if you want. All your priests and helpers

won't find him. Sempal isn't on the island,' Marna said.

'He went to fetch Marna's mother,' Fara informed her brother.

'How long since he left? When will he be back?'

'You have to answer one of my questions before you can ask another, since that's the game you want to play.' Marna was enjoying teasing Kali. She remembered him in the village as a cheeky lad who hid behind rocks to throw pebbles at the younger children. His father scolded him for it, but being at the Ness had developed his bullying tendencies and added a 'better-than-everyone-else' attitude. Kali scowled and turned towards the door. 'Sempal isn't here, but I can help with Patro's enquiry,' Marna offered. 'I'll go with you to the meeting.'

She didn't give Kali time to object. Her shawl was on the dresser and she grabbed it before striding out of the door. She was halfway to Mooth's house before Kali caught up with her.

'Hold on, you can't barge in.'

'Watch me.'

It hadn't taken Patro long to commandeer the best house and arrange the furnishings he had brought from the Ness, discarding those previously in the dwelling. When Marna 'barged' into the hut, the priests were seated on stone stools covered with decorative cushions. They might have brought their own cushions, but Marna couldn't imagine them carrying the stones all the way from the Ness. They must have borrowed them from the villagers or brought them from the shore.

A hacking cough from the side of the room drew her attention to Wandra. The old woman was bringing up dirty phlegm, but no-one was bothered by it. Borg, Serel, Froink and Serel's brother Bryne were standing in a semi-circle in front of the priests. Marna recognised them as the men patrolling the hill. She caught Serel's eye. He opened his mouth to say something, but shut it smartly when Borg looked over. Marna guessed it was about the fire in the tomb.

'Where is Aiven?' she demanded. She couldn't see him in the room and wondered who was guarding him.

Patro had been talking to Borg and hadn't heard Marna's entrance. He looked up and gave an exaggerated sigh. 'I thought I told you to find Sempal,' he said to Kali, who had followed in behind Marna and was looking embarrassed.

'He has returned to Skara Brae,' Kali said.

'Convenient,' Patro answered with what looked to Marna like a sneer.

'Should I...?' Kali gestured to the door. It wasn't clear what he meant he should do, close the door, show Marna out or leave himself.

'Go and fetch Aiven and let us hope you can do better

at that simple task.'

'Yes sir.' Kali gave a bow then departed, scowling at Marna on his way out.

'Sempal had nothing to do with the berries,' Marna blurted out as Kali left. 'He will be back soon to tell you himself. He has gone to Skara Brae to fetch my mother.'

Patro raised his eyes to the ceiling and muttered something Marna couldn't make out. It sounded like he was beseeching the gods for strength.

'Marna's mother is a skilled healer,' Wandra spoke from her corner. Her coughing had miraculously stopped, as if the mention of the name alone had cured her. 'She will be able to heal our people of their ailments.'

'Of course,' Patro snorted. 'Aiven is trained in the astronomical arts and the use of healing stones, but why ask him to help when you can call upon a woman who makes medicines from whatever grows in her midden mixed with dog's vomit?'

'Look here,' Marna took a step forward and jabbed a finger towards Patro. 'My mother's medicines are known to cure toothache, cramps, sickness and coughs. You can ask anyone and they will agree. I haven't seen Aiven's stones doing any good.'

To Marna's surprise, Serel, Bryne and Froink agreed.

'Aiven is the one causing the evil,' Borg said.

'We have already disregarded that opinion,' Patro

reminded him.

'You have,' Borg muttered. 'It was my daughter who died.'

'And you have our sympathy,' one of the other priests said, putting a hand on Borg's shoulder. Marna hadn't expected anyone from the Ness to dare speak without Patro's permission. She recognised him as the older man she had heard speak with Borg and Wandra earlier. His soft brown eyes, set deep in a bony skull, drew Marna towards him. She felt he could be trusted. His sympathy seemed real.

'Which is why we want the truth,' Patro said. 'Not false accusations born from fear of strangers.'

'We have never been accused of not welcoming strangers to our island before.' Borg said. 'However we expect visitors to respect our ways.'

'What has Aiven done to upset you?' Marna jumped in with the question.

'Excuse me,' Patro was not impressed.

'He is a mercenary,' Borg answered. 'I don't expect you to see that. Like the other young women, you are enthralled by his charm, good looks and smooth tongue.'

Marna heard Patro give a small chuckle. 'What do you mean by a mercenary?' she demanded.

'He makes people ill so that he can cure them in exchange for gifts. In our case it is valuable whale bone and oil he wants. No doubt he demands flints or coloured beads from other villages. If they refuse to pay, a few deaths make them desperate for his help.'

'Nonsense,' Patro cut him off before his men could add their voices to the charge. 'Aiven has proven he is dedicated to learning the ways of the heavens, as we are at the Ness. His knowledge cannot be doubted. Gifts are gratefully accepted, but he would not stoop to charge for his services.'

It was Marna's turn to chuckle. The community at the Ness were known for demanding offerings from the surrounding neighbourhoods and they had armed guards to protect their wealth.

'You find this amusing?' Patro accused.

'As far as I have heard from Fara, the cattle and sheep were ill before Aiven arrived.' Marna said.

'Who is to say he can't perform his sorcery from a distance?' Wandra said. 'I once knew of a hag who could spin her evil from Wyre to Egilsay and on towards Rousay.'

'Sorcery is merely a word used when the truth is hidden from you,' Patro declared.

'What do you believe the truth of the matter to be?' Borg asked.

'It is simple.' Patro stood up to face Borg eye to eye. 'This island is godless. You speak of respect. I have only been here a short while, but already I can see the people show no respect for the heavens. Where are your priests? Where are your altars for burnt offerings? What sort of funeral will your dead receive?'

Serel made an odd grunting sound that received firm stares from both Patro and Borg. He covered his mouth and pretended to clear his throat. Marna felt her cheeks burn.

'I would be happy to officiate at the funerals of Borg's daughter and the elder, Mooth,' the older priest offered.

'That won't be necessary, thank you,' Borg replied. 'The bodies have been cremated.' He glared at Marna.

'Cremated?' Patro said. He had a knack of keeping the tone of his voice even and Marna couldn't tell if he was surprised or shocked, but she guessed from the fact that he asked, that he thought the custom unusual.

'There was a fire,' Serel blurted out.

'Aye, the ground is dry through lack of rain,' Borg added.

Patro looked dubious, but the older priest spoke first. 'Surely the bones remain?' he said.

'Yes. You are free to bless them if you want, if it makes you feel happier,' Borg allowed.

'If that is settled, I can continue,' Patro said. 'Where are your sacrificial sites? What have you offered this year? Do you plan a solstice ceremony? If so, where, tell me, are your stone circles?' His voice grew louder as he asked each question and a sense of divine outrage circled the room.

Wandra choked on her cackle. Borg looked away and the other three men cowered back. Marna's chest was heaving, her throat was dry and she felt like a naughty child.

Patro was about to continue with his rant when Kali rushed into the room. His tunic was dishevelled and covered in dust. Wisps of dandelion seeds clung to his beard. He stopped when he saw Patro standing with his arms raised and stood wide-eyed, with his mouth open.

'What is it boy?' Patro snapped. 'Where is Aiven?'

'He isn't in the pit,' Kali blurted out. 'I looked everywhere. He's disappeared.'

Chapter 16

'It wasn't your fault. Serel shouldn't have left him unguarded,' Fara told her brother for the third time. Rather than suffer the wrath of Patro, Kali had decided to spend the evening with his sister. The meeting between the priests and village committee had ended with Kali's announcement. Released from their need for excuses for the lack of religion, Borg and his men stormed out to search for Aiven. Wandra made a sign, whether it was to bless or curse the priests Marna couldn't tell. Patro waved her away with a sweep of his hand and she hobbled back to her house. Marna returned to Fara's hut with Kali. Gerk was keen to know what had been decided.

'Nothing can be decided until we find Aiven,' Kali said.

'We know why Patro is here,' Marna said, pausing so that Gerk or Fara would ask her to explain. They didn't, but she continued. 'The Ness has spies and informants everywhere. The priests will have heard about your whale bone and oil. I guess Patro is keen to get his hands on it.'

'Nonsense, Patro came because of Aiven, but now he is here he is concerned about the spiritual health of the island. He wishes to improve it,' Kali answered. Marna pushed her tongue into her cheek to show she wasn't convinced.

'People like giving gifts to the Ness,' Fara said. 'It makes then feel part of the community, even if they can't be there themselves. They appreciate what it stands for. You can't stop them, Marna.'

'I didn't mean that,' Marna said. 'I don't want to stop people bringing offerings.'

'Will Patro and the others stay here until Aiven is found?' Fara asked.

'The island isn't large,' Kali answered. 'It won't take long for the miscreant to be captured.'

'You underestimate the number of caves and the vast extent of them,' Gerk said. 'Aiven could hide for months. There is a plentiful supply of food from the sea.'

'But not water,' Marna added. 'Not for drinking.'

A gloomy light lingered outside, but a wind was blowing up, creating angry roars through the passages between the houses.

'I'm glad I don't need to venture out,' Fara said. 'Do you need to visit any of your patients, Marna?'

'It appears the priests have taken the matter into their hands,' Marna answered. 'In this weather, I don't mind having a night off.'

They settled down for the night. The following morning Marna heard Kali stomp around the house looking for his ceremonial knife which she had seen Fara place on the dresser the previous evening after using it to gut fish. It

177

was early and she didn't get out of her bed until he had left
to report to Patro. Fara and Gerk stirred soon after. They
were having breakfast when Kali returned, with news that
Patro had called a village assembly.

'When Patro is ready, Lorkin will sound a call on his
horn. Everyone must gather in the centre of the village.'

'Must,' Marna grumbled.

'Horns blowing will disturb the baby. Trust the Ness
folk to make a ceremony out of nothing,' Fara said,
gathering the empty plates.

'At least we'll find out what they have to say about
Aiven,' Gerk said.

'I don't suppose there is any porridge left over,' Kali
eyed a small bowl beside the fire.

'You don't suppose correctly,' Fara answered. 'You
can scrape the pot if you want.'

Despite her complaints, Marna was eager to hear what
the Ness priests had decided. She had expected the horn to
be sounded soon after Kali appeared, but it seemed an age
until the call came. Before it did, Marna believed every
crow caw she heard to be the signal.

She was outside the village examining the pit for signs,
when she heard the blast. There were the imprints of fingers
where she deduced Aiven had pulled himself up, but that
told her little, except that his spell in prison hadn't
incapacitated him. Dust and earth had been shuffled over

the few footprints, making it impossible to see which way they led.

Pip had trotted along with her, but was reluctant to make the return journey. By the time she carried him back to the gathering ring, she was one of the last to arrive and was stuck at the back of the group, trying to see between Gora's back and Fara's shoulder.

Patro was dressed in his ceremonial skins, as were his fellow priests. The clipped eyebrows and grey-blue stripes painted on their faces made them look like predatory hawks. Kali was holding a drum. He beat it three times and Patro raised his staff. The gathering hushed.

'Listen, people of Eynhallow, your troubles are many, but we at the Ness have heard and are here to help.'

On other occasions, with a different audience, Marna felt he would have paused at this point for effect, but from his voice it was clear he wasn't sure how Borg and the islanders would receive the words.

'I have spoken with your elders and we have decided the island is in grave need of a stone circle.' During the second it took him to take a breath, mutterings rose from the crowd, but it didn't deter him. 'Work shall commence at once. A site will be found and the ground prepared. I myself must return to the Ness, but I shall advise Jolty, who will oversee the process until someone can be sent from the Ness to replace him on a more permanent basis.'

179

'We don't need a stone circle, we need answers. We need an end to the illnesses and deaths,' someone called.

Marna thought it was Neela who was speaking, but it could have been Jael's wife. Marna couldn't remember her name.

'Jolty is skilled in many areas, including healing. He will serve your community well.'

'What about the wizard?' a man shouted.

'When Aiven is found, Borg and your village elders can deal with him,' Patro answered with a nod towards Borg. 'He has spurned the support of the Ness by his disappearance.'

'Aye,' a cheer rose from the crowd. It was what they wanted to hear.

Marna wondered how much whalebone and lamp oil Borg had offered the priests in exchange for that decision. It was clear Patro didn't intend hanging around to witness Borg's judgement and justice. He signalled to Kali to beat a marching rhythm. His drumming was not as good as he boasted.

Marna wished her brother was there to hear him. Thork had been a drummer for Kali's father and was well-known as a skilled musician. He had been trying to gain a place at the Ness for years and she knew he would be outraged that someone could play so badly for the chief priest. The thought made her chuckle as she watched Patro stride back to Mooth's house. The other priests followed, except for the older man who had spoken the day before. Marna guessed he was Jolty. It seemed an apt name for him.

A group of young men and a few women moved to form a circle round him.

'I know how to lever stones,' one man said.

'I have a cousin who put up a stone at Brodgar,' a second man added.

'On his own?' one of the girls asked.

'Thank you, thank you.' Jolty raised and lowered his hands to calm the group. 'Volunteers will be needed to cut and carry stones later, but first it will be necessary to find an appropriate site for a circle then prepare the ground. It is usual to mark out the area with a ditch.'

Jolty hadn't appeared to Marna to be the best candidate to be put in charge of a major building project. She feared a gush of wind might blow him away and thought his soft voice and mild manners would be a disadvantage, but watching how the young people responded to him, she admitted she was wrong about that. He was tougher and wiser in the ways of the world than he looked.

Caught up in the enthusiasm, she thought about volunteering although in general she agreed with her mother's opinion that building stone circles was useful for only one thing - keeping the young men occupied. The work used up their spare energy and let them show off, as they positioned the larger stones. Other than that, according to her mother, they were of little use to anyone but the priests.

Her mother wasn't always right though.

Jolty seemed like the sort of priest she could ask questions and get sensible answers, without being made to feel as small as a vole or as stupid as a sea snail. She didn't know if sea snails were stupid, but she liked the saying.

She wouldn't be able to ask Jolty serious questions with his new crew of followers pouring over him, anxious to discuss the details and practicalities of building. She would find a time later. Perhaps once the other priests had left and her mother had arrived they could invite him for a meal.

For the moment she took a wander down to the shore. She hoped her mother and Sempal would arrive soon. No-one had died, but Gora's mother and Jael were still confined to their beds. She had counted the sunrises since Sempal left and convinced herself it wouldn't be long before his boat was visible pulling across the Sound. She might be able to spot it.

She hadn't gone far before she heard Pip whine behind her. He didn't like water or the pebbles on the beach and it seemed wiser to leave him with Fara. She retraced her steps. Her friend was speaking to her brother and she waited a short distance off until they had finished their conversation and Kali had departed, before going over.

'Kali will stay on the island to help with the building of the stone circle,' Fara said. Marna couldn't tell if this pleased her friend or not.

'Will he still be here to help Gerk with the autumn calves?' she asked.

'No doubt he'll be under our feet, but as for helping with manual work…' Fara gave a forced laugh.

'It looks like Patro and the others are in a hurry to leave,' Marna changed the subject. She pointed to where a group of priests and helpers were piling their belongings, ready to re-load the boats.

'Only Jolty, Kali and two helpers are staying on the island. The others have had enough of our island ways. Not that I'm sorry to see them leave. Neela told me they were using good drinking water to wash their feet.'

'I think she is making that up,' Marna said, trying to be fair. 'And they did bring their own water with them.' She looked around. 'I can't see Patro.'

His aides were rushing to and fro, sorting out the baggage, but the head priest was still indoors. The pony was being pulled towards the village gate, chewing on a mouthful of dried grass that was hanging from its lips. Marna saw a woman struggle to carry two heavy bags of whale bone.

Fara turned to go back to her house, with Pip

following. Marna walked across to the woman. 'Do you need any help?' she volunteered.

The woman was glad to accept the offer, but warned Marna to be careful.

'Patro will not be pleased if the bone is chipped.'

'Or if any of the oil spills,' Marna added, taking one of the sacks. She intended her tone to be light, but the woman took offence. Further attempts at chatting were as futile as if they both spoke different languages.

'How long have you have been at the Ness?' Marna asked. The woman glowered at her and Marna took this as sufficient response.

The Ness workers knew their jobs. They worked in an orderly manner and it didn't take long for the boats to be loaded. Cushions and skins were set out for the priests' comfort. The woman snatched the sack from Marna's grasp and handed it to a boat worker. He took care positioning the heavy load, so as not to tip the balance of the vessel.

The pony had reached the shore and was being tugged by its mane towards the nearest boat. It showed as much reluctance to get in as Pip had when Sempal and Marna set off on their journey. Unlike Pip, Hansibar was too heavy to lift up and carry.

'You're hurting it,' Marna called.

The helper ignored her and gave the animal a slap on the rump. With a startled whinny, it kicked out with its back legs, sending the man sprawling. He wasn't hurt and Marna laughed. 'Serves you right,' she said.

'Better wait on Patro,' another of the helpers said. 'The beast will do anything for him.'

The men allowed the pony to chew at the vegetation on the bank while they finished preparing the boats. Marna looked across the water. She wasn't sure at first, but as she shielded her eyes against the sunlight, she made out the bobbing of a small dot. Its movement was slow and as the waves rose it appeared to vanish, but as she watched it came back into sight and grew into the shape of a boat. She smiled and raised her arms to wave, knowing Sempal and her mother would be unable to make her out.

'What is the silly girl doing now? Is she trying to get the terns to attack us?'

Marna spun round to see Patro, and the priests who were leaving with him, march towards her. A group of villagers, including most of the children except Vern, had come down to the shore to see their visitors off. Common sense told Marna to keep her mouth shut if she couldn't answer civilly, but she was tired of the head priest and his superior attitude.

'Instead of worrying about me, you would do better to take care of your own business,' she volleyed. 'If you don't stop him, your horse will devour that whole patch of thistles. I wouldn't like to be on the boat with him afterwards.'

Patro looked over to the pony and signalled to two men to catch it. The animal out-smarted them, trotting off a few yards whenever they came close. Patro heaved a sigh and strode across. The pony stood still and allowed him to take hold of the rope halter and lead it towards the boats.

'Hansibar is a *mare*,' he said to Marna as he passed.

It was hard to tell the gender under the animal's rough coat, but Marna conceded the point to Patro. While she had been watching the pony's antics, Sempal had rowed his boat towards the bay.

'Look, it's the magic, healing woman.' One of the children pointed at the boat.

Patro's men were in their boats and the pony was coaxed on board by offering it treats. The oarsmen were ready to push off. They were waiting for Patro to climb in. He stood on the shore, showing no sign of doing so. He watched Sempal steer his craft to land. When the boat reached shallow water Sempal scrambled out and grabbed hold of the bow. Marna jogged up to helped him pull the boat onto the beach. It tilted as Marna's mother stood up and stretched her legs.

'I didn't expect quite such a distinguished welcome,' Marna's mother said with a laugh.

Patro was staring at Marna's mother, but for once he didn't look angry. He moved to offer her a hand out of the boat. 'You must be Thork's mother,' he said. 'I have heard a great deal about you.'

'And I have heard much about you, Patro of the Ness,' Marna's mother answered. 'But that is of little consequence. I'm afraid I have no time for idle chatter. You are leaving, I see, and I came here to work. That is what I intend to do. Sempal, will you bring my bag from the boat?' She took a step and wobbled as the boat shifted. To stop herself falling on her face she accepted Patro's hand, but released it when she was safely on the shore. 'Marna, will you show me to my first patient?' she said, dismissing Patro with a smile.

'This way,' Marna directed. The village children swarmed round them and she couldn't see Patro's face, but she smirked as she imagined his disdain at being shrugged aside. Her mother knew how to put men like Patro in their place.

The head priest was standing looking out to sea, as if in a daze. One of the helpers in the boat cleared his throat overly loud, to gain his attention.

'The tide is turning. We should be off, sir.'

'A fine woman,' Patro muttered, more to himself than his men, but loud enough for Marna to hear. 'Not as old as I imagined, in fact…' Suddenly aware that Marna and her mother were still nearby, Patro cut short his ruminations. He turned to address his men. 'I have had second thoughts about leaving. I feel my presence is needed to give proper ceremony to the passing of the village elder Mooth and the girl Kayleen. The island needs fitting support in its spiritual awakening.'

'We're staying here? What about our duties at the Ness?' one of the priests asked.

'I'm staying here – for a little while longer. My aides and one of the boats shall remain on the island, but the remainder of you shall return to the Ness.'

'How long do you intend being here?' the priest asked.

'As long as is necessary,' Patro sounded impatient. 'Quint will take charge of the ceremonies and administration at the Ness until I return.'

The men looked at one another. Marna heard them mutter the name Quint in a manner that suggested he wasn't a popular choice, but no-one argued with Patro. One of the musicians sounded his horn. The rowers in two of the boats began manoeuvring them into the Sound. The men in Patro's boat climbed out and dragged it up the beach.

Patro watched his party leave before turning to head back to the village. He looked startled to see Marna watching him. Her mother had followed the islanders back to the village and apart from his men, there was no-one on the shore. He hesitated then passed close to Marna on his way up the path.

'It is beyond belief how such a good-looking and

refined woman could give birth to such a clumsy daughter,' he said in a voice that sounded more questioning than cruel. Marna seethed, but before a suitable response came to her Patro marched a few steps, paused, then added with a chuckle, 'Or your gormless brother.'

Instead of the caustic retort on the tip of her tongue, Marna couldn't help laughing. She wondered what her mother would think if she told her what Patro had said about Thork, but decided she would probably laugh too.

She waited a moment until Patro was far enough in front of her before starting back to the village. She was stopped by a thunderous splash, followed by shouts. Fearing one of the boats had capsized, she looked back.

Hansibar was in the water, swimming to the shore. She clearly wasn't used to the waves and kicked her front legs wildly, struggling to keep her head above the water as her rump rose and fell. She wasn't making progress and the current began dragging her further from the shore. Marna ran to the water's edge and waded in.

The water was frozen and she shivered, but she knew the pony was in trouble. The people in the boats looked on and pointed, but not one of them made an effort to row the vessels closer to the animal in order to help. Taking a lungful of air, Marna dived deeper and began swimming towards the pony. The waves were heavy and she didn't make much headway, but turning back proved just as

189

difficult.

Fortunately the pony was in more control of its limbs than she imagined. When they met, it was Marna who needed to grab hold of its mane for support until she regained her breath. Hansibar was re-assured by the human touch. She stopped thrashing her legs and neck and was able to start swimming. Together they made their way to the shore. Back on dry land, the pony shook its sodden coat over Marna then returned its attention to munching the sorrel and meadowsweet on the bank. Someone from one of the boats gave Marna a wave of thanks or support, but they didn't turn back. She watched as the party from the Ness continued on its way home.

'Looks like you are stuck here,' she said to the pony. It gave a snort. She knew she should find her mother, but she wasn't keen to explain why her tunic was dripping wet. No doubt Patro would accuse her of trying to drown his horse.

There was a gentle breeze and she guessed it would dry her clothes. She sat on a boulder to think while she waited. The swim had shaken her senses as well as her body. It took longer for her brain to stir into action than it did to regain the tingly sensation of warmth in her fingers and toes. She didn't register the person's approach until she heard a movement to her right. She swung round with her hands raised and fists clenched.

'It's you. What are you doing here?'

'I came to speak with you,' Aiven replied. 'Is that forbidden?'

Marna relaxed her hands. 'Where have you been? Have you been spying on me? Why did you run away? What will you do now?'

Aiven laughed. 'It's never one question at a time with you, is it? Serel, who was supposed to be guarding me, went to Patro's meeting, so I took my opportunity to leave. I didn't "run away". I'm about to return to the village to explain what happened to Patro.'

'I wouldn't do that,' Marna advised. 'Patro won't support you.'

'Why not? Why else did he come here? What has he said?'

'You are the one with the questions now. Patro has made a deal with Borg. He sold you in exchange for two sacks of whalebone and five pots of oil.'

'Well, that's not a bad price,' Aiven said lightly, but his face darkened and Marna guessed what his choice of words really were.

'You have to leave the island.' Marna jumped up as an idea hit her. 'Take Patro's boat.'

'I may be strong, but it would take two good men to row that boat. Besides, I would be noticed before I got out of the bay. Patro would not look favourably on the deed.' He ran his finger across his neck.

Marna pursed her lips and looked along the shore to where Sempal had tied his boat to a boulder. 'You could manage Sempal's,' she said. 'It travels fast. You could be on Rousay before the villagers launched their boats in the water.'

'I'm sure your friend would be delighted if I took his boat.'

'He would understand. Or at least, he wouldn't try to kill you.'

'I'm not leaving yet, Marna. There is something strange going on. I mean to find out what.'

'You don't belong here. Why should it bother you?'

'Let's say that I like a challenge. I've heard you don't shy away from mysteries either. I saw the inside of the burial cairn.'

'How could you? According to Neela the entrance stone was replaced before you escaped.'

'There is more than one way to get in.'

'Oh.'

'There is a gap in the ceiling in the central chamber. You should have looked when you were in.'

Marna pretended she didn't know what he meant, but he took hold of her hands and turned them over to see the marks of healing burns.

'Something tells me you were there when the fire started.'

'It isn't wise to trust your gut instincts.'

'No, but I also found this.' Aiven opened his palm to show a yellowish pebble.'

'What makes you think that is mine?'

'It has left a stain on your tunic.'

Marna looked down, but couldn't see a mark. Any stain would have washed off in the sea. 'You're guessing,' she said.

'I'm not far off the mark though. So, will you help me find out what is going on?' Aiven asked.

Marna puckered her lips before answering. 'Don't you mean, will I allow you to help me?' she qualified.

'Have it whatever way you wish. It is my belief that whatever ails the villagers stems from the land. We would do well to examine the area where I found the berries.'

'I thought so too, but Borg and his men have been patrolling it,' Marna answered. 'The island isn't large and it lacks large groves of trees or bushes. There are few places to conceal an approach. There doesn't seem any way we can get access. Unless...'

'That sounds like you have a plan,' Aiven said.

'An improbable one, but it might work. Patro wants the villagers to begin work on a stone circle for the island. He thinks the gods are upset and need to be placated.'

'We can sneak to the spot when everyone is busy working on the land?' Aiven said.

'There will still be guards. We can do better than that.'

Aiven understood. He wagged his right index fingers at Marna. 'If Patro wanted to build his stone circle on that exact spot, no-one would be able to stop him.'

'Exactly,' Marna agreed.

Aiven looked up towards the hill and his smile vanished. 'It isn't the best place to site a stone circle, is it?'

'What's wrong with it?'

'Ritual rings need to be built on flat ground, preferably round natural hollows. There are no suitable stones we can quarry from the hilltop. They will have to be brought from the cliffs or over from Rousay. Try hauling stones uphill over heather and see how long it takes you. Besides it should be accessible to everyone in the village. You can't place it halfway up a rugged hillside and expect people to drag their sacrifices to it. Patro is an expert when it comes to designing circles that last. There's little chance of him agreeing to that spot.'

'I've done my part, coming up with a plan. You are the one knowledgeable on priestly matters. It's down to you to find a way of persuading him.'

'He won't be bribed on religious matters. He does have some integrity.'

'I thought you were serious about wanting to help,' Marna challenged.

Aiven made a tutting sound through his teeth. 'Quite a

194

feisty female, aren't you?' He moved forwards and leant closer to Marna, putting a warm hand on her waist to draw her close. She felt his breath a moment before his lips touched hers. Marna let them linger before pushing him away. Aiven laughed.

'Haven't you kissed a man before? Or are you afraid someone is watching?'

'No, but you need to wash. You smell like rotten crabs. Meanwhile I have to assist my mother, who is a proper healer. I'll bring you food after dinner and we can discuss our plan then. Where are you hiding?'

'I'm not hiding.'

'If you don't tell me, I can't bring you dinner.'

Chapter 17

Marna turned her back on Aiven and strode towards the bank. The pony was watching her and she thought about leading it to the village, but she was afraid she wouldn't be able to catch it. Aiven was within laughing distance if the animal made her look foolish.

Her mother wasn't with Fara, but it didn't take long for Marna to find her. People in Eynhallow weren't deaf, as her mother clearly thought they were. Her voice, coming from Gora's hut, could frighten the seals on Rousay.

Marna tried to sneak into Gora's house, but the door creaked as she opened it. Her mother was attending to Gora's mother, but looked up and made a face at Marna. She didn't say anything about her bedraggled appearance, but Marna knew that would come later.

'Sorry, I got held up by…' she began. 'Oh.' It took a moment to realise the figure standing behind her mother, leaning against the wall and half hidden in the shadow, was Patro. He had his eyes fixed on her mother's hands.

'Shh,' her mother signalled her to be quiet as she placed a palm on her patient's forehead. 'How does that feel?' she asked Gora's mother.

'Cold,' Gora's mother answered, giving an unconvincing shiver.

'I see. What about this?' Marna's mother turned her

196

hand over to place her knuckles on the same spot.

'Hot.'

'I thought so.' Marna's mother stood up. 'Hand me my bag.'

Marna spotted the bag of medicines at her mother's feet. She bent to pick it up and her hand reached it a few seconds before Patro's. He grunted and stood back, allowing Marna to take the bag.

'What is wrong with me?' Gora's mother croaked.

Marna's mother looked up and spoke to Patro rather than Gora's mother. 'A severe case of imaginitis, similar to Jael, would you not agree?'

Marna hadn't heard of imaginitis, but Patro obviously had. His lips twitched and for a moment Marna thought he was remembering how to smile.

'Will I die?' Gora's mother asked, reaching bony fingers towards Marna's mother.

'Not if you take this medicine, three times a day. Marna – the dock, dandelion root and willow bark powder please.'

Marna couldn't help screwing up her face. She had taken the dock and willow bark powder her mother prepared when she suffered from cramps. It tasted bitter and left a clawing dirtiness in the mouth. She reached in the bag and found the murky green powder, which she handed to her mother.

197

'It must be taken on its own, on an empty stomach,' Marna's mother continued, which Marna thought odd, because her mother allowed her to add honey to sweeten the medicine. Gora's mother grabbed at the powder. 'Only one pinch at a time,' Marna's mother warned.

'Thank you,' Gora said taking the powder before her mother swallowed the full amount. 'I'll make sure mother takes it as you said. I'm afraid we can't repay you. We did have a piglet, but it disappeared.'

'It was a runt. Mind you, it wouldn't surprise me if it had ended up as Olan's supper pot,' her mother said. 'Not that there would have been more than a finger's worth of meat to put in the pot.'

Gora blushed. 'Mother doesn't mean what she said about Olan. Gerk has promised us another pig, when his sow farrows.'

'I don't require payment,' Marna's mother insisted. 'Unless you wish to play me a tune before I leave. Come Marna, there are other patients to heal.'

Marna opened the door and held it until her mother stepped out. She gave Gora a weak smile before leaving herself, carrying the bag of potions. She closed the door before Patro could follow. 'What is imaginitis?' she asked when they were clear of the house.

'It is whatever you want it to be,' her mother explained.

'I don't understand. Is it something the villagers have eaten that has entered their blood?'

'It is something they have heard that has entered their skulls,' her mother answered.

Marna thought about her mother's words as they made their way to the next house. 'Do you mean, because Kayleen and Mooth have died, the villagers believe there is an illness on the island? Surely that can't cause the sickness and coughing?'

'Trust me, you will find these imaginary symptoms will vanish before it is time to wash again, especially when the alternative is taking my medicine three times a day on an empty stomach.'

'If there is nothing wrong with the people, I have wasted your time sending for you,' Marna said.

'I was in need of a break. Thork came over from Orphir. Caran is expecting a child.'

'That is wonderful,' Marna answered, giving a jump. 'I hope it is a girl who is as pretty as Caran. I could make her tiny tunics and shawls and show her my bone figure.'

'Yes, but I don't need to hear how great a father Thork will make twenty times a day - nor how fantastic an aunt you will be. Not when the baby isn't due until after the winter solstice.'

'I wonder what it feels like to have a baby growing inside you.'

'I barely noticed Thork was there, but you were a different story, you wouldn't stop kicking, trying to get out.' She glanced over Marna's shoulder as she spoke. 'Now, hadn't you better hurry back to Fara's house and get yourself dry?'

'Don't you need my help?'

'It seems I have a helper.' Patro had stepped out of Gora's house and was heading in their direction. Her mother gave him a wave.

'Oh, right.' Marna handed the medicine bag to her mother. 'Aren't you too old to be flirting?'

'A woman is never too old for that, Marna.'

'Perhaps you could tell 'his greatness' that his pony is on the shore eating half the island. It jumped out of the boat after he left. Everyone is frightened to go near it.' Marna took a step then added. 'You'd better humour him and call it a horse.'

Fara was re-arranging skins and heather mattresses when Marna returned to the house. There was a heap lying on the floor in the centre, gathering ash from the remains of the fire.

'Do you want me to add the bog myrtle?' Marna asked.

'What's that for?'

'It's what my mother does,' Marna replied, deciding it wasn't the time to mention she'd been feeling itchy in the mornings since her arrival. Fleas had a liking for her blood.

She would ask her mother if she'd brought any over and slip some sprigs among the heather when Fara was out. 'Oh, there it is.' She rescued her shawl before Fara stuffed it under a pile of cushions.

'I'm trying to sort out sleeping arrangements. Kali will stay in Neela's house with the others from the Ness in case he is needed, but there will be your mother and Sempal.'

'Did someone mention my name?' Marna had left the door open and Sempal hobbled in.

'Where have you been?' Marna asked.

'With Olan.'

'Not playing dice, I hope,' Fara said.

Sempal's face reddened. 'He has asked me to stay with him and his parents.' Fara made a face. 'It's not that I don't like it here, I just thought it would be a bit crushed with Marna's mother and... everyone...'

'Sometimes it would be better if you didn't think,' Marna interrupted, but Fara put a hand on Sempal's shoulder.

'You're right. You know we'd love to have you here, but there will be more space at Olan's.'

'And it is only next door. I've come to pick up my stuff.' He looked to Marna. 'How long do you think we will be staying on the island?'

'Mother doesn't think her work will take long. Jael is already out of bed and sorting wood to make a new table. A

201

couple of doses of medicine and the whole village will be dancing at Patro's mid-summer romp.'

'Patro is having a mid-summer ceremony?' Fara jumped on Marna's words.

'He hasn't actually said so, but I wouldn't be surprised if he did. What I meant was my mother doesn't think the illnesses are serious.'

Fara had stopped listening. Marna could hear her mind clicking into party mode. Gerk returned from making sure the cattle had water. A couple of the younger men had rowed to Rousay and brought back fresh water from the loch. In return, Gerk gave them milk from Fara's suckler cow. He was hardly through the door before Fara began discussing food, decorations and music with him.

'Has Patro declared a feast?' Gerk asked.

'Not yet, but Marna says he will.'

'Won't Patro be expected back at the Ness for the solstice? There was preparation going on when we were there and he didn't seem to trust the deputy head he put in charge.'

'A tallish man with a birth mark on his cheek?' Fara asked. 'That would be his brother Quint. Jona had stories to tell about him.'

'Your father had stories to tell about everyone, including me,' Gerk laughed.

'I didn't say it was definite,' Marna excused, breaking

up Fara and Gerk's conversation. She was beginning to think she would have to find a way of making sure Patro made the announcement or look like a liar.

Although he claimed only to have returned to collect his few possessions, Sempal hung around the hut, sniffing the air every so often hoping the tang of cooked meat reaching his throat would slither down. Marna found a clump of wool to dry herself while Gerk and Fara played with Terese.

Marna's hair was clumping and she hoped to have the tangles loosened before her mother returned. Her mother would take the comb and insist on reaching the back for her although she was not as careful with the combing as she could be.

She expected her mother would be tired after the journey and doctoring the sick, but on her return she bustled around the house, moving various bits and pieces that Fara had arranged. Marna felt there was something her mother wanted to say, but she knew she would have to find the right question to get an answer. It came out over dinner. Sempal had decided to stay for the meal and made a joke about the priests demanding goat's milk and honey ale.

'It's only the best for those from the Ness. They have heard about the ovens in Rousay and Patro wants someone to row over every morning for bread and fresh water,' Gerk said.

'He'll be lucky,' Marna said.

'Olan has volunteered,' Sempal replied.

'He would,' Gerk said. 'He will make sure it is worth his while though.'

'The ovens in Rousay produce wonderful bread,' Fara said, breaking a bannock and allowing the crumbs to scatter over her stew.

'I could have been staying with them,' Marna's mother said casually, taking a mouthful of stew. The others stared at her. She finished chewing and swallowing before continuing. 'Patro invited me to share their house.'

'Their house? It hasn't taken the Ness lot long to feel at home. Neela and Vern have to share with Wandra and Borg until the house is free,' Marna said.

'Mmm,' Marna's mother made an enigmatic murmur and took a bite from a bannock.

'It would be good to have an ear in there,' Gerk said. 'To find out what they are planning. Someone told me Jolty has selected a group of villagers to help him choose a site for the stone circle.'

'Would that *someone* be Olan?' Fara said.

'He has an ear for gossip. He said Borg has made sure his friends are the ones with influence - Serel, Bryne and Froink.'

'Let them plan what they want,' Fara said. 'They'll choose a site, arrange for stones to be quarried and once the priests have left the island, the stones will lie where they have been left.'

'But somebody will gain something from it, no doubt, and it won't be us,' Gerk reflected.

His remark put a dampener on the conversation, which petered out until Sempal was persuaded to stay longer and tell a story before he retired to Olan's house.

'Would you like a true story or a far-fetched fantasy?' Sempal didn't need much encouragement to launch into a tale.

'The true ones are less believable than the made-up ones,' Marna's mother replied. 'But I am in the mood for fantasy.'

'Tell us about sea monsters,' Gerk said. 'Then I can scare Olan the next time we are in his boat.'

'Sempal's rowing is scary enough without meeting krakens and giant whales,' Marna teased.

Sempal told several stories, with the ending of one running into the beginning of another, so it was late before Marna got to sleep. There was no chance of speaking with Sempal on his own that evening and she wasn't keen to tell the others about her meeting with Aiven.

The following morning she made the excuse of taking milk to Olan's mother to speak with Sempal. He was about to head to the shore to check on his boat.

'I'll come with you,' she said. 'Pip needs his exercise.'

Sempal waited while she returned to Fara's house to collect Pip. She returned a few minutes later, panting and without the dog.

'He prefers the warmth of Fara's fire. I couldn't shift him,' she said.

'I thought Pip was the one needing the exercise not you,' Sempal joked.

'Ha.' Marna strode ahead. Sempal caught up and walked beside her.

'I tried speaking with Vern, but she seemed afraid of something,' Marna said.

'Sorry, I must have missed something. Can we start from the beginning?' Sempal said.

Marna gave an exasperated sigh. 'That's just it, we must have missed something.'

Sempal scratched his head, trying to think what Marna was talking about. 'Perhaps nothing *is* going on. Kayleen ate rotten berries and sadly died. The same with Mooth; he was old and weak and everyone is short of water, which saps the body's vigour.'

'That doesn't explain why Borg and his friends are acting like island guards; accusing Aiven of foul deeds and patrolling the hillside?' Marna argued.

'Borg's daughter has died. He needs to blame someone.'

'Or he had something to do with it,' Marna suggested.

'Borg wouldn't harm his own child.'

'I suppose not, but perhaps that was an accident. Or… or…' Marna snapped her fingers. 'Perhaps Mooth was his real target.'

Sempal shook his head. 'You have my stories from last night in your head.'

'Real life is more unbelievable, as my mother said. Think about it, wouldn't Borg love to be the head man of the village? He is already acting as if he is.'

'Getting rid of Mooth wouldn't help him. Choosing leaders doesn't work the same way here as in Skara Brae. I asked Olan. He said the eldest resident is automatically made chief, in name at least. With Mooth dead, that honour goes to Olan's mother. I can't see May killing anyone to gain the position.'

'I wouldn't put it past Olan to try and persuade her,' Marna grumbled.

'We're talking about Borg, and there are a good many more people in line before he is chief. He can't poison half the village.'

'Maybe my mother is wrong. Perhaps that *is* his plan.' Marna twisted the end of her hair as she thought. 'I know, I'm being stupid, but there is something upsetting the villagers that we can't understand. There's something evil on the island.'

'The weather is the problem,' Sempal said. 'It is

affecting you too. There hasn't been a proper shower of rain for months and the air is pressing. The spring is completely dry today. Olan says that Serel and Bryne are keen to organise a grazing system for the cattle and sheep on the lower grassy strips. The shaded land there is still moist, whereas the plants in other areas have shrivelled to nothing.'

'Sounds reasonable,' Marna allowed.

'It is if you are the people making the rules,' Sempal said.

They reached Sempal's boat and Marna rested against the side. She picked up a piece of driftwood and untangled a thong of seaweed from it before tossing it towards the water.

'I know you enjoy a mystery, but it seems to me there is another reason you are reluctant to leave the island,' Sempal said.

'What is that?'

Sempal puckered his lips, mimicking a kiss. Marna pushed him lightly on the shoulder and he stumbled a few steps until he regained his balance. 'Did you think no-one was watching? Remember, this is a small island. You are never alone.'

'Friends don't snoop on one another,' Marna said. 'Nor do they let their imaginations run wild. I'm using Aiven to help me find out what is going on, that's all.'

'I wasn't judging, but don't let your feelings for him blind you to his true motives.'

'What feelings? What true motives? You know what those are?'

'Olan was gambling with Serel and Bryne. They thought he was asleep after drinking too much ale, but he overheard them talking. Aiven's name came up several times.'

'That tells me more about Serel and Bryne's motives than Aiven's. Didn't you say they were the ones plotting to get the best grazing for their cattle? You should be keeping an eye on what those two are up to.'

'Why me?'

'Because it will be easy for you, now that you are best friends with Olan. He knows all the gossip.'

'Don't be like that. I thought you would be glad to see me back, not jumping down my throat whenever I say something. I am trying to help.'

'I'm sorry.' Marna moved closer and took his hands. They felt warm and comforting, but she didn't feel the thrill she got when she touched Aiven. 'It's this island. I don't know what it is. Perhaps it is the weather, or the people. I haven't felt settled since we arrived.'

'Then we should leave.'

Marna shuffled a foot in the sand. 'I suppose you're right. I have to finish dyeing a tunic for Gora, but that should be ready by this afternoon.'

'We can leave with the late tide.' Sempal removed his hand from hers and ran it across the skin of his boat.

'Depending on my mother, of course,' Marna added.

'I thought you said she had nothing more to do here.'

Marna smiled playfully. 'I said she had no more work. That isn't the same as wanting to leave. Still, I'd better tell Fara our plans.'

'Good. Damn.'

'What is it?' Marna moved to examine the side of the boat.

'There's a tear in the skin,' Sempal explained. 'How could that have happened? It was fine when I pulled it up here yesterday.'

'Could it have ripped on a rock?'

'I was careful. This is more like a knife slash.' Sempal stuck his fingers through the gap and wriggled them. 'This was deliberate.'

'Don't be silly. Who would want to damage your boat?'

'Maybe somebody wants to keep us on the island.'

'I can't imagine anyone would want that. The islanders seem anxious for us to leave, if only to save the water supplies.'

'I know someone who might want to keep you here,' Sempal said. Before Marna could ask who, he mimicked kissing again. This time Marna gave him a hard push, knocking him against the boat. His fingers were still through the tear and twisted round the material. 'Aargh. I was joking.' He untangled his fingers and rubbed away the pain. 'No need to get touchy.'

'Sorry,' Marna said, 'But who has been telling you tales about me and Aiven?'

'No-one.'

'Really?' She stood in front of him with an outstretched arm either side of his ears, playfully pinning him to the wooden frame of the boat.

'Vern,' he confessed. I met her this morning. She was heading to Fara's house to ask if she could play with Pip.'

'Why did you stop her? I need to speak with her.'

'It was early. I didn't think you would want to be disturbed.' Marna leaned closer, her eyes narrowed. 'It was very early,' Sempal said.

Marna stood back to release Sempal. 'There is something odd about that child,' she said. 'I'm sure she is hiding something.'

'All children have secrets, or pretend they do. I remember when you were younger…'

'How long will it take to repair your boat?' Marna stopped him before he began an embarrassing story. Sempal inspected the rip again.

'The tear won't take long to sew over, but I will need

to check the willow frame then re-apply the fat layer to waterproof the lining. That will take time to dry.'

'How long?' Marna wasn't interested in the details of boat repair.

'It depends on the weather.' He looked up to the sky. 'It doesn't look like it will rain, but it will take until …tomorrow morning… at the earliest.'

Marna could tell from his hesitation he was guessing at what she wanted to hear and smiled. Her misgivings about the island could be unfounded, but since fate was offering her time to investigate, it would be foolish to spurn it.

'Try and keep out of trouble until then,' Sempal pleaded. 'I heard about your trip to the tomb.'

'I'll try,' Marna answered. She smiled as a wicked thought flashed through her head.

Someone should convince her mother to do the same.

Chapter 18

Marna left Sempal to begin his repairs, scrambling up the path to the village. Sempal hadn't been as curious as she hoped about the island's mystery, which led her to ponder whether there was some other reason he wanted to leave. Was there something at home? Or someone?

That was ridiculous. If there was someone waiting for him, she would know. There had been the affair with the Irish woman, but fortunately he had seen sense over that sorcerer. Did he think he was too old for 'childish' mysteries and secrets? Did he consider her a child, compared to Erin?

By the time she reached the village wall she was determined to solve the puzzle on her own to show him she wasn't some stupid girl. She would have to find a way of doing it that didn't involve hanging around the village otherwise her mother would find her jobs to take up the day.

Jolty was addressing a group of villagers in the central gathering area. He had his back to her and she didn't recognise him at first. Not only had he discarded his cumbersome priestly skins in favour of a tunic and leggings similar to the village men, but his beard was un-plaited and the ochre dye and scent had been washed out. Marna tagged on at the back to listen.

As Gerk had reported, Jolty had chosen Borg and his cronies, Serel and Bryne, to advise him on choosing a site for the new stone circle, but Neela was also included in the group. They had decided on the flat area of cleared land a short walk along the coast from the village. It was a sensible choice. They could quarry stones from the nearby cliffs and it was near the bay to ship in supplies from the neighbouring island of Rousay. The plan to raise five stones on the spot sounded unambitious, but manageable.

'Has anyone any further questions or comments?' Jolty asked. Marna couldn't imagine Patro showing such consideration, but the head priest wasn't in attendance. She stuck her hand up, waving her fingers above Froink's head to gain attention.

'Yes – Marna, isn't it?'

Everyone turned to look at her.

'It isn't very inspiring,' she said. 'Not compared to the circles on the mainland.'

'The older circles took a great deal of time to construct,' Jolty answered. 'The Ring at Brodgar is still barely started and work has been going on for many seasons. The idea here is to have a focal point for worship and ceremony. You know that planting stones in alignment has special importance, which wise people are continually studying.' He had been speaking to Marna, but he raised his head to address the others. 'Of course, if you feel that once ritual practices are established and you have your own trained priest you wish to enlarge the circle, then that would certainly be possible.'

His thinking was logical and Marna didn't like arguing, but she couldn't rely on Aiven carrying out his part of her plan. 'But could it be re-located?' she queried.

The woman beside her grunted and Marna supposed she shared her mother's view on stone circles and how much time should be wasted on them.

'Re-located where?' Jolty's tone implied he was aware there was more to Marna's questioning than naïve speculation, but he was willing to listen.

'There.' Marna pointed up the hill. Borg suppressed an exclamation, while Serel whispered something to Bryne. 'It would be closer to the gods,' Marna justified her choice. 'Or would that be too much hassle? Don't the gods deserve the best?'

'Now listen here…' Borg began, but Jolty put out a hand to hush him.

'What makes you think the gods live in the sky?' he asked Marna.

'Jona, the priest at Skara Brae, taught us that they did.'

'Don't you think the gods may also reside in the sea, in trees or in animals? Do not believe everything you are taught. Our knowledge grows the more we ask questions about what we sense around us. My own teachers were wise men and women, but they were convinced that one day the waters in the sea would drop down over the edge and fall away from us, leaving the fish to flounder on the sand. I am not putting Jona down. He was a man with a great depth of understanding. He believed a good many things that others disagreed with. So do I.'

He smiled and Marna smiled back. 'I haven't studied the ways of the gods,' she admitted. She wasn't sure she even believed in them, but she knew not to admit this in public. 'But if someone built a stone circle for me, I would want it to be placed in the most prominent position. I'd want it somewhere it could be seen not only from the village, but also from the mainland…and Rousay.'

This last point went down well with the Eynhallow folk. They liked the thought of having something better than their larger neighbours.

'We are wasting time,' Borg cut short the mumblings of approval. 'A site has been decided. It's time to begin work.'

'No need for haste,' Jolty reminded him. 'Patro must first agree to the location.'

'It's our island.' Marna heard Olan's voice pipe up. 'Why must Patro have a say?'

'Some sites are favoured by the gods and some are not. A stone circle must be consecrated by the head priest.' Jolty seemed perturbed by Olan's question.

'You said Patro's decision was a matter of course,' Borg said. 'You implied he would go along with whatever we agreed.'

'Patro will heed my recommendation,' Jolty said. 'But he will expect it to be well researched.' He looked up the hill. The sun was high, burning down on the heather to give a glorious sheen to the summit. He shielded his eyes with his arm, but beneath his sleeve Marna saw a set look. 'There is merit to Marna's suggestion. The hillside gives a better view for tracing the movements of the sun and moon and forming alignments. It should be considered,' he decided.

Marna felt a rush of blood to her head. Jolty had not only remembered her name, he had listened to her proposal and thought it worthy. She was brought down by a piercing glare from Borg before he spoke.

'Aye, well we've considered the girl's ludicrous idea and rejected it,' he said, turning to encourage Neela, Serel and Bryne to join in his mockery.

'She isn't from this island – what does she know?' Bryne said before giving a hearty guffaw. Serel and Neela eyed one another, but didn't laugh.

'I think we could at least inspect the area,' Jolty said.

'We can't,' Serel burst in. Jolty stared at him. 'I mean, it's out of bounds, isn't it?' he appealed to Borg.

'That is where the poisoned berries are,' Borg

answered.

'Indeed? I will be careful not to eat any of the berries I find there. Thank you for the warning,' Jolty said.

Serel opened his mouth to say something further, but a glare from Borg stopped him.

'An inspection can be arranged,' Borg conceded. 'When do you wish to make the trip?'

'There is no time like the present,' Jolty answered cheerfully. 'That is, if Marna is free.'

'She isn't on the site committee,' Neela objected.

'There is no site committee,' Jolty said. 'It is Marna's suggestion. She must be allowed to point out the advantages of her choice. Whoever wishes can accompany us and speak against it.'

'There is no point everyone trudging up the hill,' Borg said before others from the village could declare an interest. 'Bryne and Serel will accompany you.'

'What about Patro?' Marna asked.

Borg laughed. 'I'm sure he has better things to do.'

'He has **other** things to do,' Jolty qualified. 'He has placed me in charge of this project.' He turned back to Marna. 'What do you say, Marna? Are you free and able to show us your spot?'

'The sun is up, will you manage a brisk walk up the hill?' Marna asked. Jolty was not a young man. Without the dye, his face was wrinkled and his beard was silver. His bones creaked when he stood up. 'I don't mean you are too old,' Marna added, 'But you will be all right, won't you?'

'I'm not in need of a stretcher yet,' Jolty answered.

'I shall have to tell Fara and my mother where I'm heading,' Marna said. 'I won't be long.'

'We'll wait.'

Bryne gave a snort, but Serel nodded. She reached the door of Fara's house and Pip came out to greet her, nosing round her for a treat. She took hold of his scruff to make sure he didn't run off and was about to enter when she spotted Vern. The girl was standing a little way off, rubbing her arm.

'Hello,' Marna called. She would have waved, but was reluctant to release Pip.

Vern looked up. She looked like she was about to run off, but hesitated for a moment.

'No, wait. Don't you want to see Pip?' Marna said. She lifted the dog in her arms and patted his head as she walked towards Vern. The girl stood frozen to the spot as Marna approached. Her eyes were fixed on Pip. Marna held him so that Vern could stroke his nose.

'He likes that,' Marna said.

'His fur is soft,' Vern said. 'Like my mother's cloak.'

Neela's cloak was made of smooth sealskin. Marna had to bite her tongue to prevent herself from saying that she would kill anyone who tried to make Pip into an item of clothing. 'Would you like to look after him for me while I go up the hill?'

Vern's face paled and she pulled her hand away. 'Why do you want to go up the hill?' she asked. 'That is where the evil is.'

'Do you mean the evil that killed Kayleen?'

Vern nodded. 'You shouldn't go there.'

'Don't worry I will have Serel and Bryne to protect me, and Jolty the priest will guard us against evil.' Marna smiled. Vern returned it with a weak grin. She stroked Pip's head.

'I will look after Pip for you. I don't want him going on the hill.'

'Thank you. I won't be long. Perhaps you could brush the tangles out of his coat while I am gone. I'll fetch you the special bone comb I use.'

'I have a comb,' Vern said. 'I use it to brush wool from the sheep.' This time her smile was wide.

Pip squirmed to be let down. Marna gave him a kiss on the top of his head before placing him on the ground beside Vern. 'Stay,' she commanded, walking into the house before he could follow.

Her mother was out, but she explained to Fara where she would be. When she returned to the gathering spot the villagers had returned to work, leaving Jolty, Serel and Bryne on their own. They were discussing plans as she reached them, but fell silent before she could make out the words. Jolty was holding a forked hazel sapling, which seemed to be the cause of Serel and Bryne's upset.

'Ready,' she said with a smile that wasn't returned.

Marna had hoped to ask Jolty questions about the Ness on the walk, but despite her concerns about his age, the elderly priest marched ahead of Serel and Bryne, as fleet-footed as the men born on the mountains in the south lying lands. Marna puffed to keep up, drawing in short breaths when they reached the hill and started climbing through the dense layers of sun-burnt heather.

'Aargh.' Her foot caught and she stumbled forwards. Jolty stopped and looked back. 'I'm fine,' she said, her face reddening.

'Borg was right, we shouldn't have brought a girl from the mainland with us,' Bryne muttered.

Jolty slowed to allow her to keep pace while Serel and Bryne went ahead to clear a path with their stone knives. Jolty didn't speak and Marna was afraid her voice would disturb his higher thoughts. When he began whistling out of tune, the noise grated. It would be rude to ask him to stop, so she asked a question instead.

'What *other* business does Patro have on the island?' She lightened her tone, trying to suggest the question was a casual one. Jolty gave a chuckle. She couldn't see his eyes, but imagined there would be a twinkle in them.

221

'My son doesn't tell me everything he gets up to,' Jolty answered. 'He must consider the matter important, since it is keeping him from preparations for the summer solstice ceremony at the Ness.'

'Your son? You are Patro's father?'

'That surprises you?'

'I suppose I thought…because…well… I can talk to you.'

'And you can't talk to Patro? He has a position to maintain, but that shouldn't stop anyone from speaking to him.'

'He doesn't like me.'

'You don't like him,' Jolty countered.

'Mmmm,' Marna replied with a humming noise that showed he had discerned the truth.

'I can see you have your reasons, but it is my turn to ask a question,' Jolty said. 'Why are you interested in this stone circle? You don't live on this island. You won't be the one celebrating here.'

Marna was expecting the question and had prepared an answer. It was awkward lying to Jolty, and the words didn't come out as she had repeated them in her head. 'The stars…in the sky…up there.' They had stopped walking and Jolty was staring into her eyes as she spoke. She swallowed and tried again. 'I'm interested in learning. The stone circles tell us about the movement of the stars and what that means for us…don't they?'

'Mmm.' It was Jolty's turn to express his opinion without words. 'Have you spoken with Aiven?'

'Not about the stars.'

'About his healing stones?'

'Not about anything, really.'

Jolty puckered his lips and his voice became sombre. 'I fear Aiven is not a friend of our islands. He soaks in our wisdom, but guards his own knowledge as if it were a child. Learning must be shared and challenged. How else can societies advance?'

He posed a question, but Marna knew he wasn't looking for an answer, and certainly not from her. Jolty took her lack of response differently.

'That does not make him an enemy,' he conceded. 'Some people prefer to keep their own council.'

Marna suspected he was referring to her as well as Aiven. They began walking again. The hill had a gentle gradient, but they had reached a rockier section. She was excused from continuing the conversation by the need to concentrate on her footing. She watched where Jolty placed his feet and tried to follow his steps, wondering what learning he had that enabled him to stay so active. He stopped abruptly and she had to swerve to avoid knocking her nose on his back.

'Ah, these must be the berries Borg warned about.'

Jolty pointed to a shrivelled clump of early strawberries.

'I wouldn't want to eat those.' Marna knelt down to inspect them.

'No, but the ones further along are pink and plump. They should ripen in a few days.'

Marna had assumed the stick he was carrying was to aid his progress, but he hadn't made use of it. She was surprised when he held it in front of him with the forked ends furthest from his hand.

Serel and Bryne were about fifty yards in front of them. They hadn't bothered with the stragglers, but at that moment Serel looked back to check how they were. 'Hey, what are you doing?' he shouted, jogging towards them.

'I slipped on the heather,' Marna answered, grasping at Jolty's arms. 'Jolty was helping me up.'

Serel looked at the ground. Some pink campion, lovage and sorrel sprung up from the hard earth, but there was no trace of heather. 'Did you touch the berries?'

Marna inspected her palms, wiping the dust on her tunic. 'No, I don't think so.'

Bryne had joined the group. He scowled at Marna. 'We don't have time for weaklings. We need to get on.'

'Can you manage? Are you injured?' Serel showed more concern.

'I'm fine.'

Marna prepared to move on, but Jolty stood on the

spot as if his feet were snared. He gazed out across the Sound, focussing on the ripples of the water. It was a clear day and the outline of Rousay was sharp, rising from the sea. The sun hung above the hills on the neighbouring island, dangling its rays on the land like slender fingers.

'It's a beautiful view,' Marna said.

'Spectacular,' Jolty agreed. 'Words cannot describe it. We have found the perfect site.'

'Where?' Serel turned in a circle to see where Jolty meant. 'You can't mean on Rousay.'

'I mean here.'

'Here,' Bryne and Serel repeated in unison. 'That is madness.'

'On the contrary.' Jolty raised his stick. 'Marna has divined the perfect spot – and without the need of any device. She is indeed a wise woman.'

Chapter 19

The land they were standing on bobbled and was far from flat. Marna would not have considered it suitable for building on and she had the fleeting feeling that despite what Jolty said, he chose it because he didn't want to climb any higher.

'Ridiculous,' Bryne said.

'The gods have sent a sign.' Jolty pointed at the sky. 'See how the sun shines across onto this spot.'

'Only at this exact time,' Serel answered. 'I don't see why it is important. It isn't the solstice.'

'No, but it is the time we are here,' Jolty answered.

Marna could tell Serel and Bryne didn't understand his logic, but didn't want to show their ignorance.

'It will take months of work to level the site,' Bryne objected. 'Then there will be the problem of transporting the stones up the hill. We won't be able to slide them on seaweed. The stones will simply slip downhill.'

'Would you like me to tell the gods that the islanders of Eynhallow aren't willing to put in the labour for them?' Jolty asked.

'I didn't say that,' Bryne muttered. 'I am concerned that folk may be injured in the process – or worse. This land is cursed.'

'Which is more reason to build our circle here. The

stones and rituals will sanctify the earth.'

Serel and Bryne glanced at each other, but couldn't think of further objections.

'Do you have a problem with this site?' Jolty asked Marna.

Although she agreed with Bryne and Serel that the positioning was a challenging one for building, Marna suspected that wasn't their true reason for rejecting the spot. She decided to test them. 'If the gods have chosen, who are we to question them?' she replied.

'Good,' Jolty smiled. 'I shall speak with Patro this afternoon.'

'You won't need to wait until then,' Serel said, pointing up the hill. 'Isn't that him there?'

Patro's pony was plodding down from the summit, with its rider swaying like reeds in the breeze. The priest's feet were inches from the ground, in danger of getting in the way of the pony's hooves.

'Indeed,' Jolty said. He leant over to Marna and whispered, 'The more devout my son becomes; the less use he has of his legs.' Marna thought he was serious until she saw the smile cross his lips.

Jolty was first to move, striding to meet Patro with a raised arm. Not wishing to be left with Serel and Bryne, Marna followed, but hung back a little way off. Jolty was a mere three feet in front of Patro before the head priest snapped from his inner thoughts and pulled the pony up sharply with a tug on its mane. The animal gave a snort. Jolty stroked its nose and gave Patro a curt nod.

'What is wrong? Has something happened?' Patro asked, glancing at Serel and Bryne.

'Nothing is wrong. We have found a site for the Stone Circle,' Jolty said.

'The news could have waited. You didn't need to trail up here to tell me.'

'We didn't. This is our site.'

'What!' Patro's incredulity was a match for Serel and Bryne's. Marna guessed if anyone else had told him, he would have declared them mad.

'Yes. It was through Marna's inspiration that we considered the hillside and once here, we were given a sign.'

'Marna's inspiration?'

Marna heard the disdain in Patro's voice although Jolty didn't appear to. He described the appearance of the sun and the glow across the water with a gleam in his eyes. Patro kept his eyes on Marna as his father spoke. They burned through her with more power than the sun. She wanted to look away, but there was something different about the head priest. She couldn't put her finger on it, but she was curious to work out what it was. Jolty finished speaking, but Patro did not respond.

'You have business here yourself?' Jolty said.

Patro kept his gaze on Marna for a further moment before turning to answer his father. 'I spoke to you about the forecasts for the sky. Kali and I have been deciding on the best spot to keep vigil.'

At the mention of the younger man's name he came into view, struggling to keep upright on the dry grass under the weight of a heavy bag. Patro raised his snipped eyebrows and rolled his eyes at Kali's attempts to descend the hill. If he didn't hold such a dignified position, Marna would have thought he was laughing.

'I was looking for Kali earlier,' Jolty said. 'I will need his help with the organisation.'

Patro sniffed the air several times before agreeing. When Kali puffed up, he instructed him to remain with Jolty. The pony was taking the opportunity to devour a gorse bush and Patro gave her flanks a nudge to urge her on. Jolty put a hand on the beast's rump to delay them.

'Won't you need your bag?' he asked. He took the sack from Kali before Patro could answer and positioned it across the pony's back. Hansibar flicked her tail then began waddling down the hill. Jolty moved to speak with Serel and Bryne as Marna watched Patro leave. Kali's breathing was heavy beside her. She turned to talk to him.

'Hard work?'

'I can manage,' Kali replied. 'I volunteered to go with

Patro. I want to learn about the stars. One day I will know more than anyone about them.'

'I would like to learn about the stars too,' Marna said.

'Patro would never teach a girl.'

'That is his loss,' Marna said. 'I'll find someone who will.'

Kali blew air through his teeth. 'You mean the wizard?'

'Maybe.'

'Do you know where he is?'

Marna guessed Kali was smarting from being blamed for losing him and wanted to be the one who found him. She thought it wiser to change the subject. 'There was something different about Patro today…'she began.

Kali gave a chuckle before she could finish her sentence. Without answering, he scratched the top of his shaven head. Marna looked at him for a moment then laughed too. 'He's grown hair,' she said. Kali nodded. 'Why?'

'Rumour has it your mother told him she can't take a man who shaves his head seriously.'

Marna pictured her mother with her arms akimbo, speaking to the priest the same way she lectured Thork. 'Why would Patro care about what my mother says?'

Kali made a face. 'You're not a child, Marna. Can't you see he has taken a liking to her? He hasn't shaved his head since she arrived on the island.'

'You're joking?'

'Not at all,' Kali said, but was suddenly serious. 'You won't tell him I laughed, will you?'

'He wouldn't listen to me if I did. I'm only a girl,' Marna answered. She pointed past Kali to where Jolty was waving. 'It looks like you are wanted.'

'It had better not take long,' Kali sighed. 'I'm starving.'

'Make sure you don't eat any berries,' Marna warned.

Kali's stomach rumbled and he held his abdomen. 'My sister makes a delicious berry tart. I was hoping she would bake one while I'm here.'

'I think you are out of luck. It is only the berries on this spot that are tainted, but the others on the island are too shrivelled to eat.'

Jolty's waving was getting agitated. 'I'd better go,' Kali said. He walked past Marna, beginning to strut as he approached Jolty.

With the men busy, Marna hoped she could gather a handful of healthy berries without Bryne or Serel noticing, but before she found any Jolty signalled her to join them.

'Have you seen my divining rod?' he asked.

'Your forked stick?'

'I set it somewhere to lift Patro's bag, but I can't seem to find it now.'

'Is this what you are looking for?' Serel held up one piece of the stick. His brother had the other half. 'I'm afraid there has been an accident.'

Marna could tell Jolty suspected the brothers of sabotage, but he accepted Serel's word that he had stood on it unwittingly.

The men began talking about foundations and wind direction. Marna nodded or shook her head when she felt she should, but it was difficult to keep up the pretence of knowing more than she did about building.

Kali's mention of food had made her hungry and words like "stake" made her mouth water. She thought of her mother's cooking while Jolty paced the site and counted steps. The instructions he gave to Kali were rapidly delivered and Marna could tell Kali was having problems remembering steps from strides.

Serel and Bryne moved a little distance away, muttering to each other. Marna didn't venture close enough to listen, but they didn't sound happy. They were keen to return to the village, but reluctant to leave Marna and the priests unguarded. Bryne was quick to shadow Jolty when he looked like wandering off and Serel was never far from Marna.

'Kali and I can manage for now,' Jolty assured them, but Marna knew they had orders from Borg not to leave.

Eventually Jolty was satisfied and they trekked down

the hill to the village. The trip had taken longer than Marna expected and she went on ahead, anxious to find Vern and make sure Pip was fine. The dog was sitting at the entrance to the village licking his paws, but jumped up when he heard Marna approach. She hurried to him and knelt to give him a hug. The tangles had been combed out of his fur, leaving it soft to her touch. She looked round to thank Vern, but the girl was nowhere in sight.

'Vern,' she called, hearing footsteps approach, but it didn't take long to realise it was her mother coming towards her. She was in a hurry and for a moment Marna thought she spotted someone following her, a short distance behind, but when she squinted against the sun to see clearer, the shadow had disappeared.

'Thank goodness you're back,' Marna's mother said, tugging at Marna's tunic to drag her to the house.

'Why? What has happened?' Marna felt her heart jump. 'Terese hasn't taken ill?'

'She is well, as ever, but *he* has been following me for a good half of the morning, making stupid remarks.'

'Who has?'

'And when I volunteered Thork's services to help with the stones, he wasted no time in putting me in my place.' Her mother gave a grunt. 'I knew it would be many moon cycles before the ground was ready for the stones.'

'Of course,' Marna agreed. 'Who are we talking

about?'

'Who do you think?'

Marna remembered what Kali had told her. 'Oh.'

'Oh, indeed. The sooner Sempal gets his boat fixed the better,' her mother answered.

'How is Sempal getting on with that?'

'He should be on the beach working on it. You could go and ask him yourself. Show some interest.'

Marna was familiar with her mother's tone. Now that Thork was married, it was her turn to find a partner. 'Mother…you know Sempal and I are just friends. Besides, I'm tired and ready for something to eat.'

'You will have to wait. The afternoon meal is still being prepared. I offered to help Fara, but she wants to impress us with her berry tart.'

'Delicious. Wait! Where did she get the berries?' Marna snatched at her mother's words.

'Not from the pathetic specimens on this island. They would hardly fatten a vole. I brought a pot of mixed fruit over from home. Thankfully they survived Sempal's rowing.'

'You are wonderful.' Marna gave her mother a kiss on the cheek. 'I suppose Sempal told you about the berries that Mooth ate.'

'He did, and I was surprised there were any berries on the island, given the lack of rain.'

'There are a few up the hill that have survived.'

'Mmm.' Her mother often made sounds that Marna didn't understand, and she rarely explained the meaning of them.

'Maybe I will take a stroll down to the shore,' Marna said.

'You do that.'

Her feet were blistered from her walk up the hill and Marna felt she was dancing over the pebbles as she chose her steps. It took longer than usual to reach the bay. She could see Sempal's boat on the shore, but her friend wasn't beside it.

'Sempal, are you there?' she called.

She sat down on a rock and removed her sandals to rub her feet, expecting Sempal to appear. When he didn't, she got up and ambled towards the boat carrying her shoes. She kicked at the pebbles in annoyance, aiming at the boat. Sempal had started to repair the damaged wood and skin, but the work wasn't finished. She put a hand out to touch the sides. The skin was greasy with fat and she ran her fingers down her tunic to wipe them. She had left a smear on the boat skin and she tried to rub it away with her sleeve before Sempal came back. The more she rubbed, the worse it looked. She stood back to consider what to do next.

A hand grasped her shoulder and she screamed.

Chapter 20

'Steady on girl.' Marna twisted under the grasp to face Borg. He was laughing.

'Let go of me,' she snapped. Borg loosened his grip and she yanked his hand from her shoulder. 'What do you want?'

'You are a feisty one. I want to know what you are up to, snooping around our island like a dog with a fresh scent and stirring up trouble wherever you go.'

'I want to know what happened to your daughter. Don't you?'

'I know what happened to Kayleen. One of the gods fell in love with her and took her for his own.'

'Is that what Patro told you?'

'I don't need a puffed up priest to tell me what is plain to everyone – except you. This island is under a curse because we failed to appreciate what the gods have done for us. We refused to give them a sacrifice, therefore they chose their own.'

'That is rubbish and you know it. Kayleen died because she ate rotten berries,' Marna said. 'Do you think the gods sprinkled the poison on them?'

'You can make a joke of it, but nothing will bring my daughter back. At least I can make sure no-one else suffers by blocking off the area until the gods are appeased.'

It seemed hopeless trying to argue against whatever idea Patro had put in Borg's head. A different approach was needed. 'A stone circle may appease the gods, but it will take years to complete. In the meanwhile, if we find out where the poison is coming from…'

'In the meantime, why don't you gather your boyfriend, your mother and your pathetic mutt and go home?'

Marna was about to give a smart retort, but decided it wasn't worth the effort when a simpler one was at hand. 'We can't go home until our boat is fixed,' she said.

Borg narrowed his eyes. He nudged past her to examine Sempal's boat. 'What happened to it? Did it catch on a rock as your puny friend struggled to pull it up the beach?'

'No,' Marna said. 'The tear was deliberate.'

Borg forced a laugh. 'Who would need to sabotage this thing?'

'I was about to ask you,' Marna challenged.

'You think I damaged it? Why would I? I have no wish to delay your departure.'

'Perhaps you thought we wouldn't notice until the boat floundered in the Sound.'

'That is a serious accusation. You would be wise to hold your tongue unless you have evidence to support your claim.'

Marna felt words bulge against her cheeks, anxious to spurt out, but she picked the ones she wanted carefully. 'Someone on this island wants to prevent us going home. You have assumed the role of chief elder; you must know who is to blame. Or perhaps you wanted to make sure no-one else used our boat.'

'Who do you mean?' Borg asked. If he was bluffing, he was doing a good job. Marna wished she hadn't spoken. 'Ah, you mean the charmer, coming here with his 'magic' stones to cure our problems. He thought we were fools who would be tricked by shiny trinkets.' Borg ran his hand over Sempal's boat, managing to do so without disturbing the layer of grease. 'If you weren't a friend of Gerk's, I might think you were in league with the wizard. Your friend Sempal knows about boats. The repair is almost complete. I advise you and your family to leave our island before the sun goes down tomorrow.'

'And if we don't?'

'There will not be a welcome for you or for anyone who gives you shelter.'

Marna watched Borg stride off with a determined air, but after a few steps he stopped and looked back. 'If you do see the wizard, let me know. Don't try to approach him. He has a knife and is not above using it on those who have shown him friendship. He attacked the priest, Jolty, on his way down the hill. Ask Bryne and Serel if you don't

238

believe me.'

Marna tightened her nails into her palms to stop herself responding, as Borg wanted. He gave a cold smile and continued towards the village. Marna waited on the beach, listening to the swell of the tide and the seabirds squawking and mewing above her. Even they were arguing over food and the best nesting sites.

Caught up in the moment, she didn't hear the approaching footsteps along the rocky edge to the shore. Someone was next to her before she could move. She spun round, slipping on a strand of seaweed and tumbled into the chest of a man.

'We shouldn't keep meeting like this,' Aiven said, helping her to regain her balance.

'What are you doing here?' Marna said. She glanced over his shoulder to make sure Borg was out of sight.

'You gave me a mission. I'm reporting back.'

'I didn't ask you to attack Jolty.'

'Attack him? Who said that?'

'Borg. He said Serel and Bryne told him.'

'Either he is a liar or they are. I didn't attack Jolty. I approached him to offer him the berries I found.'

Marna's mouth fell open.

'Don't be silly, I wasn't trying to poison him. I wanted him to examine them. I thought he was alone, but Serel and Bryne appeared and there was a bit of a scuffle.' He swept

239

back the fringe of hair covering his right eye to reveal a bruise spreading across the skin above the socket.

'Why give the berries to Jolty. Why didn't you bring them to me?' Marna asked.

'Jolty has studied poisons at the Ness for many years.'

'And my mother has been curing people of poisons, in life and death situations, for longer than I can remember.'

'It's too late to argue over who should have seen the berries. They were trampled underfoot in the struggle. Neither Jolty nor your mother can study them.'

'I didn't know Jolty was an expert on poisons.'

'He doesn't boast of his knowledge – not like some people.'

'You mean Patro?'

'And others,' Aiven said pointedly. Marna scowled. 'So, what is your next plan? What do you want me to do?'

'Stay out of trouble.' Marna picked up a flat stone and skimmed it across the water, watching it bounce twice before sinking. 'Borg has told me to leave the island, in no uncertain terms.'

'Will you?'

'If I don't, Fara and Gerk will bear the brunt. Times are hard and they need the help of their neighbours.'

'I can solve the mystery on my own,' Aiven said. 'I'll find a way of letting you know if it is worth hearing.'

'Who is the one boasting of their skills now?'

Aiven selected a stone from beneath his foot and sent it flying across the water, bouncing seven times before Marna lost sight of it.

'Smarty.'

'You don't trust me, do you?' Aiven said.

'I trust you to look after your own interests.' Marna began searching among the pebbles for another stone, determined to outdo him. She was bent over with her eyes to the ground when Sempal hobbled up.

'Am I interrupting a lover's tiff?' he asked. Marna lifted her head. Sempal was holding a wooden rod with dried reeds binding a clump of hair round the top.

'What is that?' Marna said.

'It's a brush. Do you like it?' Sempal demonstrated the implement. 'I'll have the boat finished in no time. I got the hair from Patro's horse.'

'I hope you asked permission,' Aiven said.

'From the pony, as well as Patro,' Marna added.

Sempal couldn't tell if they were being serious or teasing. He blew air from his nostrils in a similar manner to the pony.

'Don't let me hold you back,' Aiven said. He turned to Marna, 'I'll see you again before you leave.'

'You don't have to go,' Sempal said. Aiven put his hand up to wave, but didn't look back. Sempal looked to Marna. 'What did he want?'

'To show off.'

'What's up now?' Sempal secured the brush in his belt and put his arms around Marna's waist. She wriggled away at first then nestled closer to him. His body was warm and she liked the feel of his chest against hers.

'Nothing.' She rested her chin on his shoulder. 'Aargh, what's that stink?' She drew away.

'The pony gave me a kick and I fell in its dung. I was about to wash when Fara said dinner was ready. I've been sent to fetch you.'

'After a whiff of that, I don't think I'm hungry.'

'Yes you are.'

He took hold of her hand and Marna allowed herself to be led up the beach towards the village. She spotted Borg as they neared Fara's house, but he avoided looking at her and she turned her back on him. The aroma of baking from the hut tickled her taste buds. She licked her lips and Sempal was sensible enough not to say he had told her so.

Her mother sensed Marna's mood and didn't insist that she help serve. She sat her daughter beside Gerk and placed a bowl of warm stew in her hands without speaking. The gossip over dinner revolved around Terese's activities and the baby Thork and Caran were expecting. Marna was only half listening. Her thoughts simmered in her mind, reaching boiling point when she pictured Borg and his stupid grin. The stew was good though and it mellowed her mood. By the time Fara brought out her berry tart she was ready to add her bit to the table talk.

'That looks fantastic. I wish I could bake,' she said.

'Practise helps,' her mother answered.

The berries oozed from the pastry straight into the mouth. There was silence while they munched on the tart. Marna was about to swallow a mouthful when the door burst open and she choked on the crust. Borg was first to enter, with Patro close behind, peering from behind Borg's thick-set shoulders at Marna's mother. He sniffed the air, taking in the fruity smell of the tart.

'To what do we owe the pleasure?' Marna's mother was the first to speak, while Gerk and Fara looked on in surprise.

'The priest, Jolty, has taken ill,' Borg answered. 'He has been poisoned by the wizard Aiven.'

Borg was staring straight at her and Marna jumped to her feet. 'That's a lie. Jolty didn't eat the berries Aiven showed him.'

'Who said anything about berries?' Borg said. 'And who told you Aiven gave anything to Jolty?'

'You said so.'

'I said Aiven attacked Jolty.'

'I made an assumption,' Marna countered.

'You have spoken with him since we met. I would say you are in league with him,' Borg accused.

243

'I'm not in league with anyone, but at least Aiven is trying to find out the truth. All you are doing is hindering island life from returning to normal.'

Borg took a step towards Marna. Sempal got to his feet to stand behind her and put a hand on her shoulder. Gerk also struggled to his feet, dropping crumbs from his tunic onto Fara's swept floor. He was about to confront Borg, but Patro moved between the men.

'Enough of this. While you are squabbling, my father is dying.' He turned to Marna's mother. 'I need your help.'

'What are the signs?' Marna's mother asked.

'He has difficulty breathing…'

'Aha.' Marna's mother rubbed her chin.

'And his legs are numb. This is not in his imagination. My father has never been ill in his life. I know he is old and the gods will take him one day, but I can't watch and do nothing.'

'That's not what you said about Kayleen and Mooth,' Marna said. 'It was fate when the gods took them. Why should this be different?'

'Marna, if you can't say anything helpful, keep quiet,' her mother rebuked.

'But…'

A look from her mother shut Marna's mouth. Her mother turned to Patro. 'I'll come straight away.' She handed her plate to Fara and moved to collect her bag while

Patro stood wringing his hands. He stepped aside to allow her to leave the hut ahead of him, but before she could do so Borg pushed past and stormed out. Her mother tutted. Patro reached out a hand to steady her and she brushed it away then stepped outside.

Patro nodded an acknowledgment to Gerk then made to follow Marna's mother. Fara was standing beside him, holding the plate with the remains of the berry tart. Patro paused. 'These berries…?'

'Marna's mother brought them over from Skara Brae,' Fara answered.

'Ah.' He slipped his hand out to take a piece and slid it into his mouth before exiting.

'He's got a nerve,' Marna muttered.

'No-one can resist Fara's berry tart,' Gerk said.

'I should go with them,' Marna said. Sempal held her back. 'Your mother will send for you if she needs help.'

Marna couldn't think of a reason to object, so she settled on the floor to finish her tart. She looked around the room 'Where's Pip?'

'I didn't want him in the house while I was baking,' Fara explained. 'He's in the wood shed.'

'If we've finished eating, why don't we have some music?' Gerk said. 'It will take our mind off our problems.'

Fara clapped her hands and Gerk fetched his pipes from the dresser. He wasn't such a skilled player as Gora

245

was, but he knew how to play a tune. Fara sang and later Sempal told a travelling tale. Although enjoying the entertainment, Marna wasn't musical or good at telling stories and she felt awkward until it got chillier in the evening and she was able to tend a small fire for the group. By the time everyone was ready for bed, her mother still hadn't returned.

'What do you think is keeping her?' she asked.

'I suppose, if she is with Jolty, it means he must be alive,' Gerk said. 'She may have decided to stay the night there.'

'She didn't stay with Gora's mother or Jael,' Marna complained. 'I like Jolty, but I don't see why he gets preference, just because he is Patro's father.'

'Patro is only doing what any son or daughter would. You can't blame him,' Gerk said.

'I wish I had been with my father when he needed me...' Fara's voice tailed off as Gerk put his hand round her shoulders. 'This isn't about Jolty, is it? You don't like your mother being close to Patro.'

'No...I mean...why should I...?'

The baby gave a cry and Fara turned to her. 'I'd better see to Terese.'

'You're tired,' Gerk said to Marna when Fara moved away. 'It has been a long day. Try to get some sleep. I'll wait up in case your mother returns.'

'I won't sleep,' Marna protested, but when she opened her mouth a yawn came out. Her eyes were droopy and the snugness of the cot and the skins was appealing.

'Fara takes a sprinkling of dried valerian leaves when she can't sleep,' Gerk said. 'It was one of her father's remedies.'

'No thanks,' Marna declined the herbs.

'See you in the morning,' Sempal said. 'I'd better get back to Olan or he'll be wondering what has happened to me. Thanks for the tart, Fara.'

'Here, take Olan and his parents some,' Fara reached for the dish. 'Oh, there doesn't seem to be much left.'

'There's none now.' Sempal popped the last piece in his mouth and Fara frowned. 'Olan doesn't deserve any pie,' Sempal said. 'He's been acting strangely.'

'Oh?' Marna pricked up her ears.

'He says he has work whenever I ask him to help me with the boat. Nobody can use that much rope.'

'The men will need rope to erect the stone circle,' Fara said.

'That won't be for weeks yet.'

'If at all,' Gerk mused. 'The project may not come to anything. Patro won't want to continue with it if his father doesn't pull through.'

Marna had drawn the bedding skins round her, but she felt a shiver at Gerk's words. Jolty had been skipping over

247

the rocky hillside that morning, fitter than Serel or Bryne, wondering at the splendour of the sun on the water. It seemed bad things could strike anyone on the island, without warning - even those who made it their life's work to please the gods.

Chapter 21

Her mother wasn't in the house when Marna woke the following morning. She knew she hadn't returned because if she had, she wouldn't have allowed Pip to cosy beside her in the cot, licking her face. Terese was bawling.

'Fara, Gerk,' Marna called.

No-one stirred and Marna imagined the house was empty. Someone must have let Pip in when they left, but hadn't thought to disturb her. Even so, it surprised her that she had slept over the noise they must have made.

Terese was not a quiet baby when she wanted fed. Marna got up, straightened her hair and arranged her clothes. Normally there would be a bowl of water to splash over her face to freshen her after a night's sleep, but with the current shortage she knew she would have to take a trip to wash in the sea. She debated whether to take Terese with her or not, but decided against it. Fara would be back soon and panic if the baby was missing.

'Come on,' she called to Pip. 'Let's find the others.'

Pip gave a groan before scrambling from the cot, catching his back legs and tumbling to the floor. He tangled his weak legs as he tried to right himself and Marna laughed. 'Stay here and guard the baby then.'

Jael was outside his house scraping at a piece of driftwood and a couple of the younger men were steeping pelts in a vat of bearberries, moaning at the price the traders on Rousay had asked for them. Steeping skins softened the hide and made it easier to scrape the fat and hair off, which was usually Froink's job. She guessed he was busy keeping guard on the hill. Marna held her nose as she passed.

Fara and Gerk weren't in the central yard. She thought about asking the men where they might be, but decided instead to go to Olan's house and find Sempal. As she neared the door she spotted Borg heading in the same direction. She slipped behind the side wall before he looked up and saw her. She circled round the back towards Mooth's house, hoping to find her mother there.

The door was open. In her own village, that was an invitation for anyone to enter, but she was learning that habits were different on Eynhallow.

'Hello,' she called before stepping inside. She was met by a cloud of smoke and spluttered to breathe. Patro was lighting tiny pots of oil to burn sweet-smelling herbs although the acrid fumes from the oil overpowered the mint and thyme. In the flickering light his face looked pale and his eyes were lined and reddened.

'I'm looking for my mother,' Marna said.

Patro looked up. He didn't answer, but gestured with a finger towards the back of the house. A reed curtain had been hung up to separate the area. Marna could hear her mother's voice from behind it and wondered who she was speaking to. She walked over and pulled the edge of the curtain aside to pass through. The oil and incense clung to the lining of her nose, but above it she detected the putrid scent of approaching death. It reminded her of the whales that beached on the shore and lay moaning while the gulls watched and waited. Guttural breathing rising from the corner of the room sounded like the wind trapped in a sea cave. Marna had an urge to turn and run out.

Her mother had her back to her, leaning over the cot where Jolty was lying. The morning was a warm one and the house was clammy, but despite being smothered in skins, the old priest was shivering. Kali was hunched beside her mother, listening to her advice. She was showing him how to do something. Marna couldn't make out what, but from her mother's tutting noises she guessed he wasn't her best pupil.

'Can I help?' she asked.

Her mother swung round. 'Marna, about time, what kept you?'

Marna was about to answer, but a cackling from the corner distracted her. What she'd thought was a bundle of furs was actually a person. When she leaned forwards to cough up phlegm Marna recognised Wandra.

'Should she be here?' she asked her mother in a whisper.

'I need whatever help I can get,' her mother replied.

'Jolty has been poisoned. From the signs I would say hemlock.'

'Hemlock? What is that?'

'You won't have come across it. The leaves are similar to those of various root plants, but are deadly if eaten. They attack the senses causing numbness. They stop the chest from rising and falling so no air can enter.'

Jolty gave an exaggerated sigh as the air escaped from his chest and Marna saw that Kali had pressed on his rib cage.

'Then it wasn't the berries?' Marna asked.

'Hemlock has a bitter taste, which even berries wouldn't sweeten.'

'Oh,' Marna said, glancing at the stricken priest and trying not to hold her nose. 'Where did this hemlock come from?'

'A good question,' her mother said in a voice that showed she didn't want to propose an answer.

'What can be done?' Marna asked.

'We have been breathing for him. We need to continue assisting him until the poison wears off.'

'How long will that be?'

'You are full of questions, as usual. I hope only another day at the most. We managed to make him sick and he brought up a good portion of food. If the poison stays in his system,' her mother lowered her voice to make sure

Patro couldn't overhear, 'I doubt we will be able to save him.'

Kali groaned. 'I can't press his chest and breathe air into him for another day.'

'You'll do what it takes,' Patro answered. Kali had spoken over-loudly, bringing Patro into the closed area. Her mother rose to calm him and urge him back into the main chamber.

'I'll take over,' Marna said. She knelt beside Jolty's bed and placed her hands on his chest. His body was stale and she tried not to take in the odour as she bent over to fill his mouth and lungs with her own breath, the way her mother had taught her.

'The faerie folk will not be denied,' Kali whispered to her.

'What do you mean?'

'I warned them, the faerie folk on Eynhallow demand a tribute.'

'You don't believe in faerie folk.'

Kali stood up and stretched. 'I need to get air.'

Marna continued to breathe for Jolty, but voices rose from behind the curtain and she couldn't help listening to the conversation. Patro's temper was frayed and with the other priests and helpers having been sent out while her mother worked, Kali was bearing the brunt of it.

'The boy needs a break,' her mother intervened.

Marna heard odd snorting noises and the sound of shuffling and pots being moved before Patro spoke. 'You would do well to use the time wisely,' he advised. 'My calculations show that a shooting star will pass over the island within two moons. The same star that passed when my father was a young man. He was eager to see its return.'

It seemed odd to be worrying about seeing a star – or not seeing it - at such a time, especially since there were so many in the sky. Kali mumbled a reply and she heard footsteps leave the house. A moment later her mother and Patro drew back the curtain and entered.

'I should send a message to Quint at the Ness,' Patro said. 'He will need to know about Jolty and about our delay.'

Wandra had been coughing in the corner, but she gave a hoarse cackle in response to Patro's words. 'Your gods may not delay you much longer,' she croaked.

'What do you mean? Do you foresee death? What do you know of this poison?' Patro moved towards her, but Marna's mother put out a hand to hold him back.

'I know enough,' Wandra answered. 'The question I ask you is this; what do you know about the man who gave him it?'

'The man?' her mother queried.

'You are convinced that Aiven is to blame?' Patro scratched his scalp where new blonde hairs were appearing.

'The signs are similar to those Mooth showed before he keeled over,' Wandra said.

'Aiven didn't kill Mooth,' Marna broke in. 'You weren't even at the gathering to know what the signs were.'

'Ha, listening in again, are you?' Wandra accused.

'If your voice wasn't so loud, I wouldn't hear. Aiven has nothing to do with this. Why would he wish to harm Jolty?'

'The man is in league with evil spirits.'

'Nonsense,' Patro answered. 'My father must have eaten the poison by accident.'

Wandra gave a cackling laugh in reply, leaving Marna's mother to explain. 'Hemlock does not grow on this island.'

'And never has,' Wandra added. 'Not grown naturally, in the wild at any rate. I have only seen and heard about it from traders.'

'Then you are mistaken about the substance,' Patro said.

'I don't think so,' Marna's mother answered. 'I too have heard about it and the ailments it causes. Someone has used it deliberately.'

'And who would come across a rare poison in their travels?' Wandra added.

Patro scratched his thumb nail against his front teeth before speaking. Marna couldn't tell what he was thinking,

255

but it seemed to be deep. Every so often he looked down at his father, but turned away when his eyes caught Marna's. 'There are no boats missing. Aiven can't have left the island, unless he swam across the Sound,' he said.

'He can't swim,' Marna said. The others stared at her. 'He told me.'

'Aye, when you were lying together in the heather,' Wandra said.

'That's a lie.' Marna jumped up and advanced towards Wandra.

'Marna, what are you doing? You are supposed to be tending to Jolty,' her mother stepped between them. 'Do you want to be the one responsible for his death?' Marna glowered at Wandra then returned to her post.'

'I think you need to rest, dear,' Patro moved to put an arm around Marna's mother's shoulder. 'Marna can cope.'

Marna expected her mother to shove Patro away, but instead she took hold of the priest's hand and gave it a squeeze.

'Yes, I think you are right,' she said.

'Allow me to help you back to Fara's house.'

Her mother gave him an unmistakeable look.

'I meant accompany you,' Patro corrected. 'I didn't mean you needed help.'

As her mother and Patro left, Marna heard Wandra snigger. 'I've got some cow parsley seeds if you want any.'

256

'What are they for?' Marna asked.

Wandra puckered her lips and made a kissing noise before laughing until she choked.

'I can manage fine on my own,' Marna said, hoping the old woman would take the hint and go home, or at least fall asleep.

'I know your sort,' Wandra answered. 'You think you know everything, poking into other people's business, trying to find a way to meddle.'

'Don't you want to know what happened to your grand-daughter?' Marna objected.

'Why does that matter to you? You aren't from the island.'

It was pointless arguing. Marna tried to ignore Wandra as she returned her attention to Jolty, pounding his chest over-zealously and breathing into his mouth. She could feel his heart beat beneath her fingers, but his body was cold. She took off her shawl and laid it on top of the skin. There was a fire burning in the hearth, but it was dying down and gave off little light or heat. Marna was tempted to fan the flames, but that would mean leaving her position and she wasn't sure how much time she would have.

Wandra had muttered nonsense before falling asleep and was snoring like a pig. The noise was louder than Marna thought the old woman's lungs could produce and it was driving her mad. She wanted to throw water at her to wake her. She took her hands from Jolty's chest to reach for a pot at her side, but it was empty. It would have been a waste throwing it at Wandra in any case. A cushion would do. As she moved Jolty a fraction to free one, she thought she heard him give a sigh. Her heart jumped and she laid her ear close to his chest to detect movement.

'Come on,' she muttered.

It moved. It moved.

She tried to convince herself that the patient had taken a breath without her aid, but any movement of Jolty's chest was imperceptible. She was about to inhale air into his mouth when he gave a definite groan. She jumped up, ready to shout the news to the entire village, but looking down, Jolty lay motionless and pale. She couldn't leave him.

She considered waking Wandra while she ran for help, but she didn't trust the old woman. She looked repugnant, lying in her drool. Marna could only screw her nose up. She wouldn't be surprised if Wandra allowed Jolty to die, just to blame Marna for deserting him.

She stretched and rubbed the cramp from her legs before kneeling down again. Patro or one of his helpers would surely be back soon.

Her mother had pulled the reed curtain over before leaving, blocking light from outside. The darkened room closed in on Marna and coupled with the warmth from their bodies and the fire embers, she found it a strain to keep her eyes open. Jolty gave some further gasps and each time she waited expectantly for him to come round, but the last two had been weaker. When she found herself toppling onto Jolty's body, she pulled herself up with a jerk and knew she would have find help, even if it did mean trusting Wandra.

'Hello, anyone here? Marna, is that you?'

'Of course it's me, you idiot.' She jumped up to open the curtain, but the pins and needles in her foot made her stumble. When Sempal entered she almost knocked the bowl he was carrying from his hand. He steadied himself and she gave him a hug.

'Careful, the soup is hot,' he warned. Marna sniffed the air as she caught the delicious tang of seaweed. 'It's lamb and kelp broth. I thought you would be hungry. I've brought nuts too, left over from last autumn. The shells are a bit bruised, but the nuts inside are tasty.' He offered her the bowl and a handful of hazelnuts. 'If you don't want them, they won't go to waste.'

'No, no, I want them,' Marna took the bowl, but placed it on a wooden table leaning against the side wall in the main chamber of the house. 'You have to find my mother,' she said.

'Is she lost?'

'No, but I need her here.'

'Right.'

Marna turned back to check on Jolty. Sempal stood

looking on. 'Now,' she insisted.

'Where will I find her?'

'Isn't she with Fara?'

'She wasn't when I left. I haven't seen her since yesterday evening.'

Marna gave a grunt. 'She'll be with Patro.'

'Patro isn't here? – obviously not,' Sempal added the final word before Marna could make a comment.'

'Just find them.'

Marna's raised voice woke Wandra. She sat up and glared at Sempal with glazed eyes, taking a few seconds to identify him. 'What are you doing here? Up to no good, I bet.'

'I brought Marna lamb broth.'

'Lamb?' Wandra sniffed the air. 'I'm surprised there are any left in the village. If you young folk want a mystery to solve, you should look to find out what is happening to our piglets and lambs - but maybe that is no mystery.'

'What do you mean? Sempal said.

Wandra let out an eruption of wind. 'That's better.' She squirmed to get comfortable. Sempal was watching her, waiting for an explanation. 'I mean laddie that the animals started disappearing when you and your friend arrived.'

'Are you accusing us of stealing livestock?'

'Leave it Sempal, she likes stirring up trouble,' Marna said. 'You need to find my mother.'

Sempal made a face at Wandra before leaving and Marna knelt beside Jolty to check his breathing. Wandra shuffled to her feet and trudged past, nudging Marna with her cloak as she left the room. Soon Marna heard slurps from behind the curtain as Wandra made short work of the broth. Marna wanted to make a loud comment about taking things that didn't belong to you, but managed to hold her tongue. Thankfully it wasn't long before her mother appeared.

'What's wrong? Sempal said it was urgent. Has Jolty taken a turn for the worse?'

'I don't know if it's good or bad, but he's been making noises.'

'What sort of noises?'

'Talking to the Spirits in the Afterlife,' Wandra suggested. 'He is between worlds.'

Marna's mother made a sound with her tongue to show she was unimpressed. Jolty gave a gasp and his right arm twitched.

'Fetch warm water,' her mother instructed.

'Water, you'll be lucky,' Wandra cackled.

'Sea water will be fine. It's not for drinking.'

'I'll fetch some and heat it,' Marna said, glaring at Wandra as she picked up the empty pot. Her mother put a hand on her shoulder for an instant before she left.

'You've done well,' her mother said.

Her mother's words lifted her spirits and it was a relief to be outside in the sunlight. It had been impossible to know which part of the day it was while she was nursing Jolty. There was a gentle breeze blowing as she made her way to the shore. She breathed in as much fresh air as she could, as fast as she could. It made her feel light headed - that couldn't be Pip running on the pebbles, chasing his tail? As she got closer she saw that it was and she spotted Vern close by, hiding behind a boulder.

'Come out, I won't hurt you,' she called.

Vern didn't move until Pip trotted over to the boulder. A hand appeared to pat his forehead. Marna followed him across. Vern turned away as Marna approached.

'What's up?

Pip nuzzled into the girl and she looked up. A dark bruise was gathering around her left eye and the skin round it was swollen and yellow. There was a cut on her cheek with blood clotted to the edges.

'What happened? Who did this?' Marna demanded.

'Nobody, I fell against the rocks,' Vern said, getting to her feet.

'Was it Borg?' Marna said.

'No.'

'Then who?' Marna folded her arms and tapped her foot the way her mother did when she demanded the truth.

Vern rubbed her palms against her tunic. 'It was the

wizard,' she said without looking at Marna. 'It was Aiven.'

Chapter 22

'That isn't true. You're lying,' Marna grabbed Vern's arm and shook it.

'No I'm not. He accused me of tampering with your friend's boat. When I denied it, he hit me. Now you are hurting me too.'

Marna let go and Vern fled up the shore. Pip gave a yelp and moved to follow the girl, but a look from Marna made him sit. She watched Vern disappear behind the bushes on the bank and realised she was wasting her time trying to understand the girl. It made her feel old. She ambled to the water's edge and dipped the pot under. A tiny green shore crab sidled in and she shook it out.

'Don't be in too much of a hurry to be eaten,' she warned it.

On her way back to Fara's house she kept a close lookout for Aiven. There was no-one around, but heavy footprints had trodden on the dried grasses - recently from what Marna could gather. She suspected there had been more than one culprit involved. She knelt to inspect the area. It seemed as if someone had lain on the ground. She pictured them rolling, their weights evenly spread, squashing the dandelions into the earth. If the young men on the island were anything like those in her own village, it was probably a wrestling match to prove who was strongest or to settle a quarrel over something stupid.

Fara had a fire burning in her house and some heated stones sitting next to it. Marna took care not to burn her fingers as she placed a couple into the pot of water. She could have heated them in Mooth's house, she knew, but the closed atmosphere there had left her feeling nauseous and she welcomed the openness of Fara's home. She carried the water pot back to Mooth's house without spilling any, feeling the warmth as the stones gave their heat to the water and the pot. Patro was with her mother when she entered. They were sitting on wooden stools at the side of Jolty's bed. The patient's skin was pinker, or so Marna imagined. She set the pot down beside her mother and turned to leave.

'Where are you off to?' her mother asked.

'I want to find Sempal.'

'He is with Kali,' Patro answered. 'When you find them, instruct Kali that I wish to speak with him.'

It amused Marna to think of herself 'instructing' Kali to do something. She held her face in a serious pose as she replied that she would, but outside the hut she let the laugh escape.

The village wasn't large, but she was unable to find Sempal or Kali. Fara thought Sempal was helping Gerk mend a cattle enclosure that had blown down in the wind, but when she met Gerk, he told her Sempal had gone with Kali to collect heather. Marna was too tired to stomp round the hill chasing them. She spotted Olan sitting outside his house mending a rope and strolled over to admire the deftness of his fingers as they smoothed and twisted the fibres. It was as if nature had given him three thumbs, attached to his hands by loose threads. He sensed she was watching and looked up.

'Oh.' Marna was shocked to see a sharp gash across his nose. The jagged edges of the wound were held together by clotted blood.

'It's nothing,' Olan said.

'It will require yarrow or a barley poultice. Have you spoken with my mother?'

'Your mother has more important tasks and this is only a scratch,' Olan insisted. 'What can I do for you?'

'I'm looking for Sempal and Kali.'

'They went swimming.'

'I've come from the shore and didn't see them there.'

'They said they wanted to explore the deeper caves further round the island,' Olan said.

'They went exploring caves without me?'

Olan's face suggested it wasn't something any reasonable person should undertake and he believed Marna had more sense than to join in, but Marna could feel the tickle of her temper gather in her stomach and move up her

265

chest towards her head.

Sempal and Kali could go swimming and exploring, while she had to help her mother. That wasn't fair.

Thinking reasonably, she didn't mind nursing Jolty, especially not now when it looked like he was over the worst, but her mind was full of conflicting tensions. She needed to calm down.

It wasn't a conscious decision, but her feet guided her towards Gora's house to listen to her play the pipes. Marna would have liked to ask her to teach her, but she didn't have the same feel for rhythm as her brother did. It hadn't taken Thork long to earn the role of chief drummer in Orphir. Neither did she have the patience to learn.

Before she reached Gora's house she heard a commotion in the centre of the village. Voices were raised and hearing Gora's she scurried to find out what was happening. Neela, Serel, Gerk, Jael, his wife, Gora and several others were having a heated discussion.

'Something has to be done about it soon.'

Marna heard Neela's high-pitched voice as she approached. She slipped in beside Gerk.

'What's going on?' she whispered.

'It's the beast that Patro brought over. It has eaten half the island, including the few crops we have. Had.'

'Can't you tie it up somewhere safe?'

'We would if we could catch it. No-one is able to get

266

near it. Bryne got close and it kicked him in the groin.'
Gerk rubbed the area and Marna sensed the pain Bryne
must have felt.

'You should tell Patro,' Marna said.

'He won't listen. He is too concerned about his father.'

The others had stopped talking and Marna realised
they were staring at her. She stepped forward to address the
gathering. 'I have come from Mooth's house. Jolty is
improving.' There were a few murmurs. Most of the
villagers seemed relieved by the news. 'Patro will not wish
to remain on the island once his father is fit to travel.'

A man in the crowd gave a small cheer and Marna
recognised him as the man from the Ness assigned to take
care of Hansibar. The islanders looked at him with
disapproval.

'It is almost the solstice. Patro needs to be at the Ness
for that,' the man explained.

'Even a few more days is too long,' Jael grumbled. 'I
had bere growing three moons ago.' He lifted his hand to
demonstrate the remainder of chewed stalks.

'I'll ask my mother to speak with Patro about his
pony,' Marna promised.

'Aye, he will listen to her,' Neela answered.

Since nobody was keen to tackle the problem head on,
they wagged fingers and agreed with Marna's suggestion
before beginning to disperse. Marna caught up with Gora as

she returned to her house. 'I wanted to ask if you would show me your pipes. I could never play like you, but I would love to learn.'

'I'm sorry, I don't have time today. The tide has washed in a cast of crabs, which we want to gather before the birds attack them. I would be happy to teach you later.'

Marna expected she would have left the island by then, but didn't bother explaining. Her attention was drawn to Pip, who was digging the earth beneath the door to Wandra's house. She whistled to call him over before Borg or Wandra spotted him, but he didn't respond.

'You were supposed to be with Fara,' she said, dragging him away by the scruff. When she returned to Fara's house, her friend was playing with Terese.

'Have you seen Gerk?' Fara asked.

'He was with the others a moment ago. Didn't he come back here?' The house wasn't large and it was clear Gerk was not hiding behind the dresser or inside a cot. 'I shouldn't think he will be long.'

'I'm worried about him. He has been acting strangely since he got back from the Ness,' Fara complained.

'In what way?'

'The other islanders have always been suspicious of me, because I wasn't born here. When the water cistern cracked and we lost half the water in it, they blamed me for not tending the stone. Gerk used to laugh about it, but lately he has started agreeing with the elders whenever I do something they think is wrong. Yesterday he told me to remove a hanging I had on the wall because it was too bright and today he doesn't want me to keep the stones my father gave me on the dresser, in case our neighbours see them.'

'That's ridiculous,' Marna agreed.

'He says I should learn to sing like the other wives. If he tells me "Borg said this" or "Borg thinks that" one more time, I'll…I'll…pack my things and leave.'

'Don't do that. I'm sure the situation will improve,' Marna said.

'If only it would rain. I mean a proper downpour.' Fara ran her fingers through her hair, catching her nails in the tangles. She tugged at her head and Marna could see she was about to cry.

'You're tired. Why don't you let me take care of Terese while you rest? I'll let you know when Gerk gets back.'

'Thank you.' Fara took her advice. She reached for a pot on the dresser and helped herself to a pinch of the powder in it. 'It helps me sleep,' she explained.

'Valerian, Gerk told me,' Marna answered.

'No doubt he thinks I take as many plant potions as my father.'

'Of course he doesn't. You are uptight. You'll feel

better in the morning.'

Fara lay down and Pip found a cosy spot at the bottom of the bed. Soon Marna could hear snoring coming from them both. Pip's heavy breathing answered Fara's nasal whistle in a sleepy conversation. She bounced Terese on her knee and told her stories she'd heard from Sempal. The baby was too young to understand, but the sound of her voice calmed her and she kept quiet so her mother could rest. Between stories, Marna got up and walked to the door to check for Gerk.

Fara couldn't be serious about wanting to leave him and return home. Jona's house was taken by Horen although her mother and some of the others would prefer it to be offered to Albar and Henjar. In either case, there would be nowhere for Fara to live, unless she stayed with them. There was an empty cot with Thork gone.

Marna was busy working out possible domestic arrangements when Gerk returned, accompanied by her mother. They were sharing a joke.

'Shh, you'll wake Terese. I've just got her to sleep,' she scolded. 'I assume from the laughing that Jolty is back on his feet.'

'He will be soon. The poison is leaving his body. He even has an appetite. I reckon he should be strong enough to leave the island tomorrow. A messenger has been sent to the Ness to prepare a litter at Evie for his journey. But guess what?'

'What?'

'Don't be like that.' Her mother gave her a nudge. She was in a strange mood, acting like a child. Marna was too tired to join in the game, but she made a guess to please her.

'Gerk is taking you fishing tomorrow?'

'No.'

'Have you been drinking too much ale?' Marna sniffed the air in front of her mother.

'Don't be silly. Patro has invited me to study at the Ness.'

'What? You? Why?'

'The Ness isn't just for young people and foreign students,' her mother objected. 'Patro thinks I would make a good teacher, with some instruction.'

'From him?'

'And others. Jolty is an expert on toxin antidotes.'

'Didn't do him much good,' Marna muttered. If her mother heard, she ignored it.

'Patro gave me this bracelet in appreciation for what I did.' Her mother held out her arm to show Marna the polished, stone band. 'It's jet.'

The bracelet was gorgeous, and valuable. Marna couldn't resist stroking the smooth stone. 'I suppose he has plenty of treasures at home. What will I do, if you go to the Ness?'

'You could stay with Henjar, Albar and Sempal, or move to Orphir to help Caran when her baby arrives,' her mother said, brushing back a strand of Marna's straggly hair that Terese had pulled out of place.

'Great.'

'I haven't made a decision yet. We can discuss it later.'

'Right, good, well now you're back, I'm going to find Sempal.' Marna was out of the house before she remembered she was meant to wake Fara when her husband returned. There was no point returning, her mother and Gerk's chattering and clattering would surely wake a sleeping hedgehog.

Marna made her way to the shore. There was no sign of Sempal. A breeze blew up and a few light spots of rain danced in the air as she left the village. Marna thought nothing of it, but by the time she reached the beach there was a downpour. Drops of heavy rain the size of small pebbles bounced off the hard ground and soaked into her clothing. She called Sempal's name a few times, but nothing could be heard above the thudding of the rain. She retreated to the village.

'It's raining,' she called as she entered Fara's house, dripping water onto the new felt rug.

'So Gora said,' her mother answered.

'Oh.' Marna hadn't noticed Gora, who was talking to Fara in the corner of the room, next to Terese's cot.

'I've brought my pipes,' Gora said, 'but it seems a shame to wake the baby. I'll play them for you another time.'

'We're leaving tomorrow, or the day after,' Marna said. 'That's if we ever find Sempal.'

'He's with Froink,' Gora said as she walked to the door. 'I saw them talking when I came out.'

'What does Sempal want with him?'

'I didn't hear their conversation. I imagine it was to do with gaming.'

Her mother, Gerk and Fara settled by the fire with warm ale, but Marna wasn't in a mood to join them. She lay down in her cot and pulled the seal skins over her head to muffle the sound of their voices while she thought about what her mother had said. What was Patro's plan? For years her brother, Thork, had been pressing everyone he knew with connections at the Ness to be allowed to study there. Patro always came up with reasons to deny him, yet her mother had only to…what?

She didn't have an answer before she fell asleep and was woken the following morning by a shove on her shoulder.

'Time to get up, lazy bones.' Her mother pulled the skins away.

'Why?' Marna yawned. 'Is Sempal here? Do we have to leave now?'

'No. Wandra has invited us to breakfast.'

Chapter 23

'Why?' Marna screwed up her nose and reached for the skins to pull them back over her.

'She is keen to discuss healing plants with us.'

'She's more interested in the poisonous ones, if you ask me.'

'Try to be nice, Marna. I think she is lonely and wants the company. She is a clever woman who likes to know what is going on in the world outside the island. It can be frustrating having few people to talk to with the same knowledge and interests.'

'Why does she live here then?' Marna asked.

'To be near her family.'

Marna knew her mother was thinking about Patro's offer. 'I suppose it could get boring living on a small island that doesn't get the traders and visitors we get at Skara Brae,' she answered.

'There has been too much excitement in our village,' her mother agreed. 'Don't boast about it when you are speaking with Wandra. Now, get up and make yourself presentable.'

Marna noticed her mother had straightened her hair and was wearing her new jet bracelet. 'Patro won't be there too?' she asked.

'Of course not, why do you ask?'

Marna made a face, but didn't answer. Her mother spoke with Fara while Marna got ready. She took longer than usual, trying to delay the visit and hoping something would happen to avoid the meeting.

'Can Pip come? He'll get in the way here.' Marna didn't need an answer. Her mother's face registered the disapproval.

'He isn't here,' Fara said. 'No doubt he's cadging breakfast from Sempal. I'll take care of him when he arrives back.'

Marna went with her mother to Wandra's house. The old woman was bent double, poking at the hearth fire with a hazel stick when they arrived. The rain had stopped overnight, but it had seeped into the ground and their sandals were muddy. Marna's mother removed hers at the door and Marna copied her. As she moved into the centre of the house, Marna spotted Borg and took a step back.

'Sit down.' Wandra offered them mats. Marna hesitated. 'Borg is leaving.'

'Not on our account, I hope,' Marna's mother said in a tone Marna knew meant she wasn't sorry.

'Aye,' Borg answered, nodding at his mother. 'We have Patro and his priests to thank for this rain. The elders have decided that building a stone circle to the gods is not such a bad idea.'

'Jolty is leaving with Patro and his remaining followers,' Marna said.

'I will speak to them before they go,' Borg answered. 'Patro has business at the Ness organising the solstice celebrations, but the boy Kali has relatives here. He can stay with Fara and Gerk to oversee the work.'

'I'm sure Kali will be delighted to stay,' Marna said. A look from her mother warned her to mind what she said.

'I'll be back for dinner,' Borg told Wandra before he left. Marna crouched beside the fire, with the flames between her and where Wandra stood. Her mother brought a small patch of decorated felt from her pocket and offered it to Wandra before sitting down on a stone. Marna wasn't sure what she could do with it, but Wandra seemed happy with the gift. After fussing around as old women do, Wandra produced two small pots containing warm drinks. She handed one to Marna and one to her mother. Her mother raised the pot to her nose and sniffed. Marna did the same. It smelt vaguely of blackcurrant, but there was an earthy aroma that clung to the inside of her nose, making her feel dizzy.

'It's good,' Wandra said, lifting a third pot of the liquid from the dresser. She took her time positioning herself between Marna and her mother, squeezing Marna further away. She rocked from side to side to nudge both of them, her smile implying it was intended as a welcoming gesture. Marna resisted the urge to nudge her back.

'Are Neela and Vern not with you today?' Marna's mother asked.

'I don't know where they are. They keep themselves to themselves,' Wandra answered.

'Vern is a pretty girl, she looks like her father,' Marna's mother said. There was a silence while Wandra eyed her. Her smile withered.

'As your daughter is like you,' Wandra finally said. 'Please, drink up.'

It was rude to refuse to drink, but from the smell, Marna knew she wouldn't like the taste. She was working out how she could accidentally spill it when Neela rushed in.

'Wandra, have you seen Vern? – oh, you have guests.'

'Isn't she with the other children?' Wandra answered.

'No. I sent her to collect driftwood, but that was as the sun was rising. She'll be hungry and should be back by now. The others haven't seen her.'

'I wouldn't worry about her,' Wandra said with a poorly-disguised sneer. 'She's always off on her own.'

'She can't swim,' Neela said. 'What if she waded into the sea to pick a floating piece of wood and was caught by the tide?'

'She'll be well on her way to Rousay or beyond,' Wandra cackled.

Neela's face paled. Marna's mother put her pot on the floor and stood up to put an arm around her. 'Have you spoken to Borg?'

'No. He cares as much for my daughter as his mother does.' Neela prodded a finger at Wandra. 'She knows the truth, yet she feeds him lies.'

'Don't worry. Marna will go and search for Vern. I'm sure she will find her safe.'

'I've looked everywhere.'

Marna was quick to leave aside her own pot and get to her feet. 'I'll fetch Pip. He'll be able to find her,' she said. 'He may not be a hunting dog, but he has a good nose and he knows Vern's scent.' She hurried to the door before Wandra or Neela could object and picked up her sandals. She waited before she was outside and round the side of the house before slipping them on her feet.

'Pip,' she called, expecting her dog to come trotting out of Fara's open door. He should have returned home, even after begging for his breakfast from Olan's parents, and probably Gora as well. 'Pip, here boy,' she called a little louder when he didn't appear.

'What's up?' Sempal walked towards her from Olan's house.

'I can't find Pip.'

'I guessed that,' Sempal replied. 'When did you last see him?'

'I can't remember. He was with Fara yesterday evening, I think. I left him to look for you. Gora said you were talking to Froink. What was that about?'

'Kali and I found where Aiven is hiding when we were exploring the caves.'

'And you told Froink?' Marna accused.

'He's wanted by the villagers, unless you'd forgotten.'

'He hasn't done anything.'

'You've changed your tune. I thought you said he was an arrogant charlatan.'

'That isn't a crime. The villagers want to blame him for their problems because he is a stranger. If we weren't guests of Fara and Gerk, they would blame us too.'

'You are talking nonsense Marna,' Sempal said. 'If Aiven is as innocent as you say, let him come before the village elders and prove it. Wait, where are you going?'

Marna had side-stepped Sempal, but she stopped when he reached out a hand. 'I don't have time for your pointless prattling. I have to find Pip. I need him to search for Vern.'

'Vern has gone missing? Then I think I can guess where Pip is,' Sempal said.

'Where? Oh.' Marna made a face as she realised what Sempal meant. 'Vern has taken him?'

'I can help you look for them,' Sempal offered. 'They shouldn't be hard to find. Thanks to the rain, there will be footprints in the mud.'

'There are lots of prints. How will we know which are Vern's?'

'Pip's paw prints will be nearby.'

'She'll carry him,' Marna said.

'Not for long. Have you felt how heavy he is getting?'

'Are you saying my dog is fat?' Marna said, but she was grateful to Sempal for coming up with an answer. She leant towards him and gave him a kiss on the cheek.

'Very fat,' Sempal said, offering his other cheek, but Marna had turned away.

'We should split up,' Marna said. 'You take the shore. Vern was last seen collecting drift wood. Her mother thinks she may have had an accident, but she can't have if Pip was with her.'

Sempal was about to say what he was thinking. If Vern had been pulled out to sea, Pip would have tried to rescue her and…He stopped himself.

'I'll head up the hill,' Marna said. 'That's where she and Kayleen went when they wanted to get away.'

'I'll meet you back at Fara's house,' Sempal agreed. Marna watched him head towards the shore before making her way inland towards the hill. There were several sets of footprints, some old, some new, but none accompanied by a lame dog. Vern wouldn't be able to carry Pip if she wanted to climb the hill. After searching round the bottom of the path that led up through the heather she found a tell-tale paw print. It didn't take long to find another. She increased her pace as she followed the tracks. At regular intervals the paw prints disappeared and the footprints sank deeper into the mud as Vern struggled to carry the dog.

'Serves her right for taking him without asking,' Marna muttered.

She thought she could ask Serel or Bryne if they'd seen Vern, but there didn't appear to be guards on the hill. Marna felt her heart rattle against her chest as she realised she might get to explore the area where the berries had been found. But no – she wasn't alone. Joining the set of footprints that she assumed Vern had made, was a larger set belonging to an adult. A grown man, she surmised, from the size.

Borg, she thought, but it couldn't be.

Borg didn't know Vern was missing and she had seen him in his house not long ago.

Had Vern arranged to meet someone? Aiven?

She said he had hit her, so why would she do that?

Besides, she couldn't tell if the two sets of prints had been made at the same time.

As she examined the larger prints she realised there was another mark in the ground beside them – a deeper, circular mark as if the person was walking with a stick. Some of the older folk used a stick to walk, but the prints were spaced a distance apart, implying the person was walking briskly.

The prints followed close to Vern's for a while then broke away. Marna was deciding which to follow when she noticed a number of older footprints a short way off. They weren't clear and Marna suspected the rain would still have been falling, if lightly, when they were made. The hillside was a busy meeting site and it annoyed Marna to think that this was going on when she was asleep.

She was near a small hazel copse. The branches of the trees were bent with the wind and the leaves shrivelled and ready to drop, although it was early summer. There wouldn't be many nuts to gather in the autumn. Marna moved across to check if any were developing. There was something on the ground, bunched between the trunks. She took another step. Her heart jumped and she held her mouth.

The shape looked like a body…no, she must be mistaken, it couldn't be…

She increased her pace. As she neared she realised it was too large to be Vern.

Aiven?

She didn't know what to think when she looked down at the grotesque, gaping mouth and wide eyes of Froink.

Shock, but also relief.

There was a gash on his forehead and lying near his sprawled out hands was a wooden club. She bent to pick it up then turned with it held in front of her as she sensed someone was approaching.

'What is going on here?' The voice was Patro's and Marna remembered the second set of footprints, with the stick. He stared from Marna to the body then at Marna again. Taking two steps back he raised his staff in front of him. 'Put the club down, Marna.'

Instinctively Marna opened her palm. The club fell from her hands. As it did, she saw her fingers were drenched in blood. A high-pitched scream echoed round her mouth and exploded into the air before she fell to the ground.

Chapter 24

'Don't touch me,' Marna cried. Patro was standing over her and she rolled away from him. Her foot caught his shin and he staggered back, stumbling on a rock and landing on his backside with a groan. Marna scrambled to her feet a few seconds before Patro did. They stared at one another. The club was lying on the ground between them.

'I found him lying there,' Marna explained, gasping through the words. 'I didn't...'

'I know. You have a talent for finding bodies, but hardly the strength to fell a grown man. What are you doing here?' Patro said.

Marna's head was buzzing and she couldn't think of an answer. 'Borg is looking for you,' she spoke the first words that came into her head.

'And he sent *you* to find me?' Marna assumed he wasn't expecting an answer and remained silent. 'Is that Froink?' He pointed with his staff, making sure the tip did not touch the body. She nodded and he stepped towards it. She moved a step closer too. Recovered from her shock, she was keen to look for signs of what had happened.

'He's dead,' she said.

'I wouldn't have guessed,' Patro answered. 'You have a talent for stating the obvious. I'm not convinced that makes you the wise woman you presume to be.'

'He must have been lying here all night,' Marna observed. 'His tunic is wet.'

'Mmm.' Patro bent over to examine the clothing. 'We shall have to ask questions in the village. Where did you say Borg was?'

'I didn't, I said he was looking for you.' Marna looked at the club and for a second a mad thought rushed through her shaken mind. 'What are you doing here?' She stepped back.

'Don't be silly. You don't think I would…If you must know, I was looking for the best site to watch the shooting star.'

'You won't see stars during the day. Were you here last night?'

Patro gave an exasperated sigh. 'I was with my father last night. I can see you got your brains from yours. The shooting star is due soon, but you can't turn up and expect to see it without advance preparation.'

Marna couldn't imagine what advance preparation was needed to look at the sky, but she didn't want to look any more of a fool. While she was thinking what to say, Patro was searching around.

'We need to get back. Where has your dog gone?' he asked.

'He's with Vern. I'm here looking for them.'

'You said Borg sent you to find me, now you claim to

be looking for Vern, which is it to be?' Patro queried.

Marna hesitated. She stuck her tongue into her cheeks and circled it round his mouth before replying 'Borg is looking for you, but he didn't send me to find you. You said "where has your dog gone?" Does that mean you've seen him?'

'I saw Vern with your dog not long ago. She was training him to sit and stand at her command.' Patro glanced at Froink's body. 'Vern shouldn't be out here. She is too young for such sights.'

'She has seen death before.'

'Yes I know - her friend, Kayleen - a terrible business.'

It was clear to Marna that Patro understood, possibly even cared, more about what had happened on the island than he made out. 'Someone should return to the village with the news about Froink. He will already be missed.'

'I can look for Vern,' Marna said, judging his dilemma. 'Do you know which way she went?'

Patro twisted to point behind him, round the side of the hill. Marna walked past, spotting Froink's blood on the heather.

Who had seen him last? Who had spoken with him? Sempal.

She lost her footing and her left leg slipped. Before she could react she had fallen to the ground, landing with her hands outstretched in front, her feet in the air and her nose in a puddle.

'Are you hurt?' Patro offered her a hand, but she struggled to her feet without it, brushing the heather heads from her tunic.

'Perhaps we should stay together,' Patro said.

'I'm not a child.' Marna's dignity was bruised more than her bones.

'Whatever would your mother say if anything happened to you?'

'Don't worry she would put the blame on me.'

'Nonetheless…' Patro insisted on walking with her. Despite her coldness towards him, he was keen to talk. 'The passing of a shooting star is said to bring good fortune. It is a sign from the gods. This island is in need of good fortune,' he said.

She didn't answer. They walked a little further before Patro stopped and looked around. 'Ah, the villagers have already begun to mark out the diameter of the ditch.' He took several strides, holding his stick horizontally, as if measuring. 'This will not do at all.'

Marna wasn't listening. She was searching among the heather.

'Is this where the poisoned berries were found?' Patro said.

'Yes. There are a few here.'

'Don't touch them,' Patro warned, but Marna had

already picked a couple.

'It doesn't look like there is anything wrong with them.' She held them to her nose and sniffed.

Patro thrust out his staff to swipe them from her hand. 'Whether the berries look normal or not, you can't take a risk. My father was poisoned. Your mother says so. She is a wise woman.'

Marna looked to where the berries had fallen, feeling rightly chastised. She was about to apologise to Patro, but when she looked up she saw he was walking ahead. He fell to his knees and gave a gasp.

'Are you hurt?' She repeated his words as she ran towards him. Patro hadn't fallen by accident. He was on his knees, leaning over to scoop water into his palms. Before him, a spring was bubbling from the ground.

'The gods be praised,' Patro said. He tasted the water. 'They have sent fresh water to the island.'

Marna didn't know about gods, but she couldn't deny what was in front of her eyes. She stood open-mouthed watching him. He scooped a handful and offered it to her. The water trickled through his fingers before she reacted, but she bent down to sample it from the spring herself. Patro got to his feet.

'Some movement of the earth must have brought the water to the surface,' he said in a down-to-earth voice. 'It is good news for the village.'

'We have to tell them at once,' she said.

'And about Froink's death too,' Patro reminded her. 'First we need to find Vern. I'm worried about her safety. The spring won't disappear while we search for her – and neither will a dead body.'

Marna sucked her lip. From Patro's voice she could tell he thought the two incidents were connected and she let out a gasp. 'Was Froink an offering to the gods? Did he kill Mooth and Kayleen? I have heard people talk about purging evil.'

'My priests do not practise human sacrifice, if that is what you are thinking.'

'The thought hadn't…of course I wasn't...' Marna let her voice tail off.

'Froink was one of the guards protecting the area. He must have known about the spring,' Patro said.

'And you think someone killed him because of that?'

'If they did, we are also in danger,' Patro answered. 'And so is Vern.' He looked towards the sea. 'There is a mist descending.'

'Vern knows every pebble on the island. She can find her way home, even with a mist. Pip can protect her from danger.'

Patro turned to face her and raised one of his clipped eyebrows. 'While being carried?'

'He only needs to be carried when he gets tired. Over

there, look, beside the hazels.' She gestured towards
shadowy figures about fifty feet away. 'Vern, Pip...' she
called, running towards them.

'Wait, that's not...' Patro's warning was too late. She
was grabbed from behind. Her neck was pulled back and
she clawed at the hand choking her. There was the flicker
of the smooth black ring she had admired on Aiven's hand
before she felt a thump on the back of her head and her
vision went dark.

Chapter 25

Marna's head was throbbing when she came to her senses. At first she thought she had been blindfolded, but as her eyes adjusted, she realised it was the surroundings that were dark.

Black as a tomb and twice as cold.

There was droning in the background and it took her a moment to realise it was the singing of the sea. She was lying on her back and could feel rough stone beneath her head and body. Her feet felt as if they were dangling over an edge. Wherever she was, it was damp and water crept into the fabric of her tunic. Her instinct was to sit up, but her bones were stiff and she couldn't move her arms. They were tied behind her. She wriggled her wrists against the bonds and smelt the same oil that Olan used when he wound his ropes. As feeling returned to her ankles she suspected they were also bound.

Juggling her weight sent pains up her thighs and edged her closer to the edge of the stone slab, but with care she managed to roll onto her side without falling off. A sharp beam of light shone towards her and she adjusted her vision. A pair of dark eyes watched her.

There was a splash, the light rippled and she realised it was reflecting in water. The eyes belonged to an inquisitive seal that swam off when she stirred. She was looking out towards the entrance of a sea cave. It didn't take long to work out the tide was rising.

Her ears were attuned to the sound of the sea, and over it she could pick up a grumbling noise coming from a little way ahead of her, slightly to the right. With a painful twist of her neck and head she saw another body, lying in a prone position on a boulder, nearer the incoming waves. She could see the back of a head, then behind that the tips of toes poking from sandals. The growth of spiky blonde hairs told her it was Patro that the tide was advancing towards. He didn't move and if it weren't for the groans, she would have thought he was dead. When the light caught his skull she saw there were clots of blood sticking to the light hairs.

'Patro, are you hurt?' she said. Speaking even a few words ripped at her throat. She tasted blood as well as salt in her mouth. The noise echoed against the domed walls of the cave, as if in mockery.

Patro let out a moan that sounded like a cow giving birth. Marna shivered. 'I think we were ambushed,' she said. She was going to add 'I didn't see who it was', but speaking hurt and she didn't expect Patro to answer. A vision of Aiven's ring flashed in her head.

He couldn't be in league with…whoever, could he? Or was Sempal right, had she been foolish to trust him?

It was not the time for accusations. She was trapped in a cave with the badly injured head priest from the Ness and the tide was coming in.

Think of a plan, Marna.

Her mind wouldn't function. She watched the sun's rays throwing shadows against the cave walls. It should be possible to estimate the passing of time by their movement. Sempal had explained it to her, but she hadn't been listening. The sun appeared to be going down, but what was more important was the tide coming up, no matter how much she tried to imagine otherwise.

With effort, she had twisted into a position where she could keep a watch on Patro. His feet were now floating and the water rippled towards his tunic. He was a strong man, but even without injury, it wouldn't take long for the cold to seep into his body and freeze his innards.

She failed to think of one decent plan, although her head was bursting with outrageous ones. Her hands and feet were bound and nothing could be achieved until she was free. Squirming this way and that didn't loosen them.

If only Pip were here. He had strong teeth, he could chew through the rope.

What had happened to him and Vern? They must have seen the attack. Would Vern have had the sense to return to the village for help? What if the men had captured her too?

She couldn't see behind her, but there hadn't been any noises to indicate there was anyone else tied to the rocks.

Borg would be searching for her. Could they have

killed her?

The snatches of the conversation in Wandra's hut came back to her.

How did her mother know Vern was like a father who died several years ago? What were the lies Neela accused Wandra of spreading?

Another low groan from Patro disturbed her thoughts.

Why hadn't their attackers finished the job with her and Patro instead of leaving them in a cave to drown? Did they fear the gods would curse them if they killed a priest?

A sound came from the back of the cave, behind her. With a heave, she twisted her shoulders round, slipping her legs off the rock and into the water. Her fingertips gripped onto the seaweed to prevent the rest of her body following them in. There was a dim light coming from the far end of the cave and she remembered the hole she and Sempal had found on the cliff top. There would be a passageway, however narrow, leading up to the surface.

After an initial surge of hope, she realised it didn't help unless someone stumbled across it from the other side, which didn't seem likely. She heaved her legs back onto the rock, scraping her feet as she did so. She had to keep awake and she had to keep warm. Patro hadn't made a sound for some time and she feared he had passed into the next world. Funny, she expected the gods would have put on a show for their high priest. Coloured lights and sounding horns.

Thunder and lightning at the least.

Her eyes were closing and her body was slipping when she jerked awake. There was someone in the cave, clattering over the stones behind her.

'Who is there?' she forced the words through her chilled lips.

'Marna? It's me, Aiven.'

A rush of anger brought her voice back. 'Have you come to make sure we haven't escaped? Are you going to finish the job?'

'What are you talking about? I saw your dog wandering in circles among the heather at the entrance. It was odd behaviour, even for him, so I thought I'd take a look. Just as well I did.'

'Ha, I may be weak, but don't think I'll fall for that. What have you done with Pip? If you've hurt him I'll...'

'I haven't done anything to your dog. Lie still, so I can cut your bonds.'

Marna felt a stone against her wrists. She tried to wriggle free, but her arms were numb. There was a prickly feel as Aiven rubbed them and blood rushed to her fingers.

'Ouch.' She pulled her arms from him and nursed her hands. Before she could object, he lifted her from the rock and hoisted her over his shoulders. Beating his shoulders did not help. He carried her to the drier rocks and shore pebbles at the back of the cave and put her down. She

295

struggled to sit up, but kept her feet still as he untied them. She had an urge to kick him as he stood up, but her feet were too slow to react. He handed her his cloak.

'You'll need this.'

Marna didn't take it. 'Whose side are you on?' she asked.

'What do you mean?'

'You attacked me and hit me on the head. You can't deny it. I saw your ring.'

'My ring?' Aiven seemed bewildered. He stared at Marna then gave a sigh. 'Aah, I see. I don't have it.' He raised his hands to show Marna they were bare. 'Serel took it when he was guarding me in the pit.'

'Serel?' Marna repeated, unsure whether to believe him. Aiven wrapped his cloak round her shoulders and she didn't toss it off. The wool was warm and she pulled it closer to her

'Can you stand up? I'll help you.'

Marna was beginning to feel a tingling in her feet. She allowed Aiven to take her weight as she wobbled up. He caught her before she staggered into the sea.

'You are frozen. We need to get you back to the village as fast as possible. I can carry you.'

'What about Patro?'

'Patro?'

Marna pointed a jittery finger in front of her. The tide

had circled round the raised stone and a good three lengths of water lay between them and where Patro was lying. The water had covered the stone and was rising. Patro's head was above water, but Marna couldn't imagine it would be for long.

Aiven swore. He took a stride towards the sea then pulled up.

'It's too late,' he said. 'We need to get out of here.' He urged Marna towards the shaft of light that indicated the cave exit.

'We can't leave him.'

'He's dead, Marna. He must be. His helpers will come for his body and give it a proper burial.'

'You don't know that. What will my mother say when she finds out we left him here?'

'She will be more concerned about you.'

'You can explain to her.' Marna didn't move. She watched the water trickle towards the priest's ears. 'Listen, I heard a groan.'

'That was the noise of your belly. You've swallowed too much sea water.'

Marna stood her ground. 'If you aren't brave enough to rescue him, I will,' she said. Her spirit was strong, but her body refused to move. Aiven tightened his grip on her.

'No you don't.'

He looked back at the water and gulped. It was then

Marna saw the blanket of jellyfish sweeping in with the waves.

'You are scared of jellyfish,' she accused.

'No.' Aiven took a step nearer the exit.

'They are dead,' Marna said.

'They can still sting.'

'You are scared.'

Aiven tightened his lips. 'Stay here.' He stepped into the water and made a burring sound with his lips as he waded up to his thigh and reached across to the rock. Marna watched as he tried to shift Patro's body, but the weight of the water dragged it down.

'His feet are trapped,' Aiven spluttered the words across to Marna. 'They must be trapped under the water.'

Marna waved her hand to direct him to dive below the water. He dunked his head under the water, jerking it out after a few seconds. After repeating this several times, he produced one of the ropes. A strand of kelp had wound its way round the twine. Aiven tossed it out to sea then sank his head below the surface again. Marna watched his head rise and fall as he surfaced for breath, blowing out watery bubbles. Eventually Patro's body was freed and he struggled to drag it back to land.

Marna took a few steps towards him to help, but wobbled and fell. With a heave, Aiven thrust Patro's body on the shore pebbles. He remained in the water, panting air into his chest. The priest's skin was pale and the blueness of the lips and fingernails against it was eerie, as if he had painted his face for a burial ceremony. Marna crawled towards him and ran a finger over his cold cheek, stopping when she reached his lips.

'I think he's alive,' she said, bending her head to detect movement in his chest. She beat her knuckles against his ribs, pounding water from his lungs.

'Don't be silly,' Aiven said, dragging himself out of the water and moving towards her.

'I managed to bring Jolty to life.' Marna took hold of the priest's lips to ease them apart and breathe into them.

'That was different,' Aiven said.

Marna didn't heed him. She repeated the action, massaging Patro's chest and giving him her air until he let out a heavy moan and splattered Aiven with a mouthful of sea water.

'He's alive,' Marna said.

'But for how long? He needs to be near a fire. You too, but I can't carry you both.'

'I can light a fire here.' Marna looked around for drift wood.

'Don't be silly,' Aiven said. 'The air in the cave is too damp and the driftwood wet.'

'What about your stones? Do you still have them?'

'Yes, but they aren't flints.'

'Let me try.'

'No, we are wasting time.'

Marna realised he was right. 'You'd better take Patro,' she said. 'He's in more need of heat than I am.'

Aiven opened his mouth to argue, but he could tell from the fire in Marna's eyes that she wouldn't listen. He took a moment to regain his strength before hoisting Patro onto his shoulder. The attackers had removed the priest's cloak, but his tunic was sodden and Aiven struggled under the weight.

'Stay here and don't try anything stupid,' he ordered her.

Marna watched him stumble towards the passageway. She sat down and pulled Aiven's cloak closer to her. It was important to keep warm. She wished she'd asked him how far the cave was from the village. She thought of Pip.

Was he still searching among the bushes at the entrance? Would he come if she called?

She got to her feet and took a step nearer the exit. Her legs were as flimsy as the jellyfish, but they kept her upright.

That wasn't too hard.

She took a few more steps. When she reached the passage she clutched hold of the side walls for support. She couldn't see her feet and her toes were too numb to feel the rocks. The cave narrowed. Larger stones blocked the end of

300

the passage. She leant against the side wall.

'What did I say?' A voice echoed from above her. She looked up. There was a shadow blocking the rays of sunlight.

'I didn't expect you back so soon.'

'I've left Patro wrapped in heather. His horse is here. It's eaten most of the island apart from these rocks. We can use it to get him back to the village - if you can catch it. You're pretty good with animals, aren't you?'

'I can try,' Marna said. 'Once I've got out of here.'

Aiven removed his belt and threw an end down to her. She wound it round her wrist and held on as he pulled her up. He grasped her hand to take her weight for the final feet. She fell against his chest and his body was comforting. The late evening, midsummer sun was warm enough to heat her.

Patro was lying on the heather where Aiven had left him. Hansibar was standing beside him, nudging her master with her nose.

'Is he still with us?' Marna gestured to Patro, not wanting to look closer in case his spirit was in the act of departing.

Aiven moved to stand over Patro. The pony pawed the ground and took a step back. Aiven crouched on his haunches and slapped Patro's face several times.

'What are you doing?' Marna was shocked.

'Bringing colour to his face. It helps with the blood movement.'

'Oh.' Marna stepped towards them. There was a tinge of pink on Patro's cheeks.

'We need to get him on the horse. Can you hold it steady while I lift him over its back?'

Hansibar did not appreciate being held. It thrust its head back, snorting mucus over Marna then raised its front legs. Marna stepped back smartly to avoid being kicked, but she tried again, speaking softly and stroking the pony's neck. After three attempts she quietened Hansibar to allow Aiven to position Patro across her back.

'It isn't very gainly,' Marna said.

'That can't be helped. I'll walk at the side and make sure he doesn't fall off, if you can lead the horse to the village,' Aiven instructed. 'It's that way.'

Marna's legs were weak and she was glad of the pony for support. Progress was slow and when she rested, Hansibar stopped to eat more heather. Marna gave a cry.

'What's up?' Aiven said.

'Where's Pip? You said he was at the cave entrance.'

'He must have wandered back to the village.'

'He was with Vern. I don't know what happened to her. She could have been attacked.'

'I spotted her before I saw Pip,' Aiven said. 'She wasn't hurt. She ran off before I could speak with her.'

'She thought you were going to hit her again.'

'Again? What do you mean? I haven't hit her.'

'She said you did. You accused her of tampering with Sempal's boat.'

'I caught her ripping the lining with a sharp stone. There's something not right about that girl, but I didn't touch her. You don't think…?'

'Somebody gave her a nasty bruise on her face.'

A groan from Patro cut the conversation short. 'We need to get him to the village and your mother,' Aiven said. 'We can discuss other matters later.'

Hansibar had devoured a large clump of heather. She had a branch poking from her mouth as Marna coaxed her to start walking. She finished chewing before taking a step.

'Do you want your master to die?' Marna said, as if the pony could understand. She pointed to Patro's head which was swinging close to the ground. The pony neighed and began walking, jolting Patro further over. Aiven grabbed at his legs, but he couldn't stop Patro from sliding off the pony and landing with a thud on the hard ground before rolling over. Marna gave a gasp then a laugh.

'That should bring the colour to his face,' Aiven said.

Marna gave a gasp then a laugh 'Let me help.' She bent over Patro and slapped his cold cheeks. It took a moment before she realised he had his eyes open and was staring at her. 'Oh.' She stepped away.

Patro struggled to move his arms and Aiven helped him sit up. He didn't say anything, but continued to glare at Marna with glazed eyes.

'There he is,' a voice called from behind them.

Marna twisted round to see Sempal, Olan and Kali striding towards them. It was Kali who had spoken.

'Step aside and leave Patro alone, you murderer.' He raised his arm to show he was carrying a stone axe. 'I'm not afraid to use this.'

It was clear from the well-honed flint head that the main purpose of the axe was not ceremonial.

Chapter 26

The approach of the new-comers startled Hansibar and sent her trotting off. Marna let her go. She stepped in front of Aiven, shielding him with outstretched arms. 'Stop,' she said. 'Aiven is trying to help Patro.'

The head priest gave a groan.

'It doesn't look that way to me.' Kali pushed past Marna. Sempal held her arms as she tried to prevent Olan and Kali advancing on Aiven.

'Let go of me, you idiot,' she insisted.

'I can explain,' Aiven began when Olan swung a fist, landing the knuckle on Aiven's cheek. Aiven staggered back, holding his nose.

'Get up,' Olan said.

Kali aimed a kick at Aiven's groin, but he managed to roll aside and scramble out the way. Marna wriggled to free herself from Sempal's hold, but his grip was strong. She was about to kick his ankles when he let go with a cry.

'Ouch.' He shook his leg. Pip had appeared from the path and jumped up to lodge his fangs in Sempal's backside. 'It's me, Sempal. I'm not hurting Marna. Call him off.'

'Not until you call off your thugs,' Marna said.

'Stop,' Sempal shouted in a high-pitched voice as Pip leapt towards Sempal's thighs with his teeth bared. Kali and

305

Olan looked round.

'You can settle whatever your problem is later,' Marna said. 'We need to get Patro to the village now.'

'I'll take him,' Kali said. He handed Olan his axe and strode over to Patro. Olan passed the axe to Sempal and moved to help him. Sempal looked at Marna, but didn't give her the axe. Hansibar was out of sight, but the men were able to carry Patro between them. They strung one arm over each of their shoulders and formed a chair with their hands. Patro was taller than Kali and Olan and his legs dragged as they made their way along the path. Sempal didn't follow them. He pointed the axe at Aiven, who was lying on the ground, nursing his wounds.

'We haven't finished with you,' he said.

'You've got it wrong.' Marna pulled Sempal aside. 'Aiven rescued Patro and me.'

'Rescued you? What from?'

'You mean who from. Your mate Serel attacked us. He wasn't alone, but I didn't see faces. Patro may have.'

'I don't understand. Why would Serel attack you? He has been out looking for you. We've been worried stupid.'

'He knew where I was. He is pretending to look for me and I know why, but I have to find Vern.'

'I have been doing a little investigation of my own. I know what she and Kayleen were up to and I can guess where.'

'Tell me.'

'No, you'll have to wait, like the others.'

Marna crossed her arms. 'If you are going to find Vern, I'm coming with you.'

'No you're not. You need to get back to the village and have your mother look after you. This is one job I can manage on my own.'

Aiven had got to his feet. He rubbed his jaw as he moved to stand beside Marna. He took hold of her hand. 'I'll take Marna to the village.'

Sempal glowered at him. 'No you won't.'

'You can't stop him, if you're searching for Vern,' Marna said.

'I am.' Sempal pushed past Aiven, nudging him with his shoulder. 'But I haven't finished with you,' he muttered.

Marna's gaze followed Sempal as he trudged towards the hill.

'Are you worried about him?' Aiven asked.

'Sempal's ideas usually end badly.'

'You don't say. He and that brother of Fara's were nosing round the cave where I was sleeping. They found my cloak and some of my stuff. I heard them say they were going to tell Borg.'

'Sempal can be an idiot sometimes,' Marna agreed.

They began walking. Aiven didn't speak, but Marna found the silence awkward. 'You were telling me about

Vern,' she said.

'That poor girl doesn't know where she belongs.'

'Her father died when she was young. I think she was closer to Mooth than her mother,' Marna agreed.

'I've heard rumours about the family from my gaming friends. Don't judge me - it's how I find out information. Borg, Serel, Bryne, Froink, Neela and her husband Fossa used to roll dice for sport. They drank bread ale and it went to Fossa's head. He had no strategy and a shaky hand, but if he suspected the others were ganging up on him, he couldn't prove it. One night, Fossa was losing badly and drinking heavily and he lost his senses. It was after Borg's wife died and from what Serel told me, Neela was doing a good job helping him get over her. With the ale flowing, Froink and Bryne encouraged Fossa to bet Neela. She implied she was willing. Fossa thought his run of bad luck couldn't continue and he would win back his cattle and land.'

'Did he?'

'What do you think?' Aiven tilted his head. 'You must have noticed the resemblance between Vern and Borg.'

'Borg is her father?'

'He denies it and no-one wants to argue with him, but I believe it was a constant niggle between him and Mooth.'

'What about Fossa?'

'He drank more and when he couldn't afford to pay his

debts he went out to sea to fish with his cousin. Neither of them returned.'

Marna was going to say something, but a thought bounced into her head. She stopped walking. 'Froink is dead. We found his body. It was in the bushes near the spri...' Aiven looked at her with a crooked smile. 'The spring,' she finished. 'You knew about that?'

'I discovered the spring a few days ago. It has been my source of drinking water.'

'You didn't tell me. Did you know Froink was dead? Have you seen his body?'

'Well...'

'I wish Sempal had told me where he was going. Froink's killer is at large out there. I should go after him.'

'No you shouldn't. I doubt the killer will attack again,' Aiven answered. 'Sempal is right about getting you back to the village.' Aiven looked at Pip who was digging a hole in the heather. 'Why don't you send him after Sempal?'

'He doesn't like Sempal. I think he's jealous of him,' Marna said.

'He's a dog, Marna, not a person.'

'He's not like other dogs.' She clicked her fingers and Pip cocked his head then trotted up to Marna. She stroked his head. 'Go with Sempal, and don't bite him.'

Pip sniffed the air then padded off. Marna watched him lollop across the heather.

'Come on,' Aiven said. He took her hand, but she shook it free and began walking to the village. Aiven walked beside her. He had rescued her, but despite what she told Sempal, she didn't trust him – not fully. Why, for instance, was there a blood stain on the cloak he gave her?

'You know who is responsible for the illnesses and deaths on the island, don't you?' Aiven asked her as they neared the village.

'I have a good idea,' Marna agreed. 'But some things don't make sense, like Froink's death. I won't make accusations before I speak with my mother and Wandra.'

'Wandra? What has this to do with that old witch?'

'Why don't you ask Jolty?'

Aiven was puzzling over her answer as they caught up with Olan and Kali at the village gates. Patro was weak, but conscious and Marna thought she saw a wry smile when he saw her. They walked together into the village, drawn to the centre where a group of villagers had gathered. Voices were raised.

'We have to find your mother,' Aiven said. 'We don't want to get involved in a village spat.'

'I think we'll have to. That's my mother's voice in the circle,' Marna said.

Aiven sighed. 'Like mother, like daughter.'

As they reached the gathering spot, Marna saw her mother standing on a rock in the middle of the group. Jolty was standing at her side, looking thin, but recovered, and they were facing Wandra.

'I tell you, she tried to poison me and my daughter,' Marna's mother pointed a finger. 'Jolty has examined the contents of my cup.'

The on-lookers turned to the priest.

'It is true there was hemlock in the cup that I was shown,' he said.

'What makes you think *I* put it there?' Wandra appealed to her fellows.

'More likely it was dropped in the cup to incriminate my mother,' Borg said, pointing a finger at someone in the group. Marna didn't see who.

Marna's mother was about to continue her argument when Jael, who was at the back of the crowd, noticed the new-comers. He raised a cry and the villagers moved aside to make way for them.

'What has happened?' Borg stepped forwards to greet them. His voice was steady, but Marna saw rage, or perhaps fear, in his face.

'Patro and I were attacked,' Marna said. 'We were knocked unconscious, bound and left to die in a cave with the tide coming in over us.'

The gathering made noises of disbelief and anger.

'Patro is injured,' Kali said. 'He needs urgent attention.'

Marna's mother was the first to move, stepping from the stone and rushing to Patro. She placed a hand on his forehead. 'Kali, Olan, take him to Neela's house,' she ordered. 'Make sure a fire is lit. Get him out of those wet clothes and wrap him in seal skin. Fara, bring a bowl of horsetail for the wounds. I shall prepare a potion of bugle and water mint to clear his chest and strengthen his heart.'

Kali and Olan were ready to do as they were told, but Patro managed to struggle free from their hold. He stood unsteadily and wagged a finger at Borg, trying to speak.

'You need to rest. We shall get you better,' Marna's mother said.

Patro resisted. He made some noises, but his throat was too dry to make himself heard. Marna was standing beside him and thought she could make out the words on his lips.

'He says, Borg has his staff,' she spoke up.

'This is hardly the time to be concerned about a silly stick.' Marna's mother took hold of Patro's arm. He didn't try to shake her off, but he didn't move.

'He has my staff.' The words were clearer now. 'He has no right.'

The crowd turned to stare at Borg. He tried to hide the staff behind his back, but it was obvious he had the stick. His face turned a deep purple and he gave a grunt.

'Only the High Priest can wield the staff,' Kali said.

'Where did you get it?' Aiven had been concealed at

the back of the group, but he marched forward to speak.

'I found it on the moor,' Borg said.

'You knew it belonged to Patro. We have all seen him with it. Didn't you wonder whether something might have happened to him to leave it lying there?'

'I assumed he had forgotten about it.'

Patro gave a snort. His voice was returning. 'What sort of priest forgets about his staff? Kali, fetch it for me.'

Kali strode over and grasped the staff. Borg tightened his grip, reluctant to relinquish it. Kali heaved it from his hands and there was a mild struggle. From the looks of the villagers, Borg realised they were against him and let go, thrusting Kali away from him. 'There's no need to grab. My intention was to return it to Patro when he returned,' Borg said.

Kali returned to his leader and gave a bow as he presented the stick to Patro. The High Priest accepted it and rubbed the wood with his fingers, making sure there was no damage.

'You'd rather die of your wounds than lose some silly bit of wood,' Marna's mother grumbled. She raised a hand to touch the back of his head and he flinched. 'You'll need a comfrey poultice for that, unless you want the crack to expand and your brains to fall out.'

Patro eyed the blood on her palm and allowed himself to be helped away.

'You too, my girl,' her mother said as she passed Marna.

'I thought she was never going to notice your condition,' Aiven whispered to Marna.

'I'm fine. We have to stop Borg. Look, he's left the crowd and he's talking to Serel and Bryne.'

'They are plotting something,' Aiven agreed. 'Wandra has gone too.'

'We have to confront him about the attack before the islanders return to their homes.'

'It's too late. The others are leaving and we can't face up to the three of them on our own.'

'You're not afraid of them as well as jellyfish, are you?'

'I'm not afraid of jellyfish, or Borg, but I'm not stupid enough to antagonise them. This is a small island. They can't go far. Once Patro has recovered his strength we can challenge them with his backing. The villagers will accept what he says. They won't risk having the powers of the Ness set against them.' Marna didn't answer, but the small hum showed she didn't object. 'It is time to get you patched up.'

Aiven led Marna to Fara's house. Her mother was busy with Patro in Neela's house, but Fara had returned from taking the horsetail and was able to find Marna dry clothes. She warmed ale for her and Aiven insisted that Marna drank a full beaker, although the sea water had made her stomach feel sick. When she finished, Fara applied horsetail to her wounds and ushered her to bed.

'I'm not tired,' Marna yawned, but soon after lying down her eyes were closed and she was asleep.

Aiven was in the house when she woke. He was talking to Gerk and Fara, but they stopped when they realised she was listening.

'Is it morning?' Marna asked, rubbing her eyes.

'The sun is well up,' Fara answered. 'Your mother was here, but she didn't want to disturb you. She will be back shortly.'

'How is Patro?' Marna asked.

'Out of danger, thankfully, although his temper isn't,' Gerk said.

'I wouldn't like to be the one nursing him,' Marna said.

'Your mother knows how to deal with him,' Fara answered.

'Where is Pip? Is Sempal back yet?' Marna asked. She pushed back the skins and sat up.

'Back from where?' Fara asked.

'Isn't he with Kali and Olan?' Gerk said.

'He went looking for Vern,' Marna said, 'But that was yesterday evening.'

'He said he knew where she was and what she was up

to,' Aiven added.

'She's a strange one,' Fara said. 'She would rather play with the village dogs than the other children.'

'Her father's death affected her,' Gerk said. 'Not that they were ever close.'

Fara cleared her throat at the mention of Fossa. 'She is still getting over Kayleen's death and her grandfather's.'

'That's Pip,' Marna interrupted. 'I know his bark anywhere.'

'His whimper more like,' Aiven laughed.

Marna hurried to the door and opened it. Sempal was coming towards the house. Vern was walking at his side cradling two piglets in an apron she'd made from the folds of her skirt. Behind them, Pip shepherded three lambs in a line.

Chapter 27

'Sempal and his band of warriors,' Aiven said. He had
moved to stand close to Marna with a hand on her shoulder.
He watched the parade with amusement.

'Isn't that our lamb?' Fara said. 'The one we thought a
hawk had taken. I remember it had a black mark on its neck
that looked like a footprint.'

'Yes, and one of those piglets could be Gora's,' Gerk
said.

Sempal waved and Pip ran as fast as he could towards
Marna, tumbled over at her feet then jumped up to greet her
with a lick.

Fara and Gerk stepped outside to face Vern. She didn't
look at them, but played in the dirt with her foot.

'You took our lamb,' Fara said.

'It was Kayleen's idea,' Vern said. 'We didn't hurt it.
We wanted to play with it.'

'It was weak. It needed to be with its mother,' Fara
said.

'We looked after it,' Vern protested. 'We looked after
all the animals. We made them strong.'

Fara had to admit that the lambs and piglets looked in
good health.

'Where did you get food and water for them?' Gerk
asked.

Vern looked at Sempal, but didn't answer.

'I think I can make a good guess,' Marna said. 'I'll explain later.' She turned to Vern. 'Wouldn't the other children play with you and Kayleen? Is that why you took the animals?'

Vern nodded. 'They called us names. Kayleen said we had each other, we were sisters and didn't need the other children.'

'You can help me look after the animals, if you want,' Fara said, 'As long as you promise you won't take them from the village.'

'I promise. Sempal told me it was wrong. I'm sorry.'

'Did you damage Sempal's boat?' Marna asked.

Vern looked like she was about to cry. She sniffed and wiped her eye. 'That was to stop you taking Pip away.'

'Pip doesn't belong here. He has a home with me in Skara Brae.'

Vern made a sullen face.

'We'll return the animals to their owners then it will be time to get you back to your mother.' Sempal stepped in, reaching for Vern's hand.

'No.' She stamped her foot.

'We spoke about this,' Sempal said. 'I let you stay in your secret place last night because you promised to go home today. You and your mother will get your own house back soon.'

'Will **he** be there?'

'Patro and his followers are leaving,' Marna said.

'I don't mind them. Jolty makes silly faces to make me laugh when I'm sad and Patro let me ride his horse. It's Borg I hate. I hate the way my mother cuddles up to him and let's him touch her. She wouldn't if she knew.'

'Knew what? Was it Borg who hit you?' Marna asked.

Vern nodded. 'Wandra told him to. She blames me for Kayleen's death. I wish she would leave our village - and Borg too.'

'Why does she blame you for what happened to Kayleen?' Marna said.

'I left her alone on the hill. I was cross with her after she said…she said Fossa was not my father. She said we were real sisters, not just pretend. Borg had told her, but I knew he was lying. If I hadn't hit her, she would have returned home for dinner and wouldn't have needed to eat the berries. She knew they were bad.'

'What do you mean? How could she know?' Marna asked.

'We met Wandra on the hill gathering berries. She told us not to touch them. She said the tonic she makes for the animals had been spilt on them and that it was bad for people.'

'The tonic for the animals?' Fara looked to Gerk. 'Didn't she give you some for our cow after it calved?'

319

'Why didn't you tell anyone this before?' Marna asked, but she guessed Vern was afraid to.

Neela came out of Wandra's house and spotted them across the yard. She rushed up to her daughter and smothered her in a hug.

'Where have you been?' I thought you had had an accident,' Neela said, with tears in her eyes. 'Are you hurt?'

'Vern was with the animals she has been looking after on the hill,' Sempal said. 'She isn't harmed.'

'But you must be starving,' Neela stroked Vern's hair. Vern nodded and her mother was about to lead her away when Marna stopped her. 'You can't go back to Wandra's house.'

'Why not?'

'Those bruises were caused by Borg. He hit your daughter. '

'No…but we have no choice. While the priests are here, we have nowhere else to go.'

'Gora has room. She will be happy to have you stay with her and her mother,' Fara said. 'I'll speak with her. It will only be for a day or two.'

Fara, Neela and Vern walked to Gora's house. Pip had finished licking Marna's legs and was ready for his afternoon meal.

'I'm pretty hungry too,' Sempal said.

'Come in,' Marna offered. 'Fara has made sweet

dumplings, although without the honey, I'm afraid. There are pignuts to go with them. There should be plenty for everyone.'

'I've business to attend to,' Aiven said, side-stepping Sempal. 'I'll catch up with you later.'

Sempal followed Marna into the house. She was keen to know how he had worked out what Vern and Kayleen were up to, but he toyed with her, inventing elaborate stories to avoid the truth. Marna had picked up a felt cushion and raised it above her head to threaten him when Fara returned with Marna's mother and Aiven. Marna stuffed the cushion on a stool and sat down. 'Everything all right?' she said.

'Neela and Vern are settled with Gora,' Fara reported.

'And Patro is out of danger. He is leaving tomorrow,' Marna's mother said. 'Neela will get her house back, with rich, new furnishings.'

'Patro likes living in comfort,' Aiven agreed. 'He had Olan bring in wall hangings from Rousay and craftsmen to build an oven at the back.'

'That sounds good to me,' Gerk said.

They sat down to eat. The house was full, but they managed to find space for everyone. Marna sat between Aiven and Sempal. Her mother was opposite her next to Gerk. Fara served the dumplings and pignuts before sitting between Sempal and Marna's mother.

'Has Patro said anything about what happened on the hill?' Marna asked.

'He said he needs to speak with you first,' her mother answered. Marna stuffed a pignut in her mouth, swallowed it and got to her feet. Her mother put out a hand. 'Whatever he has to say can wait until after we've eaten.'

Marna sat down and stuck a dumpling in her mouth, gulping it in one bite and choking on the crumbs. She was keen to know what Patro was planning.

Why hadn't he said anything about finding the spring? Had the blow to his head wiped the events from his memory? Was that why he wanted to speak with her?

She finished the meal and looked to her mother.

'Go if you must,' her mother said. Marna rose.

'Do you want me to come with you?' Sempal asked.

'I can go. I need to speak with Patro before he leaves,' Aiven put in.

'I don't need either of you to hold my hand,' Marna said.

Pip was waiting for her outside. He followed her across the village despite her sending him back three times.

'You can't come in,' she told him as they reached Mooth's house. Pip sat down and gave a 'yup', but when Marna turned to go in he was at her heels.

'Marna, come in. I trust you are recovered,' Jolty greeted her at the door. He was drinking a cloudy liquid

322

from a clay beaker. 'Bread ale with a spoonful of Rousay honey, would you like some?' He offered Marna the beaker, but she refused.

Patro was reclining in bed surrounded by skins and resting his head on his hand. He looked up as Marna entered. Her mother had bound comfrey leaves to his head with a felt band. His new hairs popped out from the top like bere stalks. Marna bit her cheek to hold back a snigger.

'I'm glad you are feeling better,' Marna said.

'And you too,' Patro answered.

'My mother said you wanted to speak with me.'

'Yes.' He turned to his father. 'Would you mind leaving us for a moment?' Jolty made for the door. 'Leave the ale.' Jolty placed the beaker on the side of the bed next to Patro. 'And take the dog with you.'

Marna didn't expect Pip to go, but Jolty offered him some crumbs and he left with his tail wagging.

Patro waited until his father was out of the house before speaking. 'Sit down. You make me feel like an invalid, standing over me.' Marna looked around for a chair. She couldn't find one, so sat cross-legged on the floor. 'I have a theory about who attacked us and why,' Patro continued, 'But we need to agree on our facts before we accuse anyone.' Marna nodded. 'First, we found Froink's body.'

Marna gave a shiver as she recalled the look of fear

stuck rigid on the dead man's face. 'Aiven saw him too,' she said. Patro frowned at the interruption to his narrative. 'Then we did find a spring, didn't we? I'm not imagining that?'

'It was no vision,' Marna said.

'Do you remember where exactly? Could you find it again?'

'I think so.'

'You only think so?'

Marna made a face.

'Very well,' Patro accepted her ability. 'So were we attacked because we found the body or because we saw the spring?'

Marna wondered if Patro broke everything into steps before making decisions. 'I think it was because we found the spring, as you mentioned at the time,' she answered. 'Borg and his men have been trying to stop me going to that spot since I arrived on the island.'

Patro ran his tongue round the inside of his mouth. 'You said nothing of this before. Is that why you suggested the hill as a site for the stone circle?'

'I knew Borg wouldn't stop a priest from going up the hill.'

'And my father was poisoned to stop him building the stone circle on the spot you chose.'

'I didn't mean that to happen.' Marna felt her face

redden. 'I suppose if I'd thought about it, I should have known. It makes sense.'

'Poisoning people does not make sense,' Patro said. 'Neither does killing a young girl and a village elder.' He paused, rubbed his bandaged head and winced. Marna took the opportunity to have her say.

'Mooth was poisoned to throw the blame on Aiven. Everyone at the gathering saw him give the berries to Mooth, but there is no proof that the berries were poisoned – only rumours. Aiven had eaten some earlier and apart from stomach cramps he was fine.'

'You said earlier that Borg and Wandra weren't at the gathering,' Patro said. 'How could they know Aiven had given Mooth berries and how could they poison Mooth?'

Marna hadn't thought of that, but an answer came to her. 'Bryne, Serel and Froink were there. Everyone was paying attention to Sempal and his tale. One of them could have reported back to Borg unnoticed. Wandra could have added her poison to a sweet meat and had it delivered to Mooth.'

'Mmm.' Patro showed his agreement with a murmur. 'But what about Kayleen?'

'I fear her death was an accident. Vern thinks she ate the berries on the hillside, but she could have returned home and ate the poisoned ones in Wandra's house.'

'Jolty believes that Wandra tried to poison you and

your mother,' Patro said. 'She gave my father a honey bannock when he returned from the hill. He has a sweet tooth which I have warned him will kill him, but not in that way. I don't understand why she or Borg would want to hide the spring though? Surely this is marvellous news for everyone on the island.'

'Some people are greedy,' Marna said. 'They want to keep the good things for themselves.'

Patro clasped his fingers and raised his hands to his mouth. 'You are wiser than you appear,' he admitted. 'Have you told anyone of the spring?'

'I haven't, but Vern knows about it and so does Aiven.'

'What about that simple friend of yours?'

'Sempal isn't...' She stopped as she saw a wry smile creep onto Patro's lips. 'I think he knows. He found Vern. The spring was how she and Kayleen were able to tend the animals they took. I don't think he has told anyone else.'

'I have spoken with my father, but that is all,' Patro said. 'I have said nothing to your mother, but I believe she suspects there is a hidden source of water. How else would the berries flourish? We need to arrange a village meeting.' He sank back against the skins her mother had placed in the bed for him and reached to finger the staff positioned against the wall within his reach. 'I don't feel strong enough yet.'

'I could do the talking,' Marna said.

'I'm sure you could, but we need the right words and back-up muscles on our side, in case things get nasty.'

'We can rely on Gerk, Kali, Olan and Aiven,' she said.

'You trust Aiven?'

'He was the one who rescued us.'

Patro laughed. 'You believe his actions were heroic?'

'Weren't they?'

'Don't get me wrong, I am grateful to him, but it may be that he didn't want to draw attention to the cave. His presence there was not a coincidence. My aides have not been idle while we have been on the island. They have been my eyes and ears. Aiven has secured enough whalebone at the back of that cave to make him a rich man.'

'No. How?'

'Every time Olan has rowed across to Rousay for bread and water he has taken potions Aiven has made to trade with the farmers there. They are having problems with the sheep losing their appetites. Your mother believes Aiven's medicine is no more than dried gentian roots, but the people on Rousay like it.'

'I can't believe...'

'Still, there is no harm in trade. I have no reason to think Aiven is involved with Borg, other than at the gaming tables, where I am told he has accused certain people of using weighted dice. He is keen on you, I believe.'

327

Marna blushed and quickly changed the subject. 'Will four strong men be enough?' she asked.

'I have two helpers who will fight if necessary and your mother knows how to use a heavy stone, if needs must. Yes, I think we are ready to make our accusations. Would you ask my father to come in on your way out? I imagine he is listening at the door.'

Patro reached out to take the beaker of ale and Marna took that as her dismissal. She heard Jolty scuttle from the other side of the door as she opened it. He was feeding Pip the remains of a bannock when she stepped outside.

'Patro says you can go in.' She pretended she didn't know he had been listening. As he walked by her she put a hand on his sleeve. 'Is my mother really going to stay at the Ness?'

'I don't think so. Patro pleaded with her to go, but I believe she has decided against it,' Jolty said.

'Thank you. Come Pip.' Marna walked off with a smile.

Chapter 28

Patro had his helpers spread the message and a meeting was arranged for later that day. Marna spent the afternoon going round the friends she'd made in the village. They knew she was keeping news from them and it was difficult to ask for their support without telling them, but she had promised not to mention the spring until the gathering.

'Is this about the Stone Circle?' Jael asked. 'Someone said Kali was staying to oversee that.'

Marna assumed by 'someone' he meant Fara. 'I'm not sure,' she replied. 'But Patro thinks the gods are favouring the island again.'

'Do you know what happened to Froink?' She had tried to avoid Bryne and Serel, but Bryne cornered her as she made her way to Gora's house. The skin round his right eye was swollen and dark, showing signs of a nasty bruise developing. It was roughly the shape of Patro's right elbow.

'She won't know,' Serel pulled his brother away. 'It's Sempal we need to speak with.'

Marna made a note to warn Sempal. Neela and Vern were not in the house, but Gora and her mother were excited to learn of the gathering.

'Borg is not popular,' Gora's mother said. 'Most of the villagers hold a grudge against him and his mother. He makes new rules whenever he has a headache.'

'Which is often,' Gora agreed. 'He drinks too much berry spirit.'

'Rules which suit him and his friends,' Marna put in, but didn't explain what she meant. On her way back she avoided Borg's house although she could hear raised voices from inside. She met Sempal as she was about to enter Fara's hut.

'Are you going to tell me what this is about?' Sempal asked.

'You haven't told me how you found Vern yet.'

Sempal looked over his shoulder. 'Let's go for a walk.' Marna was happy to go with him to the shore. They walked in silence until they were out of the village.

'So?' Sempal asked.

'So what?'

'What are you going to tell this gathering?'

'I can't tell you yet, I promised Patro.'

'When did you start trusting Patro enough to make promises?'

'Since he started growing his hair,' Marna answered. 'I admit I may have misjudged him.'

Sempal narrowed his eyes, thinking about what she said. 'Growing his hair? Kali said he did that because of your mother. Oh, you don't mean your mother is going to marry him?'

'She refused to go to the Ness, but I don't think Patro

will give up.'

'What will Thork say?'

'Thork has other things to think about now he is going to be a father.'

'He is lucky to have Caran,' Sempal said. He paused before asking, 'What do you think about it?'

'I want my mother to be happy. After Wilmer…'

'At least Patro isn't likely to kill anyone…or is he? Froink wasn't poisoned. Who killed him?'

'That's what I want to speak with you about. Serel and Bryne think you are to blame. You were the last person to speak with Froink. What was that about?'

'He was cheating at dice. He had a way of twisting his hands to get the throw he needed. We all knew, but nobody would stand up to him. Olan said something as a joke and got a stone across his nose. He laughed when I accused him and told me to go back to playing with the children if I couldn't handle men's games.'

'What did you do?'

'I didn't kill him, if that is what you are suggesting. He was twice as big as me, remember.'

'Where did he go when you left him?'

'He was heading out of the village.'

'You didn't think that was odd, so late in the evening? Did you see anyone following him?'

'I was glad to see him go. I didn't kill him, but it

wouldn't have upset me if he'd fallen over a cliff in the half-light.'

Marna made a tutting sound with her teeth, feeling she should be shocked, but in her heart she agreed with Sempal.

They walked on across the shore.

'I remember what I was going to Fara's house for,' Sempal said. 'Olan's mother has been baking. She sent me to ask you to have a meal with them.'

'That would be nice,' Marna answered. 'I need to speak with Olan.' Her eyes caught movement in the sand dunes and she recognised Aiven signalling to her. He ducked out of sight before Sempal looked round. 'You go ahead, I'll catch up.'

Sempal loped back to the village and Marna realised she hadn't asked him how he knew about Vern. She pondered the matter as she strolled towards the bank and concluded the other children must have given him hints. Aiven was examining his hands and she sneaked up behind him, hoping he would jump when she tapped him on the shoulder. He turned to see her before she was close enough.

'No dog today?' Aiven said.

'He's at home with Fara. Why did you wave?'

'I heard you have called a meeting. I want to know what you intend saying.'

'I can't tell you.'

'Don't you trust me?' Aiven raised an eyebrow.

'Why should I? You didn't tell me about your little medicine business with Olan.'

'How do you know about that?'

Marna rubbed the side of her nose.

'Olan wouldn't have told you,' Aiven surmised. 'Unless he let something slip to Sempal after he'd been drinking.' Marna shook her head. 'Nobody else knew.'

'You're forgetting someone who has spies everywhere.'

'Borg?'

Marna continued to shake her head. Aiven wasn't going to guess and she was tiring of the secrecy. 'Patro,' she said.

'I should have known. What else does he know?' Aiven asked, furrowing his brows.

'What doesn't he know? I could ask him about your ring. He might be able to get it back from Serel.'

'It isn't important,' Aiven said in a manner that convinced Marna that it was.

'We will need the help of strong bodies at the meeting,' she said. 'Can we count on you?' Aiven nodded. 'I'll see you there then.'

The gathering was planned for the early evening. Apart from a few villagers who were unsteady on their feet or too young to stay still and listen, the whole village turned out. Marna and Sempal arrived together.

'Are you going to tell us a story?' Jael called to Sempal.

'Perhaps later,' Sempal answered and received a frown from Marna.

'What's wrong with that?' he asked her.

'This isn't time for telling magical tales, this is serious.'

'I know, I said "later".'

Patro was dressed in his priestly robes. He had abandoned the head bandage and his scalp was shaven once more, revealing the extent of the crack to his head. It made him look severe. The deliberate procession from Mooth's hut gave him an air of authority. He held his staff aloft as he and his party paraded round the village passing each house in turn, with Jolty and Kali a few paces behind carrying small pots which held smouldering, sweet-smelling herbs. He stepped into the centre of the circle.

'I'm surprised he isn't riding his horse,' Sempal said.

'He's showing everyone he is in good health,' Marna answered. She was looking round the crowd, trying to spot Borg, Serel and Bryne. Borg was whispering to Wandra at the back of the group. It was a warm evening, but both were dressed in several skins. Serel and Bryne were together near the front. Bryne's tunic bulged. Weapons were prohibited at such meetings, but Marna suspected he was concealing an axe. Olan and Gerk were standing close to the brothers.

She couldn't see her mother in the crowd, but Fara was with Gora and Neela.

Kali had a drum slung round his neck and shoulder and with a nod from Patro he handed Jolty his incense pot and began beating it. The crowd fell silent. Patro looked round and spotting Marna, he signalled her to come beside him. The villagers parted to allow her through. When she was in position on his right side, he banged his staff on the ground three times and uttered some odd words.

'Is he talking to the gods?' a boy at the front asked his mother and was warned to keep quiet.

'I bring wonderful news,' Patro began, raising his arms in the air.

'You're leaving?' Bryne said, over-loudly. Patro sent a cold glare through the air, as penetrating as an arrow.

'I am indeed leaving, because my work here is over. I have interceded with the gods on your behalf. I have abstained from the rich food that is strewn before me at the Ness. I have lived a simple life in the village, sharing in your hardships, in order to focus my mind and plead with the gods. They have tested me in many ways.' Patro flicked his hand to show that he was above whatever trials were sent. All eyes followed the movement with awe. 'The gods have heard my prayers and have looked down to see your dry land and withered crops. The sight has made them weep tears of rain.'

Marna had to admit that he knew how to capture an audience. The villagers, few of whom had seemed interested in the gods beforehand, were ooh-ing and aah-ing in wonder.

'They have sent a spring of fresh water bubbling from the hillside,' Patro declared.

The 'oohs' intensified.

'Here on the island?'

'Where?'

His words had the desired effect and Patro stood back to allow the villagers to chatter. After a moment he raised his hands aloft again.

'The spring will bring new life to the island, but there is evil in Eynhallow. Evil that needs to be plucked out before the gods are satisfied.'

Serel and Bryne shuffled their feet. Marna looked to where Borg and Wandra had been standing, but she couldn't see them.

'The evil is such that I cannot speak of it.' Patro closed his eyes for a second before opening them and staring at Marna. 'The gods have chosen Marna to be their mouthpiece.' Marna didn't move and he gave her a nudge. 'She will explain.'

Marna wished she had Sempal's ability to hold a crowd with her voice. She felt she was speaking too fast. Her tongue was stuck to the top of her mouth and her words

sounded muffled and in the wrong order. 'When I first...
with Sempal... visiting Fara...'. When she looked round
she saw the villagers were listening to her. Olan had put a
hand on Serel's shoulder and she spotted Aiven in the
crowd, preventing Bryne from reaching for his axe.

As she became involved in the story, her tongue
moved freely and the words came. She told of how she had
been prevented from investigating the deaths, how she had
been barred from the hillside and made to feel like a
criminal by Borg and his friends.

'Wandra used poison on the animals and spread
rumours of evil to keep anyone from wandering on the
hillside so that nobody could find the spring. Kayleen's
death was a terrible accident. After that, Borg set his patrols
in place.'

She hesitated before mentioning the incident in the
cairn, but taking a deep breath she related what happened in
the tomb. 'Someone knew I was there.' She stared at Bryne.
'Someone didn't want me to leave.' The villagers started to
pass comment to each other, but nobody spoke loud enough
for their voice to stand out. Marna continued her tale and
the mumbling subsided.

She wished her mother would stand forward and
support her when she declared that Jolty had been poisoned
with hemlock, a plant not found on the island and one that
few people knew about. The woman standing in front of her

337

had her mouth open, listening in disbelief and when she accused Wandra of trying to poison herself and her mother, the woman's eyes popped and she let out a gasp.

A drop of rain fell on her shoulder, which encouraged her to finish before everyone got soaked. She rushed through the details of finding Froink's battered body to get to the revelation of the spring and how she and Patro had been attacked and left stranded in the cave to drown. The emotion of the event was too much. Her throat tightened and she had to stop. There was a brief hush then the whole village started talking at once.

'What about the wizard? What has he to do with things?' someone shouted.

'Aiven has nothing to do with it. He rescued Patro and me.' Marna felt she would be repeating these words for many days to come. Not everyone agreed and the gathering was in danger of getting rowdy, stirred up by Bryne. She looked to Patro. 'You have to say something. The people expect it. Aiven is the reason Mooth sent Olan and Gerk to the Ness.'

Patro stepped forward and raised his voice. 'Quiet everyone. Where are Borg and Wandra? Marna has made serious accusations against them. I do not doubt her words, but we should hear what they have to say.'

The villagers stopped talking and looked round. Wandra and Borg were not among them.

'They were standing next to me a moment ago,' Neela said. 'They must have gone home.'

Patro signalled to Kali and the villagers watched as he ran to their house. He returned to declare it was empty. 'I checked behind the dresser and in the cists,' he informed Patro before the head priest could accuse him of neglect.

'It's a small island and Wandra is not steady on her legs. They can't have gone far,' Olan said.

Jael rushed towards the village gate and looked towards the shore. 'There,' he called. 'I can see a boat heading over the Sound towards Rousay.'

A number of villagers ran to stand beside him.

'He's right. That's Borg's boat. Wandra is with him.'

'They must have been prepared for the journey.'

'We have to stop them,' Gora declared.

'Borg's father was a master boat builder. His boat is the fastest on the island,' Chifa said.

The mutterings increased, but no-one moved towards the shore. Marna had followed Jael and was staring out at the boat bobbing on the water. Like everyone around her, she jumped when she heard the bang.

Thunder, she thought, but the rain cloud had passed and the sky was clearing. It wasn't until Patro banged his staff again that she realised what the sound was. The villagers turned their attention to the priest. Patro looked weary and was preparing to call the meeting to a close.

'What about Serel and Bryne?' Marna said. 'Perhaps they would like to explain why they attacked us.'

'I don't explain anything to a girl,' Bryne said. Aiven was beside him and he twisted Bryne's arm behind his back.

'We were only doing what Borg told us,' Serel said.

'You knew about the spring and kept it a secret,' Olan accused. 'You knew what hardships we were facing.'

'We weren't the only ones,' Bryne answered.

A number of villagers moved closer to Bryne and Serel with their fists raised.

'If I can speak?' Serel glanced at Patro. The priest gave a nod and the villagers allowed Serel to step forward. He appealed to his neighbours. 'We were acting in everyone's best interests. We found the spring on the same morning that the stranger arrived. Bryne and I wanted to rush and tell Mooth, but Borg was with us and he warned against that, so we covered it over.'

'Why?' Olan demanded.

'He said we should wait until the mid-summer solstice. I argued that our cattle wouldn't last until then.'

'Your cattle seemed to do all right.' Gora voice was heard above the general disgruntlement. Patro raised a hand for silence and Serel continued.

'Aiven arrived, Kayleen died, then Mooth. Borg said there were too many upsets on the island, what with people taking ill, the arrival of the priests and building a stone circle. Everything got confusing.' Serel put his hands on his head and ran his fingers through his hair.

'Borg said…when did we start listening to that bone head?' Jael said.

'You didn't call him that to his face. What Serel says makes sense,' another villager replied.

'Why attack Marna and the priest?' Chifa asked.

'We found Froink's body and panicked,' Serel answered. 'Borg was the one who wanted to kill them. I persuaded him to leave them in the cave, intending to rescue them when Borg had gone.'

'They would both have drowned long before you got round to rescuing them,' Sempal accused.

'I saved Marna from the fire in the cairn.'

'And who started the fire?'

'When I heard the terns make a racket, I saw Borg and Wandra coming out from the tomb.'

'They aren't here to deny it.'

Some of the villagers accepted what the brothers said, while others were suspicious of their motives. It looked for an instant as if a fight would break out. People moved to take sides and Marna could see Patro make a gesture towards Jolty. The older man raised his arms.

'Please, please. I ask for calm.' His voice had an effect on the group and opponents stepped away from one another. 'The spring has been discovered, that is what matters. We must all work together to organise the gathering of water and to secure the future of the supply.' The murmur from the islanders was favourable.

'The gods are appeased,' Kali added, concerned that Jolty had forgotten to mention the fact.

'What must we do to keep them happy?' Jael asked.

'The building of the Stone Circle shall go ahead under my supervision,' Kali responded.

'Kali has my support and guidance,' Patro added. Kali puffed out his chest and was about to expand on his announcement when Jolty spoke.

'To mark the start of the work, we shall organise a grand feast with cattle and ale brought over from the Ness,' he said with a smile.

The word "feast" had the desired effect. Any residual thoughts of fighting were washed out to sea. Marna licked her lips and for a moment she wished she could stay to enjoy it. Gerk was standing near Jolty and encouraged the villagers to raise a cheer.

Jolty's and Patro's names were chanted and, typical of the islanders, musical instruments appeared from folds in tunics, to be blown, strummed or beaten. The younger folk wanted to lift Jolty onto their shoulders, but he managed to avoid that celebration. Kali was strutting about like a well-fed bull, giving instructions. Having no success with Jolty, four of the youths hoisted him into the air and marched round the wall singing.

'I'm not sure the gods would appreciate the words,' Patro moved to whisper to Marna. 'I think we should retire to the house.'

'Wait, you are going to let Serel and Bryne get away with hiding the spring so they could use it themselves.'

'I think we can leave it to the villagers to deal with them.'

'What about the fact that they attacked us?'

Patro didn't answer.

'You still haven't said anything about Aiven and what about his ring? You promised you would get it back.'
Patro put a hand in a pouch attached to his belt and drew something out. He opened his fist to show the smooth black stone.

'Your friend was not honest with you. Serel didn't take it from him. Aiven lost it in a gaming match.'

'Why didn't he tell me that?'

'He may have been wary of your disapproval. It appears that while most of the village were searching for him as an outcast, he was throwing dice with the renegades. He even gambled away his healing stones.'

'But he had them when he rescued us.' Marna remembered.

'Then he must have won them back from Froink,'

Patro said.

Marna took a moment to think. 'How did you get the ring back from Serel? You didn't play dice for it. You made a deal with him, didn't you?'

'I considered all options and thought that the best one. How else could I get Aiven's ring back?'

'Was it that important?'

'The ring is to Aiven.'

'And what deal have you made with Aiven?'

Patro gave a patronising smile. 'Don't concern yourself with things you don't understand.' He began walking towards Neela's house. Marna followed.

'I would understand if people told me what was happening,' she complained.

They walked a few more steps before Marna had another thought. 'We didn't come to a conclusion on who killed Froink.'

'Didn't we?' Patro answered.

'No, we didn't.' Marna stopped walking. They were almost at the house. Patro walked on a few paces, but realising Marna was waiting he stopped and turned to face her.

'I thought you would have worked it out. Froink's death had nothing to do with the others. It was the result of a gambling dispute. The parties squabbled and Froink raised his weapon. I have been assured it was self-defence and have no reason to doubt it. The club belonged to Froink.'

'Sempal confronted him about his methods, but he wouldn't have been able to defend himself against Froink.'

'I didn't mention Sempal.' Patro was about to give a name, but caught the words and smiled. 'I'll give you time to work it out.'

Chapter 29

Despite further questioning, Patro refused to tell her who he believed was responsible for Froink's death. Her mother was waiting for them in Neela's house with hot broth, fresh bread and ale. Jolty and Aiven joined them and it wasn't long before Sempal, Gerk, Fara and Olan arrived.

'Kali is minding Terese,' Fara said.

'We managed to rescue him from being thrown into the sea,' Gerk explained. 'He owes us a favour.'

'It's time he got to know his niece,' Fara said.

When the food was finished, they sat back in front of the fire. No-one was keen to leave. 'Will you tell us a tale, Sempal?' Olan asked.

'Well...' Sempal looked to Patro.

'Be my guest,' Patro replied.

'We'll need some more clots for the fire,' Marna said. 'Sempal can talk for days and nights. Pity Gora isn't here and we could have some music.'

Before she had finished speaking, Gora and her mother appeared, with Olan's parents. They held the door for Jael and his wife. Each of the visitors brought a delicacy to eat and Patro greeted them by offering beads, coloured threads and small gifts from the Ness. Marna looked at her mother, guessing she was the one who had arranged the celebration.

Some time during the evening, Pip managed to sneak

in and curl up at Marna's feet.

'This is as good as our mid-summer celebrations at the Ness,' Patro said as the gathering edged to a close. He had drunk a good share of ale and his face was fixed in an awkward smile. He turned to Marna's mother who was sitting next to him with an arm round his waist. 'I can't persuade you to change your mind and return to the Ness with me?'

'With a grandchild on the way, the harvest to think about and your ideas to brighten up our village, I have plenty to keep me busy in Skara Brae.'

Patro sucked his lips. He glanced at Marna then rubbed his chin with his finger. The party was ending and the guests were taking their leave and retiring to their homes. Patro acted as the perfect host, but in a free moment he sidled beside Marna and bent down to stroke Pip.

'He bi...' Marna began.

'Bites? So I've heard. Rather like his mistress.'

Marna didn't answer, but inside she felt pleased and for once she didn't mind Pip allowing the priest to fondle his ears.

'Aiven tells me he intends travelling on to Westray,' Patro said. Marna looked across the room to where Aiven and Olan were laughing together.

'Really? I thought he came to Orkney to study at the Ness,' she answered.

'That was the original arrangement, but we have had a discussion. Given what has happened on this island and his reactions to it, Aiven has changed his plans. He wants time to think about his future.'

'You don't sound too unhappy about it.'

'He has given us fine whalebone pieces in compensation for the inconvenience. He gave me the personal gift of a beautiful new ceremonial mace head. As luck would have it, I have a perfect block of oak – a gift from the people at Stonehenge – which the chief craftsman at the Ness can fashion into a handle for it.'

'Wonderful,' Marna pretended to sound enthusiastic.

'Yes.' Patro hesitated before continuing. 'Have you a mind to go to Westray with him?'

'He hasn't asked me.'

'He will.'

Her attention was distracted by Sempal stumbling against a side bed, swearing then apologising to her mother as she gave him a hand up. Marna smiled. 'No, I don't think so,' she answered.

'Of course,' Patro said. He had been watching her watch Sempal. He didn't continue the conversation, but he remained beside her so that Marna could tell there was something else he wanted to say. Eventually he said, 'Aiven told me that he thought I was dead – in the cave. He was prepared to leave me to the sea spirits.'

'And the jelly fish,' Marna put in.

'Yes. If it hadn't been...'

'It's all right, you don't have to thank me for saving your life,' Marna said.

The side of Patro's mouth began to twitch. He caught Marna's mother watching them from across the room and muttered something under his breath that may have been a 'thank you' of sorts. Marna smiled.

'If you are returning to the Ness tomorrow morning, I don't imagine I shall see you again,' she said rather formally. She glanced towards her mother and added in a teasing voice, 'Unless you decide to visit Skara Brae for any reason.'

Patro cleared his throat and Marna started to move off, but he stopped her. 'You haven't considered studying at the Ness yourself, have you?' he asked.

'Me?'

'We don't take many students at a time, to allow for individual attention, but since Aiven will no longer be studying with us, we can make room. You have more wits about you than I thought at first - certainly more than your brother, who Kali tells me is still in possession of Jona's staff.' He shot another look at Marna's mother. 'Which is no concern of mine, they can argue about it between themselves.'

'Our village doesn't have a priest,' Marna said. 'I have

been called upon to act in matters of judgement. I am needed there.'

'The Ness isn't so far from your village. We wouldn't be holding you hostage.'

Marna hoped that was Patro's attempt at a joke. She was suspicious of his intentions, but the offer was tempting. 'I'm not shaving my hair off.'

'That won't be necessary.'

'I'm not interested in shooting stars or poisons. I don't know what I could study.'

'I'll think of something,' Patro dismissed her excuse.

'What about Pip. I can't leave him.'

'Naturally he can come too,' Patro had answers to all her objections. Marna was about to say 'yes'. She even thought about hugging him. 'And I'm sure your mother would come to visit you as often as she could,' he added.

So that was his real reason. He was using her as one of his deals, but he underestimated her. She knew how to make deals too.

'About my brother Thork, I would say you were in need of a skilled drummer...'

Also by B K Bryce

Maeshowe Murders
The first in the Marna Mystery Series.

Made in the USA
Columbia, SC
10 October 2018